Posterity

By

Jess Newton

Posterity

By Jess Newton

Published by Gurt Dog Press

Editing by Nem Rowan

Cover design by Nem Rowan

Cover photography by Tasos Mansour, Neida Zarate & NASA

Digital ISBN 978-91-987425-1-0

Hard Cover ISBN 978-91-987425-2-7

Soft Cover ISBN 978-91-987425-1-0

POSTERITY

Jess Newton

To my children (and their children), in the hope they don't have to live in this future.

Chapter One

Captain Nina Brooke blinked as the haze lifted and everything started to come back into focus. Warm air rushed over her, soothing away the chill lingering in her fingers and toes. The face of her Chief Medical Officer pixelated into clarity, dark curls framing her serious face, then her words started to register.

"Welcome back, Captain. Remember to take it slowly."

Nina eased herself into a sitting position and rubbed her eyes, chasing the last shadows from them. Dr Caimile backed up slightly to give her room as she stretched and looked around her. The cryobay looked exactly as she remembered it, enormous and sterile. It felt like no time had elapsed since she had lain down in her pod.

"Whew. Any idea how long we've been out?"

"Not yet," the doctor replied, shaking her head. "I've been awake five minutes longer than you; I just had long enough to run checks on myself before I got the alert that you were waking up. Now, if you don't mind…"

She gestured to the medical unit in the wall and Nina got down from the table that had been her cryopod, crossing gingerly to the recess and stepping in. She felt the familiar tingling sensations as the unit assessed her but ignored them, focusing instead on running through her next tasks in her head. After years of preparation, it was about to begin. The thought gave her a pleasant adrenaline rush as she tuned out the physical. After a moment, the unit bleeped and a small receptacle containing a number of pills emerged from the wall next to her. She threw them back and stepped down, grimacing as she swallowed them.

"Alright, Doc. Prepare to wake the rest of the crew. I'm heading up to the bridge to check it's not a false alarm. I'll let you know when we're good to go."

"Aye, Captain. Try not to overdo it."

The ship was eerily quiet as she walked the hallways to the bridge, and she wondered again how much time had passed. It seemed like only a few weeks ago she had been supervising the final checks on the *Posterity* and readying it for this journey, but providing there hadn't been a malfunction and they were indeed nearing their final destination, that had been over fifty years ago now. How much had changed, back on Earth? Assuming there still was an Earth, of course.

Chiding herself, she firmly pushed away the bleak thought and concentrated on the here and now. She reached the doors to the bridge and swiped her hand over the access sensor, letting it read the chip embedded in her palm. The doors opened and lights sprung on, illuminating the large, empty room and the sleek control consoles spaced evenly around it. She made straight for her chair in the centre of the room and checked the date and their position, flicking the toggle to hail Dr Caimile down in the cryobay when she had finished.

"Brooke to Caimile, are you there?"

"I'm here, Captain. Go ahead."

"It's not a false alarm. We're right where we should be, about a week away from our new home. I'd like you to start waking the crew. I'm going to stay up here and read up on what's been happening a bit more, but call me back down before they're awake, I want to be there."

"Understood, Captain. Caimile out."

Nina skimmed through the mission briefing on her console, reminding herself what was next on the agenda. They'd have a week before they arrived at the planet to check through everything thoroughly and there were people on her team with specialities that made them more suited to the job than her, so she contented herself with scanning the list instead of absorbing it. After less time than she thought possible, Dr Caimile's voice rang through the empty bridge.

"Caimile to Brooke. You've got about five minutes until the crew start to wake up, Captain, I'd recommend you get down here."

She pushed herself to her feet, flicking the toggle to reply as she did so. "On my way, Doctor."

Caimile greeted her with a nod as she walked back through the door of the cryobay; a huge, hangar-like room right in the belly of the ship, with rows upon rows of units stretching off into the distance. Those set to wake up first, like her, the doctor and the rest of her crew, were positioned at the front of the lines, nearest the door. The rest of the colonists were carefully arranged in groups, their cryopods on tracks for ease of movement, ready for waking when their time came.

"I've staggered them slightly, so I can get them all into the med unit in turn. Liu is first."

Nina crossed to the table she was indicating and saw her First Officer going through the last stages of waking from the enforced sleep. She stood back as Caimile stepped forwards, enough to be out of her way but still obviously visible should Liu look for her. She could tell the moment he woke fully from the way his whole body tensed, even before his eyes snapped open.

"Are you all going to do this?" the doctor asked, exasperated, as she pressed firmly down on the man's shoulders to stop him from sitting up too fast. "Lie back down; you need to take it slowly."

Nina let out an amused snort. "We are soldiers," she pointed out. "At ease, Liu," she added, raising her voice so the still prone man could hear her. "There's no rush."

His eyes found hers and he relaxed as he took in her casual stance. After a moment, Caimile released him and he sat up slowly, swinging his legs over the edge. He looked smaller than she remembered, having spent fifty years unable to look after the muscles he had worked so hard to maintain before going to sleep. Liu was relatively short, but made up for what he viewed as a deficiency by looking after himself meticulously and keeping himself in prime physical and mental condition. Nina had known him for years and trusted him implicitly, both on and off duty. He grinned up at her and she smiled back, more relieved than she cared to admit to have him awake again.

"How're we doing, Captain?" he asked, rotating his wrists in front of him.

"All according to plan so far," she returned. "Now go get in the med unit, I'll debrief everyone together."

He nodded and hopped off the table and she turned her attention to the next pod.

They went through the same drill seven more times until the rest of the team had been woken and checked over. Things progressed without a hiccup until Ramin Chaudhary, the Quartermaster, woke up, and exclaimed loudly that he couldn't move his legs. The newly woken Nurse Taylor, a young attractive black American man, came rushing to his side in a panic, only to see Chaudhary grinning broadly as he pulled himself into a sitting position.

"That wasn't funny," reprimanded Dr Caimile, as she helped Chaudhary into his wheelchair. "He's only just woken up himself;, he could have done serious damage rushing over here."

"Sorry, Nurse," Chaudhary said sheepishly. "But it was too good an opportunity to pass up."

"What do you bet he planned that one even before he went to sleep?" Caimile muttered aside to Nina, as a still uncertain Taylor accompanied Chaudhary to the med unit.

"Oh, without a doubt."

When everyone was finally awake, and the medical assessments were done, the doctor pronounced everyone fit for duty. At last, Nina stood proudly in front of her crew. The mission was a global effort, so Nina had been lucky enough to take her pick of the people she wanted from all over the world. They were all specialists, experts in their field and chosen with care to form a cohesive team and avoid clashes in personality. They looked ready for action, smartly dressed in their military uniforms; grey jumpsuits with the orange logo of the United Earth Space Force embroidered on the top left pocket, black undershirts and black boots. They were all slightly paler and thinner than they had been, but otherwise unchanged. She smiled at them and took a breath.

"Welcome back, everyone. It's been fifty-three years since we left Earth, and we're a week away from our destination. So far it seems everything has gone according to plan. The ship's log has recorded the release of all the planned communications satellites, and we've been getting regular updates from Earth. Kjeldsen, I'd like you to take a look over those, please."

The Communications Officer, a tall young Dane with their blond hair combed neatly out of their dark eyes, nodded.

Nina turned her gaze to her chief engineer; an elegant Russian woman with a knack for machinery she'd never seen matched in anyone else. "Pavluhkin, I'd like you to check the status of the ship. We're arriving in a week, which means if there's anything that needs fixing, we need to do it now. Everyone else, stick to normal routine until we know what we're dealing with. Liu, with me. Dismissed."

The crew saluted and left the cryobay, leaving Nina and Liu alone amongst the sleepers.

"How're you feeling, Dan?"

Liu grinned at her. "Surprisingly okay, thanks. How about you?"

"A bit achy, but alright. I want you to keep a close eye on everyone in the next few days. I'm sure the doctor will be doing so as well, but it might just take everyone a while to adjust to the fact that so much time has passed and I don't want anyone to slip through the cracks."

"Of course, Captain." Liu nodded his agreement. "It is kind of weird to think of everyone back home being older, isn't it?"

"That's exactly the kind of thing I mean. Some people may deal with that knowledge better than others and I don't want anyone suffering in silence."

"I suppose it depends on what they left behind," Liu mused, his eyes roving over the endless lines of cryounits. Nina squeezed his shoulder in sympathy; she knew that Liu himself had nobody in particular to regret leaving, following the recent death of his father, but that in itself was a form of regret. Nina had no family left either; both parents had passed away years ago and she had been an only child. The military had been her family for a long time now.

"Come on, let's get to the bridge and start going through it."

All the other bridge stations were occupied when they reached it a few moments later and Nina slipped into her chair as the pilot, a young Maori woman in her twenties named Samantha Fraser, announced the customary "Captain on the bridge" from her position at the helm.

"Carry on," Nina responded, waving her hand in a gesture of dismissal. She loaded up the document listing the protocols on preparing for arrival at their destination and absorbed herself in that, making sure she was as familiar as she could be with what was to come. She lost track of time until a gentle cough jolted her out of her work and she noticed Kjeldsen, the Communications Officer, in front of her. "Yes, what is it?"

The young blond fidgeted and Nina, looking closer, saw that they looked noticeably distressed. "Alright, let's take this somewhere else," she said, standing. "Liu, you have the bridge." She gestured for Kjeldsen to precede her towards the doors, then ushered them into the small meeting room adjacent. "Okay Kjeldsen, I'm listening. What's up?"

"It's Earth, ma'am."

Nina took a sharp intake of breath, cursing herself for not reading the reports from Earth earlier when she had had the chance. "What's happened to it?"

Kjeldsen shook their head, tears shining in their eyes. "It's in a bad way, ma'am. I've gone through all the communications from Earth, and to start with, they were as expected. They hung on for about ten years after we left. But after that, the entries are different. Both polar ice caps have completely melted and ninety percent of the previous landmass is now underwater. There have been riots, uprisings, coups; even wars. There were some big nuclear blasts when people started placing the blame. They estimate the remaining population is around ten million people."

"Christ." Nina exhaled, turning away. "Did they manage to get any more ships off?"

Kjeldsen nodded, but their face remained grave. "Ten. The situation escalated too quickly for any more to be organised. We can expect two here, one in thirty years, one in twenty-five. From what I've gathered, they've been sent with a lot less equipment than we have, too. They just didn't have the preparation time."

"We don't need to worry about that yet," Nina said firmly. "We'll bear it in mind, certainly, but if we've got twenty-five years before they arrive that's more than enough time to get this planet up and running first." She sighed. "I'm sorry you had to go through all that. If I'd known, I'd have tried to spare you."

Kjeldsen squared their shoulders and looked her in the eye. "With all due respect, Captain, it's my job."

Nina nodded, impressed by Kjeldsen's professionalism. She didn't know much about the young Dane; she had worked with them on one previous mission and remembered them as being calm, capable and in control, but this was beyond what they had dealt with in that job. Christ, it was more than any of them had ever dealt with. "You're right. Would you please make me up a report that I can deliver to the rest of the crew? I'd like them to hear it from me."

"Of course, Captain. I'll get right on it."

She nodded and they saluted, leaving her alone in the dingy grey room. When she heard the doors close behind them, she sagged, finding the back of the nearest chair and leaning on it for support. Ten million people left on a planet that had held billions. Ten thousand more on each colony ship, of which there were now fifteen. She struggled for a moment, unable to comprehend the destruction of her species on such a large scale and grateful for the chance to deal with the information in private before she had to present a brave face to her crew. She remained a few minutes longer in the meeting room, composing herself before returning to the bridge. Liu met her eye with a worried gaze and she shook her head.

"Not yet."

He turned aside, knowing her better than to push her before she was ready, and she attempted to return her attention to her preparations. Two hours before the day's shift was due to finish, Kjeldsen handed Nina their report. She read it thoroughly, impressed with the concise nature of their work and feeling more prepared to break to the news to the crew.

Due to the automated nature of the ship, it wasn't necessary to keep a watch at all times, so the crew ate together in the mess. It was Monique Leclerc, the Chief Science Officer's turn to cook first, and the galley buzzed with energy as the crew chatted, getting to know each other and praising Leclerc for her culinary prowess. Leclerc was a round brunette with a razor-sharp mind and she had prepared a simple pasta dish with the same attention to detail that she gave her work.

"I'm afraid I have some bad news," Nina announced after the plates had been cleared. She stood, walking up to the head of the table so she could watch their reactions as she delivered Kjeldsen's report. One by one, their faces fell and she watched as they cycled through shock, denial, anger and too many other emotions to name. She gave them a moment to process the information before she straightened her shoulders and continued.

"This news only serves to strengthen the purpose we have here. Our mission to this planet is now more important than ever. We hold a wide range of people in our ship and our job now is to give humans a new home, one we can continue to develop the best of humanity on. When we arrive, we begin again, and this time, we build to last. Humanity will go on and we are the ones who will make it so."

Liu raised his glass. "Hear, hear."

There was a murmur of agreement from around the table as everyone imitated him. Tears shone in more than one pair of eyes but the atmosphere around the table had changed, and the crew had gone from defeated to determined.

"Let's call it a night, then, and I'll see you all in the morning." Nina nodded at the table in general, making eye contact with a few people and striding swiftly from the room. She knew they'd want to discuss the news she'd just imparted and Kjeldsen would be glad of the opportunity to recount the information too. It was better for everyone if she left them to get on with it while she went and got some sleep while she could.

The next few days passed swiftly, with a sense of nervous anticipation running underneath everything the crew did. Although some of them had worked together in other positions before, they were a new team and Nina was pleased with how well everyone fit together. She had taken extra care with her crew appointments, knowing it was essentially a position for life, and had been pleased that all but one of her first choices had accepted the posts.

As they neared their new home, she found herself planning almost constantly. Leclerc had been scanning the planet since they had woken up and had been able to put together some information about it, which she was adding to all the time as they got closer. It had three large continents and one smaller one, with a similar ratio of landmass to oceans as on Earth in the previous century. The atmosphere was as they had predicted, suitable for sustaining life and with a variety of weather conditions across the continents. The topography would have to be studied in more detail when they arrived, but from what they could tell at this distance, it seemed there would be a number of locations suitable to start settlements.

On the sixth morning after they had woken up, Nina took her position on the bridge as usual, her nerves jangling. She noted the presence of the entire crew, rather than just those with workstations there, and smiled to herself; she obviously wasn't the only one excited about this. Her heart pumped faster as she thought about what they were about to do.

"Alright, everybody ready?" She scanned the room, noticing the grins on the faces of almost everyone there. "Fraser, begin planetary approach procedures and take us into a high orbit."

"Aye, ma'am," the pilot responded, and Nina felt the thrum through the decks as the ship began firing braking engines to slow them down.

As the ship slowed, their destination finally became visible through the front viewport, slowly growing from amongst the stars surrounding it until it filled the screen. It was not unlike Earth, with a mixture of blues and greens shrouded in wreaths of white cloud, but the arrangement of shapes was different and filled Nina with an odd mixture of excitement and nostalgia.

"Ooh, shiny," Liu muttered from his seat to her right, quietly enough that only she could hear him. She threw him a glance and returned his grin. After what felt like hours, Fraser relaxed and turned to face her.

"Approach complete, Captain. We're in orbit." Her massive smile belied the formality of her words and Nina couldn't blame her.

"Excellent work. Welcome to your new home, everyone." There was a round of applause, with some whoops and cheering. "Now let's get out there and start exploring."

Chapter Two

Several hours later, the exploratory shuttle headed out on its first trip. Despite having an entire week to prepare, Pavluhkin had insisted on giving it one final check over before it left the ship. Eventually though, even the meticulous Russian woman was satisfied and gave her permission for the shuttle to leave. Crewing it were Liu, Fraser, Leclerc and Nanako Sakamoto, the Chief Security Officer, with Taylor along just in case.

"Expecting trouble, Captain?" Sakamoto asked with a grin as she geared up. She was a stocky woman with a jovial manner and long hair that she kept back in two tight braids while on duty.

"You know the regs," Nina responded, watching the shorter woman strapping a knife to her leg.

"I do. And I agree. No telling what we might meet down there." She handed a knife to a slightly startled Taylor, who attached it to his belt with his emergency medical kit. "Don't look at me like that, what if you're the only one left standing after an attack by some terrifying local predator?"

"Then we're all in deep shit," Fraser called from across the room, and everyone laughed. Taylor mimed throwing the knife at her head and Nina intervened.

"Okay folks, let's focus for a minute here. You're taking the shuttle down for a preliminary survey, to investigate two of the possible landing sites we've identified. You know what you're looking for. I know you're all excited but I don't want anyone taking any unnecessary risks; nobody goes anywhere alone and you err on the side of caution at all times. I'd rather still be scouting in a month than someone get hurt because we took things too fast."

"Understood, Captain." Liu nodded, and the others all followed suit.

"Alright then. Happy hunting."

They filed into the shuttle and Nina returned to the bridge, where Pavluhkin was monitoring the shuttle and Kjeldsen was keeping an eye on their comms. Nina again noted the presence of certain crew members who didn't strictly need to be there, but she understood their desire to be involved and instructed Kjeldsen to play any audio communications out loud. The shuttle entered the atmosphere with very little fuss and Nina relaxed minutely as they touched down at the first of the potential landing sites. Leclerc sent out nodules to take samples of the air and analyse it, reporting back before long to describe a slightly cleaner version of the atmosphere on Earth.

"Okay, Liu checking in!" came the cheerful voice of her First Officer, followed shortly by those of the rest of the landing party as they activated their headsets and prepared to exit the shuttle. "Landing party all standing by and we're opening the hatch." The hissing of hydraulics came over the channel, followed by gasps of appreciation from the entire party.

"Ooh, it's pretty!"

Nina chuckled; the very unscientific assessment had come from Taylor.

"It sure is," agreed Liu. "Okay, Leclerc, you stick with Sakamoto; Fraser, Taylor, you're with me. Record everything you see."

Nina saw five video feeds activate on Kjeldsen's console, and couldn't resist moving to stand behind them for a glimpse. All five feeds currently showed the same picture: a cloudless sky above a large expanse of shrub-like vegetation, with several small trees dotted about. Mountains were visible in the far distance but as far as the eye could see in front of them the ground was covered with brownish-orange plants, mostly growing no higher than waist height. Several species of larger plant were covered in what looked like flowers of many different colours, and a gentle breeze caused some of the taller vegetation to sway slowly. Here and there, what looked like birds fluttered in and out of the bushes and the occasional unrecognisable chirrup was audible.

Taylor was right; it was pretty.

Nina asked Kjeldsen to mirror their console onto the large screen at the front so everyone could watch without cramming in behind them.

Soon the feeds were full of first-person views of the team taking samples, scanning the horizon and other activity. Nina and Leclerc had decided on a location a few miles north of a large river, on what Leclerc had dubbed 'the third continent' for their first outing, on the basis that the flattish plains would be an easy spot to build on. Liu took Fraser and Taylor for a walk while Leclerc stayed closer to the parked shuttle, testing everything she could get her hands on and taking more samples than she could carry. Only Sakamoto's feed remained somewhat static and Nina could tell she was still on highest alert, waiting and watching.

After a couple of hours, during which time Nina had retaken her seat and the others had drifted back to their duties, Liu returned with his half of the team. After a brief conference with Leclerc, they agreed to pack up for the time being and move on. They set up a number of cameras to monitor the site, then climbed back into the shuttle. Nina had a moment's view of the backs of everyone's heads before Kjeldsen tactfully suggested they deactivate their video feeds for the duration of the flight. The shuttle lifted off smoothly and Fraser set a course for their next destination.

"Initial thoughts, Monique?" Nina asked once the shuttle had gained cruising altitude.

"Mostly positive, Captain, though hard to tell at this stage," responded Leclerc. "Nothing obviously wrong, looked like there was a good range of flora and fauna. That's about all I can give you until I've analysed these samples."

"Understood. Anyone else have any thoughts?"

"It was nice and warm—I liked it!" piped up Fraser, after a pause.

"It *did* seem a good temperature for farming," agreed Taylor hesitantly. "Not so hot that crops won't grow, but pretty comfortable."

Nina knew from Dr Caimile that the young man had grown up on a farm in rural Oklahoma, so was more than happy to hear his opinions on the subject.

"Good to hear, Taylor. I appreciate the input." She grinned to herself at the silence that followed, imagining him blushing and looking at his knees as she had noticed him do on other occasions after receiving unexpected praise. After a moment, she heard Liu clearing his throat.

"Great. So first impressions favourable all round?" There was a murmur of agreement, but Sakamoto raised her voice.

"I don't know, it felt a bit too warm to me," she commented warily.

"It was fairly humid," agreed Leclerc, "and remember, we don't know what season we're currently in. We won't know what we're dealing with until I get a chance to look in more detail at everything we found."

There was a pause while everyone digested this, then Liu spoke up. "Okay. What's next, Leclerc?"

"Landing site number two is in a large bay on the first continent. It's a bit further north, so I'm expecting it to be a little colder, but it'll be interesting to find out how different it is."

"Arriving at the coordinates now," Fraser chipped in, and the conversation petered out as they landed. Nina listened eagerly as the same procedures were followed as before, and the crew opened the shuttle doors and gasped for the second time that day.

"Well?" she prompted, when no information was immediately forthcoming.

"It's *gorgeous*, Captain!" breathed Sakamoto.

Nina exchanged a surprised glance with Dr Caimile, loitering next to Nina's chair.

"Well, don't keep us waiting. Let's see it!" Caimile demanded, and Nina hid her laugh.

After a moment, Kjeldsen's console flickered to life again and the small group already surrounding it eagerly let out an "Oooh!" as one. The shuttle had landed slightly inland, on top of what looked to be a small cliff, giving them a fantastic view of the curve of the bay as it swept around to the north-east. Black sand sloped gently down to the sparkling sea, which looked closer to green than blue as it lapped lazily at the shore. Cliffs sheltered the bay on both sides, leaving a gap of several miles of unbroken beach in between. Beyond the sand, they could see vegetation made up of similar colours to that on the third continent. What looked like a small copse stood a way off to the north, and to the west the ground sloped gently upwards towards some low hills. She could hear more birdsong here, though she couldn't see any movement, and what might have been a hum of insects working in the vegetation.

"Let's get stuck in, folks!" Nina heard Liu say over the comm and the view-screens split again as the teams moved off to investigate. Liu took Taylor and Fraser down to the sea and the younger two took samples of the water and sand while he kept watch.

"Volcanic, do we think?" Nina addressed the team as they worked. Fraser's feed showed an extreme close up of the sand as she gathered a sample to take back, and it reminded Nina of the beaches she had visited in the Canary Islands once with her family.

"Yes Captain," responded Leclerc, as she dug a small hole next to a bush. "According to my scans, that whole mountain range used to be active volcanoes, though most of them are extinct now."

"Most?" pitched in Taylor, his voice higher than normal.

"One or two are dormant still. Nothing is active right now, if that's what you're worried about."

Back on the ship, Chaudhary turned to Nina. "Surely that's an instant 'No!' to this site if there are volcanoes nearby?"

"Not necessarily," countered Caimile, turning what Nina privately termed her 'stern physician look' on him. "There were plenty of civilisations on Earth that prospered in close proximity to volcanoes."

"Yeah, like Pompeii," Chaudhary muttered under his breath.

Nina chuckled. "Don't be so dramatic, Ramin. You know perfectly well the early warning systems we have now are advanced enough to mean there's virtually no risk to human life by living close to a volcano. And the soil is great for farming. Very fertile."

"I agree, Captain," came Leclerc's voice, as her viewscreen filled with a close up of her gloved hand holding up a vial of earth. "This looks better than at the other site and the range of wildlife here is far greater. I'll obviously need to do a lot more analysis but so far this one has my vote."

"Mine too!" chimed in Fraser, who looked to be right down by the water's edge. "Can I paddle?"

"No!" shouted Nina, alarmed, at the same time as several other people. She heard Fraser snicker and relaxed, even as Liu's screen filled with her smiling face.

"Spoilsports," she pouted, still grinning.

"Okay team, let's wrap it up. Set up your cameras and get yourselves back here before sundown," Nina ordered, noticing the disc of gold starting to dip towards the horizon on Sakamoto's feed. There were murmurs of "Aye, Captain" as the team set about their final task of the day, before piling back into the shuttle.

The return journey was a lot quieter than the trip out; barely two words were said as the adrenaline wore off and the team started to droop. Nina packed Chaudhary off to the galley to start preparing the evening meal and oversaw the safe docking of the shuttle before heading down to greet the travellers.

"Nice work everyone. Grab a shower and we'll do an informal debrief over dinner; I'm sure the rest of the crew are just as curious as I am."

Weary smiles greeted her statement as the team stripped off their expedition gear, handing their weapons back to Sakamoto and gradually dispersing to their respective quarters.

"Anything to tell me, Dan?" Nina asked her First Officer quietly, once all the others had left.

Liu shook his head. "Don't think so, Captain. Everything seemed as it should do. Nothing shady or off colour, just a bunch of plants and insects going about their business. Looked pretty good to me."

Nina nodded, satisfied. "Great. You go clean up and you can tell me all about it over dinner."

Dinner that night was a lively affair. Revived by the shower and the flawless meal cooked by the quartermaster, the team recounted the minutiae of their first mission to the planet's surface.

"It was the weirdest thing I've ever seen!" Fraser enthused, waving her arms around with her mouth full of food.

"What, Chaudhary's cooking?" Dr Caimile smirked, and they all laughed. Chaudhary threw a bread roll at her and she grinned, unrepentant.

"No, seriously," Taylor said. "It was like, logically, we know it's a different planet. But it didn't look that different."

"Except that it did," interrupted Fraser.

"The little things," agreed Taylor, nodding.

"Like the shapes of the leaves on the bushes were all wrong, and the sea wasn't quite the right colour."

"And the sounds!"

"And smells!"

"It was just…"

"Weird!" they finished in unison, and everyone laughed again.

Nina turned to Leclerc, grinning. "Monique, anything more scientific to add to that analysis?"

The scientist shook her head emphatically as she swallowed, almost choking in her haste. "Not yet. I'll have results tomorrow, come down and see me then. I'm excited though, I can tell you that."

"We can tell," remarked Chaudhary drily, looking at Leclerc's wide eyes and slightly frantic demeanour.

"The second site was lovely," chipped in Sakamoto. "I could live on either of them, though I prefer the temperature at the second."

"Me too," agreed Liu. "I'm glad we haven't ended up with no choice but to live somewhere frosty; fur doesn't suit me."

"You never know, this could be the height of summer and the rest of the year might be freezing," pointed out Pavluhkin, waggling her eyebrows.

Chaudhary glared at her. "Thanks for that," he groused and they both laughed.

Nina helped herself to another roll and watched her crew interacting. It was still early days and some of the team had only known each other for a week, but she felt like they were a good mix. The louder personalities like Fraser and Chaudhary were nicely balanced out by the quieter types and everyone had a real passion for their specialism. The camaraderie was already evident and Nina enjoyed the banter as the meal continued.

"Just one more thing before we all go to bed," Nina announced, after the last plate had been scraped clean. "I'm going to start thinking about when we wake up the Union leaders." Several people looked as if they were about to ask questions and she held up a hand to stop them. "I know it seems early. But they're important people in the community we're building and we need to make sure the location we choose works well for everyone. There's no sense in getting our hearts set on somewhere if it's not going to be possible to farm there, for example. I want to get a bit more exploration done first, then when we've got some concrete information to offer them, we'll think about starting to get them involved."

"Where will they sleep?" queried Sakamoto.

Nina permitted herself a wry grin. "Good question. We have a few quarters left onboard and could make more space if some of you didn't mind doubling up." Out of the corner of her eye, she noticed Taylor and Fraser shoot a glance at each other, and made a mental note to ask Liu about it later. "But my intention is, after a few nights of observation, we'll start setting up a preliminary base at one of the locations. We can send a few people down and start setting up some basic dwellings to see if it would actually make sense to build there."

There was a moment of silence, then Chaudhary snorted. "So what you're saying is, we're guinea pigs and we're going camping?"

Nina grinned. "I hope you remember your Scout training." Chaudhary afforded her a sloppy salute and everyone laughed. "Let's get some rest. See you all tomorrow." She stopped Liu on his way past. "Got the energy for a quick drink before bed?"

He smiled and nodded. "Sure thing, Captain."

They helped themselves to a small glass of military brandy each, which was drinkable even if not completely enjoyable, then went to sit at the far end of the galley. Away from the dining table and the cooking equipment was a small grouping of more comfortable chairs, arranged around several side tables and one larger coffee table. The ship had been designed to accommodate a small number of people living on it for some time; it had two sections, and when they eventually separated from the sleeper section, the main part of the ship was intended to be used for further exploration.

This room served as common room as well as kitchen; the shelves at the side of the room held a limited selection of books and games, with space for additions by crew members, and there were cheerful, if abstract, pictures on the walls. Nina chose a pair of bulbous armchairs in the corner and sank into the faded orange one, leaving Liu to take the green one next to her. They clinked glasses, then Liu settled back into his chair.

"So, what do you want to know?"

Nina wasn't surprised that he knew exactly why she'd asked him to stay behind. They had climbed the ranks together; he had been her first choice of First Officer for ten years now and she had often wondered why he didn't aim for promotion and his own ship. Now, though, she was glad he'd never moved on. She grinned.

"It's like you've met me before. I don't know, what is there you think I'd like to know?"

Liu frowned, thinking. "Hmm, where to start." He took another swallow of his drink. "Crew seems in good shape. You did a good job picking them—no obvious oddities that'll rub against the others. Chaudhary likes a joke but hopefully by the time they get old, we'll have enough other company to dilute them a bit." Nina nodded and he continued. "The young'uns all seem good, if a little excitable." He snorted. "Especially Fraser. But then, a bit of natural youthful exuberance will probably do us all good."

Nina laughed, then sobered. "I'm not sure excitable is the word I'd use to describe Kjeldsen."

Liu frowned again. "No. But then, they're probably still shaken from the news about Earth."

Nina nodded. "I think we all are, but let's keep an extra eye on them, just in case. They're very professional, I like them." She paused, then changed tack. "Did you pick up on any... interesting vibes between Taylor and Fraser?"

Liu raised his eyebrows. "Interesting in what way? They seem to be getting on very well, if that's what you mean. There was a lot of banter planet-side. But I think that's just her personality, rather than being aimed particularly at him."

"I thought I noticed something over dinner. But it might have been nothing. And after all, we *are* building new lives here, so if they do like each other then I'm all for it. I'd just rather they kept it in their pants until we've got slightly more breathing room."

Liu laughed out loud. "Seconded."

Nina refilled their glasses, and for a moment they sat in silence.

"I like Sakamoto. But then, I always have done," said Liu.

Nina nodded in agreement. "She knows her stuff. I'm glad we got her on board. I've known her almost as long as I've known you and Dr Caimile. I trust her as much, too."

Liu smiled. "I'll take that as a compliment. Leclerc seems very competent as well. Haven't had much contact with Pavluhkin, but no warning signs so far. I like that everyone is taking their job seriously, even when there isn't much to do."

"That's one of the reasons I picked you all. I need a team behind me that can do what needs to be done, no matter whether that's dangerous and exciting, or boring but necessary."

Liu laughed again and stretched. "Pretty sure I know which category the next few days are going to fall into," he grumbled, standing up and twisting his back. His spine clicked and Nina winced.

"You do know how bad for you that is, right?"

He grinned back. "I know, but it feels so good!"

Nina chuckled, getting to her feet as well. "Thanks for doing the rundown with me tonight, Dan. I'll see you tomorrow."

Liu clasped her shoulder as he left. "Night, Nina. Try to get some sleep."

Chapter Three

Nina woke abruptly the next morning, the insistent beeping of her alarm eventually piercing her dreams at a volume that told her it had been going off for a while. Her mind had taken a long time to quiet enough to fall asleep, with constant jobs lists and questions running through her brain and stopping her from dropping off. She found Liu staring blankly into a large coffee in the galley and guessed he'd had the same problem. Ordering the same from the drinks machine, she joined him.

"You look like I feel," she quipped.

Liu grimaced. "I have ten minutes of notes playback. They start making less sense as you get to the end."

Nina laughed and sipped her coffee. The ships' brews had come on a lot since she had first joined up and now they were almost recognisable as the drink she used to enjoy out of a cafetière at home. Still, she'd like to plant some real coffee plants sooner rather than later. Biology permitting, of course.

As they gradually caffeinated themselves to awareness, Nina working through a bowl of porridge and Dan shovelling protein supplements into his mouth, the rest of the crew started to filter in. They looked bright and excited, full of the joys of exploration and free from the burdens of command. Nina envied them slightly, but got over herself quickly; she wouldn't trade the opportunity to be leading this mission for anything. Once everyone had gathered, Nina raised her voice. She had decided early on to keep things casual with such a small crew and the formal morning debrief had been replaced with a much simpler catch-up after breakfast in the galley.

"Good morning everyone!" She waited until the last of the chatter had died down before continuing. "Today is going to be very busy for some of you and less so for others. First priority is to get those samples analysed, so anyone with any relevant experience report to Leclerc and let's see if we can speed that up at all. If anyone still finds themselves without a job, see if you can give Chaudhary a hand digging out the things we'll need to start setting up camp. Any questions?" A mixture of silence and head shakes answered her. "Alright then, dismissed."

Nina made her way to the bridge, where Pavluhkin was already at work, having somehow made it there before her. She made a mental note to check the schematics of the ship and make sure she wasn't taking longer routes than necessary; the corridors were already winding enough without adding extra length to her journeys. They were joined a moment later by Kjeldsen, who sat down at their station and tuned into the live feeds from the cameras the teams had left at the two sites. Most of the screens instantly filled with images—a turquoise sea, distant mountains, scrubby orange undergrowth—but the bottom left one was mostly obscured by a large dark blur. As Nina leaned forward in confusion, the shape moved, the image resolved and the blur turned into a very hairy nose. Nina leapt back, her heart hammering. Kjeldsen let out a small cry of surprise as they, too, jerked back from the screen.

Pavluhkin swung around on her chair. "What the...?"

A moment more and they both relaxed, laughing, as the creature moved back far enough to see properly. It was a small, shaggy, rodent-like creature, with a disproportionately large snout, floppy ears and thin, wiry legs. Pavluhkin, who had come round the console to see, shook her head at them, smiling slightly, and headed back to her station. Nina shared a look with Kjeldsen.

"Well that's a relief!" She sighed, and they nodded fervently.

"Although my brother won't agree. He hates rats."

"Your brother?" Nina queried.

Kjeldsen nodded. "He's one of the farmers on board. It's just the two of us so we wanted to stay together."

Nina squeezed their shoulder. "He'll be awake soon."

Kjeldsen grinned. "I know. I can't wait to tell him what he's missed. I'm considering ion storms and volcanic eruptions."

Nina laughed. "Poor chap. Just don't put one of those," she indicated the now blessedly rodent-free screen, "in his pod for him to wake up to." Kjeldsen laughed too, and Nina patted their shoulder once more before stepping back. "Send anything like that over to Leclerc to catalogue, but otherwise let's just keep an eye on things."

"Yes, Captain."

Nina spent a few minutes at her console, then popped down to Science. The lab was state of the art, or had been when they left, and was usually a quiet, serene space with glowing monitors and gently bleeping machinery. Today it was a hive of activity, with many of the crew there to help out. Leclerc was calmly supervising, a trait of hers Nina particularly admired. As she watched, Taylor approached with a list of results. Leclerc ran a quick eye over them and nodded.

"Good. Add that to the database please, and then if you wouldn't mind taking a look at the images Kjeldsen sent over, I'd appreciate it."

Taylor nodded. "Of course."

Leclerc saw Nina watching and beckoned her over to where she stood at the large central console. A selection of test tubes stood in a blue, glowing chamber in front of her and she kept one eye on the constantly scrolling readouts as she talked to Nina.

"Nothing unexpected so far, Captain. Soil and plant composition exactly what I'd expect, similar to what you'd find in the appropriate regions of Earth. The second of the sites is more fertile, comparable to somewhere around the Mediterranean—the first is hotter and drier, maybe more like the South-Central part of the USA."

"Explains why I felt so comfortable there." Taylor smiled over his shoulder as he scrolled through images.

"Quite," replied Leclerc, nodding. "There's a wide variety of plant life, with a little crossover between the two sites, conforming to all the rules of plant life on Earth. Everything is a little more on the orange side than we're used to, but to my mind, it's like having acers or something of that ilk as the dominant plant life. On more detailed investigation, the plants at the first site all seem adapted for growth in an environment where water is less readily available, whereas the ones by the sea aren't as site-specific and are probably found in more places. That fits in with the fact that we found a stream at the second site, but the nearest obvious water source at the first is the river to the south."

Leclerc paused, and tapped at her screen to bring up some charts. "The weather appears temperate at both, with no obvious signs of extreme heat or cold. I'd guess we're in Spring at the moment at both sites, with more constant temperatures year-round at the first and a bit more variation at the bay, mainly because it's more northerly. It might get pretty warm at both in the height of summer, but the bay was cooler than the plains and I think the sea breeze will help there too."

"The second site is sounding better so far," Nina commented, and Leclerc nodded in agreement.

"I haven't had much of a chance to look into wildlife yet, but we've already identified at least ten different species of birds, again with more variety at the second site. Many, many insects at both sites. Sakamoto is getting acquainted with those for us at the moment."

Nina looked in the direction Leclerc had indicated and saw Sakamoto, a frown wrinkling her forehead, peering at a console on the far side of the room. She crossed to have a look and saw two pictures of beetles, slightly blurry from extreme zooming, side by side on her screen. Sakamoto turned to her.

"What do you reckon, Captain? Two different species of beetle or the same species with slight variation between them? Male and female, maybe?"

Nina raised her hands in a gesture of surrender. She had taken only the minimum amount of biology required at school and since joining the military—first as an engineer, then in command—had had very little need to be reminded of what she had forgotten.

"I have no idea, I'm afraid. I am amazed at the hidden skills of everyone in this room!"

Leclerc, who had joined them, frowned over Sakamoto's shoulder.

"Different species, I think. See the shape of the pronotum on the one on the left?" She pointed and Sakamoto nodded, tapping at the console to file the new species. With a newfound respect for the surprising depths of her Chief of Security, Nina nodded to her and moved away. Leclerc followed, leaving Sakamoto to squint at two new pictures of what looked a bit like centipedes on her screen.

"Did you see the creature Kjeldsen and I had the misfortune to get introduced to this morning yet?" Nina asked.

"The rat-dog? Delightful." Leclerc wrinkled her nose, and Nina laughed.

"A very apt description."

"We've only catalogued a couple of types of mammal so far, that being one of them, but the cameras will pick up more as we go."

"I'm seriously impressed with the amount you've managed already," Nina remarked, and Leclerc smiled a genuine smile.

"It's one of the most exciting things I've ever worked on. Thank you for giving me this opportunity, Captain."

"I can't think of anyone else I'd trust to do it," Nina replied sincerely.

The next stop on her to-do list was the stores. Nina let herself into the apparently empty vestibule, wondering if it was worth giving Chaudhary a call. Moments later, however, the doors to the warehouse opened and the Quartermaster wheeled himself out. A lot of wheelchair users opted for fully motorised models these days, but Nina knew that Chaudhary preferred the old-fashioned, user propelled style as it helped him to keep in shape. She got a brief look at the vast, hangar-like room beyond before the doors slid shut behind him.

"Hey Captain," he greeted cheerily, flicking his head slightly to get his dark fringe out of his eyes. "What can I do for you?"

"I want to build the first temporary housing unit this week. Can you get me one ready?"

Chaudhary seemed unsurprised. "Of course. I've got the droids pulling a couple out now and we're prepping a temporary science station too. Thought it might be easier for Leclerc to do a lot of her work down there, rather than lugging everything back here all the time."

Nina nodded. "That's great, thank you. I imagine she'll still want to move between the two for quite a while, but no harm in getting something set up."

"Will you be wanting any of the garden kit out to get started on growing things?" Chaudhary asked.

Nina pondered for a minute. "Just the basics, for now, I think—nothing too specialised. We'll wait until we've woken up the farmers to start on that properly; no sense in wasting resources getting things wrong when we've got the experts on hand to do it right."

"Sounds good, Captain. Want to come see the housing units?"

Nina agreed and Chaudhary led the way back through the double doors towards the stores. She had been in here plenty of times during mission prep but it still amazed her just how much it contained. Officially named Cargo Bay One, the gigantic room had been nicknamed 'the stores' early on and as the entirely appropriate nickname was much quicker to say, it had stuck. The bay was lined with row upon row of shelves, starting with smaller, day to day objects like clothing, food, medical supplies and other necessities. As one progressed further into the stores, both the shelves and the objects got bigger. They passed crate after crate of household supplies, from crockery to curtains, in every colour available. Furniture was also prevalent, with boxes of flat packed beds, chairs and tables stacked to the ceiling.

Right down the other end, where Nina and Chaudhary were headed, was the big stuff. Prefab units designed to be housing, work areas and community spaces filled a huge area at the back of the stores. There were more doors here; two docking bays had been built to enable the droids to load units straight onto transports. Two droids were in action now; these ones were specifically built to work in the stores and were programmed to handle anything and everything stocked. As Nina watched, they finished positioning one of the smaller temporary housing units against the wall by the loading doors and headed back for another. Nina walked up to inspect it.

"Thanks Ramin, these'll be perfect," she said, running her hands over the hard-wearing yet light finish of the wall. The temporary units were built of a different material from those designed to be put in permanently; the composite they were made from was just as durable as the permanent dwellings but lighter, so they were easier to take up and down. This flexibility meant they were also slightly more expensive than the long-term units, so the number on board was small.

"Awesome," said Nina finally, stepping back. "I'll leave you to it. If you could pull out all the usual gear to go in there and check with Monique to see if there's anything she specifically wants that'd be great, but you seem to have things under control."

Chaudhary grinned as he wheeled back towards the entrance. "Always do, Captain."

Nina allowed herself to smile back. "I know. That's why you're here."

He laughed and she left.

The next day, while preparations continued for the start of work on the planet's surface, Nina gathered a small team to do some fly-bys of the planet. Fraser had put them in an orbit that took them in a criss-crossing pattern across the planet's surface so they could continue to gather information from above, but Nina thought it wise to take a closer look. Leclerc had agreed, pinpointing some areas that she particularly wanted to investigate, so at 10.00, Nina, Fraser and Leclerc gathered in the shuttle bay. Fraser took them out smoothly and Nina barely felt the motion of the shuttle as they descended to the heliopause. She couldn't take her eyes off the planet as they approached; watching it grow closer out of the front of the ship reminded her of her first views of Earth from space as a young trainee. Her stomach flipped pleasantly as she wondered about this new planet that they were soon going to call home.

Leclerc wanted to start at the poles, so Fraser piloted them neatly to the 'top' of the planet, where the northernmost tip of the largest continent extended far enough that it reached into the polar region. This continent had been dubbed 'Continent One' and was the one on which they were planning to start building. They flew slowly overhead, Fraser maintaining a height of about thirty thousand feet and trusting the incredibly high spec cameras on the shuttle to pick out the details for them. The ground looked dark, with very little vegetation, and the snow and ice extended southwards into the large expanses of land.

"Could be permafrost," Leclerc murmured, poring over the images. "We'd have to come back later in the year to find out."

"That sounds sensible," agreed Nina. "We can come back in a few months once we've learnt a bit more about the seasons and take some more readings then."

They continued over the area, Leclerc muttering to herself and Nina trying not to blink as her eyes ran over the constantly moving images on her screen. After a while, Leclerc sat up, seemingly satisfied.

"Okay, let's go south now."

Fraser obediently lifted them away from the surface, increasing her speed once they were at a safe height and dropping them back down when they were above the opposite polar region. If she had questions about Leclerc's methods, she kept them to herself and Nina was impressed by her focus and the slickness of her flying. She hadn't worked with Fraser before as she was a recent graduate, instead taking her on the recommendation of one of her tutors that Nina knew well. She was pleased to see that her friend's confidence in the young woman's skills hadn't been misplaced, and made a mental note to send her a message to say thank you. Her stomach lurched as she remembered the time jump, realising that the friend in question was probably dead by now. She swallowed and tamped the thought down.

The second largest of the continents, again imaginatively called 'Continent Two' for the time being, stretched almost all the way to the pole at this end of the planet. It was a long, fairly thin landmass and by the time the tip tapered to the southernmost point, it was hard to tell what was land and what was ice. Leclerc took what readings she could and agreed again that they would come back.

"It's not urgent for us to know," she conceded, "as we aren't planning on settling here. But further down the line, I would be very interested to find out more about the polar regions on this planet and how they compare to Earth."

"All in good time, Monique," Nina reassured her. "We will definitely be studying as much as we can about the entire planet, but for now, our main job is to find somewhere to settle and as much as I love a good snowball fight, this isn't high up on my list of contenders."

Fraser grinned and Leclerc showed a hint of a smile.

"I see your point, Captain. Let's continue up this continent while we're here, and then we'll go to the smallest one."

They continued up the enormous landmass, flying low over undulating plains, scrubby heathland and a huge desert.

"This actually looks pretty inhospitable," Nina commented, as they flew over great swathes of burnt orange nothingness.

Leclerc nodded. "Yes. Although I would like to investigate in more detail, at a later date of course. It's amazing how much life you do find in places like this, often adapted in fascinating ways to their environment."

Nina nodded, but privately preferred the heathland further south. It reminded her a little of rural England where she grew up and she smiled ruefully, nostalgic and unusually homesick.

Next they went to Continent Four, which reminded Nina of Madagascar, then headed towards Continent Three, the first one the team had visited. After logging the details of both, one humped and covered in rainforest, the other huge and divided down the middle by an enormous mountain range, they crossed back to Continent One. This one was far less regular in shape than some of the others, with a long, vertical, diagonal section and a curved, thicker part across the top, almost like the letter 'r' or a backwards seven. As they flew over, Leclerc pointed out their chosen spot for the base.

"See how sheltered it is? That accounts for the good weather we had there, despite it being further north than some of the other possible sites."

Nina looked and saw what she meant. The bay the team had visited was in the nook from which both angles protruded, like being safely in the continent's armpit. The top section of the continent curved around above it, protecting it from the large amount of open water to the east, and the diagonally sloping bottom section meandered down past it to the south. From above, it looked like an ideal spot to start a settlement. Further inland, the terrain varied between rolling hills, higher mountains and large, flat plateaus, and a number of lakes were scattered across it. From this high up, they looked like puddles. Right at the bottom, around the line of the equator, they encountered another stretch of desert similar to the one on Continent Two, leading Leclerc to speculate that the two had once been joined but had since broken apart. They certainly would have fitted together nicely, Nina thought, looking at the lines of both.

Continents all neatly catalogued, Leclerc suggested they do a quick fly-by of the oceans. Nina agreed, so Fraser set a course. They registered two separate archipelagos, and descended slightly to get a proper look. By the time they had finished, Nina's eyes were blurred from staring constantly at the rapidly moving images on her screen, but they had a much more complete picture of the overall geography of the planet and Leclerc was pleased with a good day's work.

The next few days continued in the same vein, with people focusing on their specialisms and working hard to prepare themselves for the next landing. The energy on the ship was almost palpable. Even though none of the crew remembered the years they'd lost to sleep, they were all glad to be back in action and there was a fresh, back-to-school atmosphere to the work. Leclerc had plenty of volunteers helping her out in the science lab; Nina was pleased to see Fraser especially broadening her knowledge and mucking in, and the analysis of the samples they brought back had been finished pleasingly quickly as a result. The maps they had gained from the fly-bys were mostly put aside for now, as the crew focused on the more immediate future, but had been added to the ever-growing database of information they had discovered about their new home.

The team seemed to be gelling well and Nina had come to enjoy the evening meals where everyone could kick back, relax and enjoy getting to know each other. Tonight was the fifth evening since they had arrived at the planet and Nina was finally confident that they were ready to start setting up on the surface. She cleared her throat to get everyone's attention and the crew looked up from their various conversations around the table.

"Sorry to talk shop so late—I just wanted to confirm that we're aiming to leave for the planet at 09.00 tomorrow morning, so make sure you get some rest tonight." Her eyes lingered on the younger members of the crew, who had stayed up late the last couple of nights chatting. Kjeldsen blushed, but Fraser met her eyes and nodded.

"Affirmative, Cap. We'll be ready."

"I have no doubt that you will be. See you all in the morning." She nodded in response as several of the company wished her goodnight, rising from her chair and hoping that she might, against all the odds, actually get some sleep tonight.

Chapter Four

"Captain on the bridge."

The formal greeting rang out as Nina stepped onto the bridge at 08.00 precisely the next morning, after a surprisingly restful eight whole hours of sleep. The bridge crew was assembled, excitement in their eyes and eagerness on their faces.

"Good morning." She took her seat and flipped the switch to call down to the shuttle bay. "Bridge to shuttle bay. Are you all there?"

Pavluhkin answered. "Yes Captain. We're ready to commence pre-flight checks when you are."

"Excellent. Get started, comm me when you're happy." Pavluhkin replied in the affirmative, and Nina turned to the bridge crew. "Just checking there haven't been any surprises overnight?"

Kjeldsen shook their head. "No, Captain. The usual small creatures have wandered past a few times, and there was some pretty heavy rain about 03.00, but nothing else remarkable."

Nina nodded, satisfied. "We'll be able to get a better idea of everything once we've got a base down there."

The next hour passed slowly. Nina resisted the urge to wander the bridge and peer over her colleagues' shoulders, knowing how irritating that would be. Instead, she reviewed the plan for the mission, double- and triple-checking details that she already knew by heart. Eventually, her comm chimed.

"Shuttle bay to the bridge. We're all fired up and ready to go." Everyone sprang to attention as Fraser's voice came through.

Nina grinned. "Music to our ears. You are cleared to launch; move out at your leisure."

"Copy that, Cap. Launching in 5, 4, 3, 2, 1..."

Everyone watched on the main view screen as the tiny shuttle launched itself out of the rear of the ship and started towards the planet. This first trip consisted of Fraser, Sakamoto, Pavluhkin and Chaudhary who, with the help of some of Chaudhary's droids, would commence construction on the first of the units. Once the shuttle had been unloaded, Fraser would return for Nina, Leclerc and Taylor, who had volunteered his services as a builder. Nina didn't blame him; she was itching to get out and stretch her legs and she didn't even have the disadvantage of Taylor's extreme height. Liu would stay on board with Dr Caimile, who hopefully wouldn't be needed, and Kjeldsen, who was monitoring from the ship. After a short trip, Fraser announced their safe landing and everyone on the bridge relaxed.

"Good work, team," Liu said from his spot by Nina. "Get started on the unloading and let's build ourselves a village!"

"Yes sir!" came the cheery response from the shuttle crew. Nina settled back in her seat, prepared for a good few hours of watching the feed before her turn came.

"Coffee?"

A heavenly aroma wafted over Nina's shoulder, and she turned to see Dr Caimile standing with a large pot and a number of cups on a tray.

"Have I told you recently how much I like you?"

Caimile grinned. "Not in detail. Do expound." She poured Nina a cup and Nina sighed, inhaling the fumes. The doctor had a secret recipe that she usually reserved for special occasions; Nina appreciated her breaking it out now.

"I'll put it on my to-do list."

Caimile laughed, moving around the bridge and handing out cups. For a while there was silence, as the crew sipped their drinks and watched the droids unloading. The general layout of the site had been agreed beforehand; one temporary science lab, flanked by two four-berth sleeper units. The sleepers each had a bathroom attached, a definite step up from some of the other military accommodations Nina had stayed in, and they all generated their own power from solar panels on the roof. The team on the ground worked efficiently and in less than two hours, the shuttle had been cleared of its cargo. Nina flicked the switch on her chair to broadcast shipwide.

"Taylor, Leclerc, we're up," she announced, standing and stretching. "The shuttle is about to head back up here for us, so let's get down to the bay. Leclerc, any last-minute additions you need a hand with?"

"I'm okay Captain; Taylor had the same thought and has turned up with a trolley. Apparently I'm predictable."

Nina laughed as the scientist's voice came over the comm. "Good to know. I'll meet you both at the shuttle."

Sure enough, as Nina rounded the corner to the shuttle bay, she heard a strange clanking sound. Leclerc and Taylor were approaching slowly from the other end of the corridor, pushing a trolley laden with various scientific apparatus Nina didn't know the names for. Taylor gave her a wry grin as they approached.

"If I'd known 'assistant to mad scientist' was going to be such a big part of this job, I might have reconsidered."

Leclerc jabbed him in the ribs. "Oh pooh. You're having a lovely time."

Nina laughed but was saved from replying by the doors to the bay chiming, announcing the completion of the recompression sequence. Nina swiped the panel and entered, biting back a laugh at the look of horror on Fraser's face as she noticed the extra gear.

"Don't tell me. This is all very important, very fragile and completely irreplaceable."

Before Nina could react, Leclerc reached out and picked up one of the test tubes, lifted it up to head height and then let go. The tube fell before Fraser's shocked gaze, bounced gently a couple of times then rolled to a stop at Nina's feet.

Leclerc bent to retrieve it. "No, I think they'll be okay. Just don't crash the shuttle." She pushed the trolley past Fraser towards the loading ramp. Nina followed her, partly to hide the fact she was fighting laughter, leaving the speechless Fraser to Taylor. When she got on board, Leclerc was strapping the trolley into the cargo storage at the rear.

"Was that strictly necessary?" she chided gently.

Leclerc smirked, straightening up. "Maybe not. But it was fun."

Nina sat next to her. "Go easy on her. She's only young, and this is her first proper mission."

Taylor and Fraser came up the ramp, Fraser looking slightly less wild-eyed than before.

"All set?" she asked.

Nina nodded, smiling in what she hoped was a reassuring manner. "Ready when you are."

Taylor took the passenger seat behind Nina, and Fraser settled in the pilot's chair. Nina watched as she took the shuttle through its initiation sequence with confident, practised hands.

"Fraser to the bridge. Shuttle ready for launch."

It was Liu who answered. "Copy that. You are clear for launch. Take her out."

"Yes, sir."

Nina felt the barest hint of movement as the shuttle lifted from the bay floor and proceeded slowly to the launch doors. Once they were clear, Fraser increased their speed and Nina again peered eagerly over her shoulder as the planet grew larger in front of them.

"Pretty, isn't she?" Fraser threw back, when she noticed Nina's attention.

"She sure is," Nina agreed.

"What are we going to call her?" asked Taylor, curiously. "And why is the planet female?"

They all laughed.

"Both good questions, Taylor," Nina replied.

They were flying low over the planet's surface now, fast approaching the landing site. Nina could see hills, or maybe mountains, in the distance, with the ground gently sloping from the foothills to the bay they had chosen. The shuttle slowed and Nina's heartbeat sped up. She pressed her face to her window as Fraser began the landing, stretching her eyes downwards to see as much as possible. She had spent so much time tied up in the details that she had almost forgotten what they were doing here, but now it all came rushing back; she was about to set foot for the first time on a new planet—their new home. The ground rushed up to meet them and Nina's stomach swooped. Her breath hitched as the shuttle bumped gently onto the earth, settling with a rumble.

By the time Fraser announced the landing was complete and they were free to unstrap, Nina was grinning from ear to ear. The team got to their feet and Leclerc, also grinning, gestured for Nina to precede her down the ramp. Nina squared her shoulders and stepped out of the shuttle, onto the surface of her new home planet.

Warm fresh air caressed her body, blowing her long brown hair gently about her face and tugging at the fabric of her uniform. It smelled clear and sweet, with a hint of salt coming off the sea. She didn't recognise any other smells and realised with a jolt that was because everything else was new to her. She turned slowly, running her eyes over the unrecognisable plants, the blurry hills in the distance, the black beach only a few metres away, and the wide sparkling sea continuing out to the horizon. She could hear the sound of the waves rushing up the shore and retreating again, the chirping of insects and the excited chatter of birds she didn't recognise.

"Beautiful," she breathed.

"Isn't it."

Nina turned. Sakamoto had joined her, and was standing next to her, facing out to sea in the same direction. Nina smiled and looked back out.

"It's hard to believe it's real, isn't it, after all this time."

The other woman nodded. "Maybe we're still asleep, and next thing we know, the doctor will be standing over us saying we're nearly there."

Nina snorted. She had never heard her say anything quite so whimsical. "Let's hope not. I'm not sure I want to start all over again now I'm here."

"I don't think they'd be best pleased either." Sakamoto jerked her head past the shuttle, in the direction Nina knew the first buildings were being put up.

"True." She turned to head over. "How are they getting on?"

Sakamoto fell into step beside her. "Good, actually. They've been working hard this morning." As she spoke, they rounded the shuttle and Nina's eyes fell on the first of the new buildings; Chaudhary was supervising a droid who was installing the ramp up to the door, but otherwise it looked complete.

Fraser and Taylor had immediately got stuck in and were helping Pavluhkin assemble the base for the second. It was standard procedure for all temporary units to be raised slightly off the ground, unknown wild animals and flooding being just two of the possible hazards this was designed to help protect against. These units had a strong alloy base, constructed of interconnecting sections that raised it to about a foot off the ground. Taylor was currently jacking up one section while Fraser held it still for him, and a droid was fixing the already assembled pieces together while two more moved the next pieces into position. Another droid drifted over and Nina's eyes swung back to the first unit, to see Chaudhary checking the ramp was secure by rolling himself down it freefall. She laughed and crossed to him.

"Sometimes I'm not completely convinced you take your job entirely seriously."

He turned puppy dog eyes on her with a hand over his heart. "Captain, you wound me."

"You know I'm only joking." She turned back to take in the rest of the site. "Actually, I'm very impressed."

He grinned. "Nippy little things, aren't they? And the droids aren't too bad either."

Nina laughed. "You've all done a good job. Have you eaten?"

Chaudhary shook his head. "We were waiting for you— please tell me you didn't forget to bring lunch."

Nina shook her head with a smile. "We've got sandwiches on the shuttle. Let's take a look in here and then grab some food." She was too curious not to have a quick look inside the first piece of her new settlement before eating and Chaudhary knew it. With a chuckle, he waved her up the ramp, so she led the way and entered the small building with anticipation.

It was slightly disappointing. As yet, it was just four walls, a floor and a roof. Nina berated herself for expecting anything more and moved to look out of a window. The first one she chose looked west, inland towards the hills, where long swathes of vegetation sloped gradually towards the distant peaks. She crossed the cabin to look out of the front and her breath caught. From here, the curve of the bay caught the eye at just the right angle, the black sand running round to the headland in one sweep. The waves rippled lazily, movement visible on the closer ones but fading to a white blur as they followed the shore around.

"Nice view," murmured Chaudhary, and she turned to smile at him.

"Very," she agreed.

They left the unit together, gathering the rest of the crew as they went and heading to where Leclerc had laid out an impromptu picnic with the supplies sent down from the ship.

The rest of the day passed quickly. With so many hands, both biological and mechanical, the other two buildings were finished well before sundown. The days were two hours shorter here than a standard Earth day and Nina had been concerned that the difference would cause them problems. However, with everybody pitching in, they had time to finish all three units, including hooking up the solar panels, getting the bathroom facilities working and most of the inside of the housing units prepped. There were a few last jobs to finish off, but the ground team were aiming to finish those after their evening meal. Nina looked around at them as she prepared to head back up to the ship with Fraser.

"It's going to be weird without you all at dinner tonight," Fraser laughed sadly, her eyes lingering on Taylor.

Nina agreed. "This is the first step of the next part of the operation. It won't be long before we're all dining down here together, but it will be strange for a while with the team based in two places. You should all be very proud; you're the first humans ever to spend a night on the surface of our new planet. Good luck, and don't forget to call us if you need anything."

The more military-minded amongst the team saluted as Nina, Chaudhary and Fraser turned to head back into the shuttle. The journey back to the ship passed quickly and in relative silence, and Liu met them as they disembarked.

"Welcome back. Excellent timing; Kjeldsen's just finished dinner."

Nina smiled wearily. "Wonderful. We'll be there right away."

Over dinner, Nina filled the rest of the crew in on what they had missed on the surface. Fraser helped, chiming in with cheerful observations on everything, which Nina appreciated. It had been a while since she'd done any manual labour and, even with the droids doing most of the work that involved taking any kind of load, it was a different sort of tired to what she was used to. Before she could let herself switch off totally though, she asked Kjeldsen to ring down to the surface for her. The call was answered at the other end by Pavluhkin.

"Go ahead, Captain." Everyone else around the table leaned forward to hear.

"Just checking in before we clock off here. How's it going down there?"

"Good, thank you. Leclerc and Sakamoto are just finishing up attaching the bunks to the walls. We've opted to all sleep in one this evening, as there's only four of us."

"Good thinking," Liu agreed. "We're all officially running to planetary time now, so we'll give you a call at 09.00 to check in."

"Although call at any time if you're in trouble!" Kjeldsen piped up.

"Seconded," said Nina firmly.

"Don't worry, Captain, I'll be screaming for help if we need it, you can be sure of that." That was Taylor, and Nina heard the rest of the surface team laughing.

"Alright then. Get some rest and we'll check in tomorrow. *Posterity* out."

They hung up. Liu had volunteered to be on call for the first night, for which Nina was exceedingly grateful after her day on the planet, so Nina said goodnight to the rest of the crew and headed to her cabin for some much-needed sleep.

Chapter Five

The first night was done. Nina woke early, intending to check in with Liu before the ground team were up, but instead found him in the galley with a cheerful Leclerc updating him over comms. Nina dropped into a seat next to him and he swivelled his notepad so she could see the screen. Usually ground-to-ship communications would be done through the ship's consoles, but after a night on watch, Nina didn't begrudge Liu the opportunity to take the call on his personal equipment from a comfy chair instead.

"Morning Captain!" Leclerc greeted her, livelier than Nina had ever seen her. "I know it's a bit early but we all woke up here so thought we'd check in with Liu so he can get some sleep."

"Much appreciated, I assure you," he mumbled blearily.

Nina nodded to him. "Go get some rest, Dan. I'll see you later." She patted him on the shoulder and he rose, shuffling towards his cabin in the manner of a man urgently in need of some sleep. Nina returned her attention to the screen. "So how'd it go?"

"Nothing of note, really. Sakamoto snores," (Nina heard a distant shout of 'Do not!' and a muffled snort) "but other than that, a fairly standard night. Sunrise was beautiful—we had coffee on the beach watching it and Taylor's just sorting breakfast now."

"Sounds idyllic. Don't get too settled though, we'll be down in an hour or so."

"Thanks, Captain. I don't know what we'd do without you."

Nina laughed and signed off. True to her word, the shuttle touched down on the planet just over an hour later. Today's mission was to investigate the sea; having such a promising potential site right by the coast was an unexpected boon, but if it turned out the sea was full of enormous predators that made their way onto land every night in search of dinner, that was going to be a problem. They stopped just long enough for the ground team to pile in before lifting off again and proceeding slowly out to sea. Fraser kept them low, at Leclerc's request, skimming neatly over the surface of the water. Every fifty metres, they paused to take a water sample and drop an aquatic communications module with sensors and a camera on.

Once they were a few kilometres out to sea they sped up, keeping their eyes out for anything odd even as the onboard cameras filmed everything. When nothing was immediately apparent after an hour or so, they turned back and headed towards the bay again.

"Hold it here," Leclerc commanded, when they were almost to the shore. Fraser slowed down, stopping them at a hover a metre over the water. Leclerc ran her fingers over her console and a sensor nodule lowered itself into the water from underneath the shuttle. "Excellent. Now open the hatch."

Fraser shot Nina an alarmed look. "Captain?"

Nina grinned. She had no idea what Leclerc was up to, but wasn't going to let Fraser know that. "You heard her. Open us up."

Fraser raised her eyebrows but complied, swinging back around to her console and entering the commands. The hatch hissed open, aquamarine water sparkling invitingly underneath them. Leclerc rummaged in a bag then pulled out what looked like a small bloody carcass. Smiling at the aghast faces of her colleagues, she removed it from its cooling chamber and held it aloft.

"Synthesised meat. If there's anything carnivorous like a shark in these waters, this should tempt it to show itself." She tossed the carcass out of the hatch and they watched as it sank slowly beneath the water. Leclerc turned to her monitors and almost immediately one of them started beeping. "Watch out, something's there."

Nina kept her eyes trained on the spot where the bait had disappeared and thought she saw a large shadow moving swiftly under the surface, but before she could be sure, the beeping had died away.

"Did you get it?" Taylor asked, looking anxiously away from the hatch.

Leclerc frowned. "We registered something. Whether we have enough information to work out what it was remains to be seen. For now, let's close up the hatch and head back to shore. Nobody goes swimming until we've worked out what that was."

"For sure," agreed Fraser fervently.

Once they were back on land, Leclerc headed straight into the newly furbished lab to get started on analysing the latest results. Since Nina's last visit, they had added a central console in the middle, workbenches around the edges and a number of chairs. A large amount of the equipment they had brought down was already set up, arranged on the workbenches in readiness for today. Nina was impressed with Leclerc's efficiency and watched as she crossed immediately to the central console to start work. The samples would be easy enough, but the modules they had planted would have to be part of a longer-term investigation; they would only show results when anything came close enough to register.

While Leclerc set up the instruments to look at the water samples, Nina dialled up the feed from a module dropped to a few metres below sea level and about 500 metres out, then watched curiously. There was plenty of movement, but Nina couldn't tell if it was from life-forms or just the water. After a moment, a fish swam past.

"There!" she exclaimed, and immediately felt foolish for doing so. The fish was remarkably unremarkable, maybe ten centimetres long and a light grey colour. The others all turned to look, and she pointed at the screen. "This one would fit in on Earth."

Leclerc nodded. "It turns out blueprints for life are surprisingly similar across the galaxy." They watched for a few more moments but the fish turned out to be the most exciting thing anyone would see all day.

Nina made sure she checked in personally with the team in the morning again, worried that Monique might have stayed up all night in her excitement. However, the call was answered by a bleary-eyed Taylor, who explained that they had all been up a little later than intended and Leclerc was still asleep. Nina wasn't sure whether they had been working or socialising and decided not to inquire.

"Don't forget to do some work while you're down there," Nina remarked as she signed off.

"Oh we won't. Leclerc has an itinerary for today that my mother would be proud of."

Nina laughed. "Keep in touch, then. We're going to start thinking in more detail about waking up some more people later on today, but we'll let you know before we action anything."

Taylor nodded and Nina signed off, grabbing herself a quick breakfast before making her way to the bridge. Kjeldsen was already there and Nina nodded to them before taking her station.

"Cancel the 09.00 call, I've already checked in this morning and all is well. If you could give them a buzz about lunchtime that'd be great, if only to remind them to take a break and eat something. I'm worried Leclerc will get so wrapped up in her investigations that food will take a backseat for a while."

Kjeldsen nodded. "Any updates for the weekly drop?"

Nina checked her wrist unit and raised her eyebrows. "Another week already? That went fast. How did I manage to lose track of the days again? Can you give me an hour to record something to send over?"

Kjeldsen nodded again and returned to their station. The ship filed a weekly report, sending it home via the array of communications satellites they had deployed periodically on the journey here. Theoretically it should take about a month for messages to reach Earth, but if they stuck rigidly to the schedule then at least the updates would be in real time, despite the lag. There was quite a lot to go in this one, but then Nina imagined there would be for some time to come. She made her way into the small office connected to the bridge and recorded as concise an analysis of the week as she could manage. Once she had finished and okayed Kjeldsen to make the drop, she went in search of Dr Caimile and found her, to her surprise, with Chaudhary in the stores.

"Good morning," Nina greeted them both. "Should I worry you two are up to something?"

The doctor faked affront. "Never. I was just checking with our good quartermaster about portable medical units. If we're getting to the stage where people are sleeping, exploring and working on the surface, I want something more comprehensive down there than that first aid kit Taylor's got strapped to his belt."

"Are you anticipating a lot of injuries?" Nina asked, worried.

Chaudhary raised his eyebrows. "You've got a bunch of keen young things bouncing around on a planet with unknown hazards. Captain, *I'm* anticipating a lot of injuries and I'm not even medically trained!"

"Good point. Youthful exuberance and alien planet could be a recipe for disaster," Nina agreed.

Caimile raised her hands. "I'm not expecting anyone to do anything stupid. They're all military trained, after all. But we know literally *nothing* about this planet. They could touch the wrong bush and go into anaphylactic shock."

"Thanks for that reassuring thought, Doc," Chaudhary muttered. "That's really going to help me relax when I'm next down there."

Caimile scrunched her face. "Sorry. But we don't want people relaxing, not yet. We want people alert and safe until we know what we're dealing with."

"Point taken. I'll dig a unit out and send it down the next time we're taking a shuttle."

"Thank you." Caimile turned to Nina. "Did you need me?"

"Yes, as a matter of fact. Let's take a walk."

They said their goodbyes to Chaudhary and left, Nina directing them in the direction of the cryobay.

"Aha. I see where we're going with this. You think it's time to wake up some more of our sleepers." The doors to the bay opened and Nina marvelled yet again at the sheer size of it; all those people packed tightly in, ready to wake up to a new life when the moment was right.

"Yes." Nina crossed to a wall unit and brought up a manifest. "The crew is all awake," she started, indicating the short list on the right-hand side of the screen. "Due up next are the rest of the colony leaders. I'd especially like the head farmers awake soon, but if we're waking them up, we might as well wake the others to avoid conflict later."

63

Caimile nodded sagely. "Nobody wants accusations of decisions that were made while they were sleeping coming back to bite us in the bum."

Nina shot her an amused look. "Precisely. No bum biting."

Caimile waggled her eyebrows. "Unless it's consensual, of course."

"Focus, Sarah!"

Caimile pouted and Nina tried not to laugh, glaring at her until she relented. "Okay, okay. Talk me through it."

Nina smiled once more before returning to her professional demeanour. Dr Caimile was a bit younger than Nina, a short curvy black woman with cropped hair that curled around her ears and lively, intelligent eyes. Some people thought she was abrupt but Nina found her manner refreshing, especially compared to some of the smooth-talking diplomats she had served with in the military. Caimile had trained with Liu and he had introduced her to Nina after they'd served together on their first mission. That was over twenty years ago now and she'd served with her on a number of occasions since then, as well as counting her among her best friends off duty. Nina had always found her attractive, and the thought had crossed her mind that once they were a bit more settled on this planet, there might be scope to explore things a bit further. But for now, they had a job to do.

"Right. We've got the Johnsons. They're in charge of farming; he does animals and she does arable." Nina swiped the screen as she talked, searching for and selecting the names off the seemingly endless scrolling column to the left and compiling a new box in the middle. "We want to get them involved as soon as possible to make sure we're getting started on the right foot." Caimile nodded, and Nina continued.

"Our head of construction is Mira Saeed. Again, it seems kind of obvious that we want her around to make sure we're doing things right." At Dr Caimile's nod, Nina added Mira's name to the box as well. "I'd say those are the essentials for what we're doing right now, but it makes sense to wake some of the others up too and I'd suggest at least the whole of the Union."

The Union was the group of people who had been elected by their various factions as the colony leaders, and would be the governing body of the colony for the foreseeable future. It was a small group, but the people on it had all been handpicked for their expertise in their field and their ability to work well with others. "So, we've got Nehemiah Lovell, who will run the school, and his husband Patrin; I'd rather wake them together, though I think it's better to wait a little longer before we wake their daughter up."

"He may have some very useful opinions on how we go about things—it's easy to forget to make allowances for children when there aren't any about. Definitely hold off on the little one for now though."

"Agreed," said Nina. "What do you think about Jerry?" she asked, naming the older Canadian who was due to be Caimile's partner in running the hospital.

Caimile waved her hand. "Oh, wake him up; he'll only grumble if we don't." Her dismissive words were belied by the affectionate smile on her face. "And he can actually be fairly useful when he puts his mind to it."

"A glowing recommendation indeed, coming from you," Nina remarked tartly as she tapped the screen.

"Oh hush," Caimile chided. "You know perfectly well I'm only nice to people I don't like."

Nina laughed as she brought up the final name on her list. "The last member of the Union is Saima Rayat, who is our arts representative."

Caimile frowned. "Really? It seems a bit early for that to me."

Nina grimaced. "I agree that there won't be much for her to do yet, but she is in the Union and if she's not included in the early conversations, it'll be harder for her to get involved later."

"I'm not sure how I feel about having a flouncy artist lady floating around while we're trying to do actual work, you know."

"Shush you. I'm sure she'll be just as willing to muck in as the rest of us."

Caimile's expression remained unconvinced. "We'll see. How soon do you want them waking up?"

"I'd like to check in with Dan when he wakes up, see if he has any major objections, but then I think we could go for it first thing tomorrow morning."

"Unless, of course, the good commander has thought of something you haven't."

"You're very snappish this morning." Nina frowned, settling herself on a nearby packing case. "Is something the matter?"

Dr Caimile sighed. "Sorry. You know I don't mean it." She crossed to where Nina sat and Nina scooted across to make room for her on the crate. "I'm just not used to being so completely out of my comfort zone. I'm highly trained and that should prepare me for anything, but I've never faced so many unknowns before. And then just the fact that I'm feeling discomfited is making it worse, because I don't normally feel like that and that's new too!" She sighed again, rubbing her face and looking at Nina. "Sorry," she repeated.

"Don't be," Nina replied, putting an arm around her. Sarah leaned into her, her body soft and warm against Nina's. "We're all there with you. Everything is new, and sometimes that's exciting and sometimes it's terrifying."

"Exactly. I just feel like I'm getting more of the terrifying side, like I'm waiting for a disaster that's about to happen."

"You read too much."

Sarah smiled self-deprecatingly. "Probably. But what else am I supposed to do while I wait around for the first ion storm, or sulphuric geysers or toxic swamp slugs or whatever?"

Nina laughed. "Right, that's it; I'm confiscating your science fiction collection and giving you gentle historical romances to read instead."

"Oh hell no! I had enough bustles and decorum in school to last me a lifetime." Dr Caimile laughed as she sat up and disentangled herself. "Thanks, Nina."

Nina smiled. "Any time." Then she frowned. "Though you have made me wonder, is it worth waking up Ana Romero in this group as well?"

"The head counsellor? I think that's a good shout. People are likely to have trouble adjusting and it'd be good if she's got at least half a foot on the ground before she gets her first clients."

Nina nodded, crossing back to the console and adding Romero's name to the list. "That's settled then. Let's get some lunch, check in with Dan and if we're all in agreement, we can get started on the preparations for waking them up tomorrow."

Chapter Six

Liu was in agreement, so the next morning Nina found herself in the cryobay at 10.00. They'd had to send Fraser down quickly to the planet's surface to bring back Taylor so he could do his actual job instead of acting as lab lackey to Leclerc. She'd taken Pavluhkin down as a trade-off, as the engineer had a slightly more advanced first aid course than the other team members on the surface. She was also, in Nina's opinion, due a bit of fresh air. Dr Caimile finished briefing Nurse Taylor and the two of them crossed back over to where Nina was waiting just inside the door.

"Ready?" asked the doctor.

"Yes ma'am." Nina grinned, and Caimile swatted her with her notepad.

"Don't start. We've got work to do," she admonished. Nina opened her mouth to reply just as the first pod bleeped, its sides swinging back to reveal the person inside. The three of them moved closer to it, with Dr Caimile in the lead.

"Feels like just yesterday we were all getting out of one of those," Nina muttered aside to Taylor, and he grinned.

"I dunno; we've done a lot since then, Captain."

"True," Nina agreed. The person on the table sat up slowly, guided by Dr Caimile, and Nina stepped forward. "Welcome. I'm Captain Nina Brooke."

The man grinned and stuck out his hand. "Jarli Johnson, farmer." He was maybe a few years older than Nina, with dark creased skin worn dry by years in the sun and short tightly curled hair. His accent would have confirmed his identity as Australian even if Nina hadn't read his file. His hand, when Nina took it, was calloused and he had a firm grip. "Is the wife awake yet?"

"She's up next. You're the first of today's group to wake." She stepped back and indicated Taylor. "If you'll just go with Nurse Taylor here, he'll get you checked out to make sure you're all healthy and then we'll let you know when Lowanna's ready."

Taylor stepped forward and Jarli hopped down, staggering a little on landing. Taylor steadied him and they crossed carefully to the med unit on the far wall. Jarli stepped into the recess, standing still so the machine could scan him, and Taylor kept an eye on the readings as the unit did its work.

Chaudhary had dug out a few spare chairs and set up a low table with a few drinks and what passed for biscuits on military vessels, so next to the med unit there was now a comfortable seating area for the newly awakened. Liu had suggested this as the civilians were likely to have been less physically fit on entering the tubes and were therefore more likely to need a bit more assistance. Nina liked it; the room looked much more welcoming than it had done when she had woken. They had considered putting a jar of native flowers on the table to brighten things up further, but Dr Caimile had mentioned allergies and the idea was quickly quashed. The next pod bleeped and she turned back towards it.

Lowanna Johnson was just as cheerful as her husband. Her skin was a shade lighter but equally sun-scorched and she wore her hair in longer curls that had been dyed red. She waved at Jarli as she was escorted for her scan then went to join him in the chairs, helping herself to a biscuit as they greeted each other with a kiss.

"I suppose it doesn't feel like fifty-three years since they last saw each other," Taylor commented as he joined Nina at the next tube. "Weird, isn't it?"

"I try not to dwell on it too much," Nina replied truthfully.

"You can't shut it out forever, Captain," Taylor warned. His eyes, when Nina turned to him, were uncharacteristically serious and she looked away quickly, not yet ready to have this conversation.

They repeated the process until all of the chosen batch were awake and sitting comfortably in chairs at the side of the bay. Some were clutching mugs of tea or coffee, others looking around them or chatting to their neighbours. Nina smiled around at the group and was pleased when they all smiled back. She could do without hostility from the people she was going to have to work most closely with over the coming years.

"Welcome everyone!" she repeated. "I can't tell you how exciting it is that we've got to the stage where we're waking more people up. It feels like just yesterday we got here but it's actually been three weeks since we woke up and we've managed to get quite a bit done already, so we didn't want to proceed any further without getting you all involved too."

She gave them a quick rundown of the mission so far, mentioning the two landing sites they'd investigated and their choice to start building a temporary base at the second, and some of the more significant scientific discoveries. Her audience was attentive, asking sensible questions but not interrupting and Nina was pleased with how things were going until Saima Rayat asked about Earth. Nina sighed internally and looked her in the eye before answering.

"I'm afraid I have bad news on that front. Earth is in trouble. They had a lot of problems after we left and the planet has suffered. I don't think it would much resemble the place we left anymore."

Nina answered the inevitable follow up questions to the best of her ability, her heart sinking as she looked around at the shock and horror on the faces around her. She'd been doing her best to put Earth's fate out of her mind, focusing instead on the positives of what they were doing here, but now she realised that she was going to have to go through this process with everyone they woke up. Taylor's earlier comment about not shutting things out forever came back to her and the realisation slammed into her; she was going to have to face up to the realities of everything she had been trying to ignore, and soon. She shared a look with

Dr Caimile, standing sombrely next to her, and saw her watching her.

Caimile nodded slightly to Nina and cleared her throat to address the unhappy group. "I know it's a shock, and not what you want to hear when you wake up. So I'd like you to try to focus on yourselves for now as your bodies get used to being awake again. Spend today exploring the ship, eat regularly and try to fit in some gentle exercise. We've got plenty of stuff to read about the planet on hand now if you fancy sifting through some information, so get stuck in as much as you'd like to. If you feel up to it, everything about Earth is on the system as well. Look after yourselves, let us know if you need anything and we'll take you down to the planet tomorrow to get your first look at it."

Nina smiled at her, grateful for her input, then turned to the people in front of her. "I agree. We'll leave you to get settled in, and we'll see you all at dinner at 18.30."

Chaudhary had arrived to show all the newly woken to their quarters and make sure they had everything they needed, so she introduced him and left with Dr Caimile, leaving him in charge of the group. Nina exhaled heavily as they left the cryobay and Dr Caimile threw a glance at her, before suggesting they stop by the galley for a coffee. Nina complied with relief.

"Well? What do you think?" she asked, trying to get back to business. They were both safely ensconced in armchairs, hands around mugs of Caimile's best coffee. Caimile huffed.

"I knew you were going to say that. How do you expect me to form an impression so quickly?"

Nina smirked. "Then why did you suggest we stop for coffee if you didn't want me to quiz you? Safer just to retreat to your medbay, I'd have thought."

Caimile narrowed her eyes at her. "I suggested it because I thought you looked like you needed a break. Having to tell the Union about what's happened on Earth shook you up, and I wanted to check you're ok."

Nina's heart skipped a beat and she dropped the smirk. "Sorry."

The doctor's gaze softened. She reached out and put a hand on her knee, which Nina covered and squeezed. "It's just, I've been focusing on the here and now and trying not to think about anything else, and I realised in there that that's not a healthy way of dealing with things."

"You're right, it's not," agreed Dr Caimile. "We're all in the same boat here and it's okay to talk about it. Bottling your feelings up is only going to end badly in the long run, you know that."

Nina sighed. "I do. I just don't feel like I've got the time to process anything about Earth or deal with the fact that all my friends are probably dead, or at the least very old and decrepit."

"It's not going to get normal overnight," replied the doctor. "Nobody's expecting anybody to have dealt with everything yet. You just need to start thinking about it and accepting it, rather than pushing it out of sight every time the thoughts come up. That's as good a place as any to start."

Nina nodded slowly. "Okay. I'll bear that in mind. Thanks, Sarah." She took another sip of her coffee and squeezed Sarah's hand again before releasing it. "Can we talk about the newbies now?"

Dr Caimile laughed. "Okay." She paused and took a sip of her coffee, thinking. "The farmers seem the most relaxed. I don't think we'll have any trouble with them. Jarli was concerned that the years in stasis might have had a detrimental effect on his hormone treatments, but they don't seem to have done; I'm going to give him a more thorough check up this afternoon just to be sure though."

Nina nodded; Jarli Johnson was very open about being transgender and Nina knew he had raised the same concerns before he signed onto the project, so this wasn't a surprise to her. She was glad, however, that so far his fears seemed unfounded. She could only imagine the effect that waking up to discover years of treatment had been undone in what felt like overnight would have on someone.

"Thank you. How about the rest of them?"

"They all seem nice, from my limited interactions. I introduced Jerry to Ana, the counsellor, and they seemed to be getting on well. I think they'll both be good additions to the team."

Jerry, or Dr James to his patients, was a large bluff man with mostly white hair that he wore in a low ponytail, who was going to be Caimile's partner in running the planet's medical provision. He had a background in administration as well as in medicine and his cheerful, optimistic disposition was enough of a contrast to Sarah's to make them a good match. He was Anishinaabe and had originally trained in Canada, but had travelled extensively and worked all over the world. Nina had never met him before but had heard Sarah talk about him many times; she had worked with him on multiple occasions and Nina trusted her judgement implicitly.

Ana Romero, on the other hand, was unknown to both of them. She had signed onto the mission with excellent credentials, having been practising as a counsellor for twenty plus years; first in her hometown of Salta then in the Argentinean capital, Buenos Aires. She had an air of quiet competence which Nina admired. Her hair was cropped short, she was on the muscular side of toned and watched everything with intelligent eyes that missed nothing. Nina was expecting her to have her work cut out for her and was keen to get her settled as soon as possible.

"I agree. I think the four of you should sit down this afternoon and have a chat between you all, start getting the team up and running properly."

"Aye, Captain." Caimile smirked.

Nina rolled her eyes and checked her wrist unit. "I'll stop quizzing you now; I know you've got to get back to work."

Caimile grimaced. "Thanks, Nina. We can all get together over dinner and find out about everyone then."

"Very sensible, Doc. I'll see who's rota-ed in to cook tonight and remind them that our numbers have gone up. And thanks again, for looking out for me."

They cleared up their coffee things and headed their separate ways, with Nina feeling grateful to have Sarah onboard and wondering what on Earth—or off it—she'd do without her.

Dinner rolled around quickly and before she knew it, Nina was back in the galley. The Lovells were there already, sitting in the chairs that she and Sarah had stopped for coffee in earlier, and after helping herself to a drink, she crossed the room to join them.

"Do you mind if I join you?"

The taller of the two indicated the chair opposite. "Not at all, Captain. Please, sit." This was Nehemiah, the head teacher. He was quite tall, around six foot Nina guessed, with thick dark hair and a kind face. His husband, Patrin, was shorter, with similar colouring but startlingly bright eyes. Both of them were dressed in checked shirts and jeans, not quite matching but similar enough that Nina wondered how they managed the laundry without mixing everything up.

"I hope you're not finding it too strange without your daughter awake yet," she said as she sat down.

Patrin smiled. "It is quite odd. But I agree it would have been too early for her—I think she'd have been a bit freaked out by everything as it is at the moment. Plus, she'd have been into everything on the ship trying to find out how it all works."

Nina laughed. "I'm glad I made the right decision then."

Nehemiah nodded. "I'd like to have a chat to you at some point about your plans for introducing children. How far down the line were you thinking?"

Nina frowned. "I'm not sure. My initial thoughts were to wake them in groups as we expand. I want to make sure their parents and carers are settled and that they have homes to move into before they're woken up."

"I agree."

"I'd also like to make sure we've got proper support systems in place so they have people to talk to if they have trouble adjusting. Our lead counsellor is awake, but we've got a couple onboard who have more experience of working with children, so it would be sensible to get them woken and settled before the kids wake up. What do you do, Patrin?" Nina asked, because he was nodding.

"I co-ordinate the SEND teams for the schools for children with learning disabilities or other needs."

"That's great, I had no idea!" Nina enthused, slightly embarrassed. "My apologies, I should have found out—there's so much going on at the moment, I just didn't realise you worked in the same area. I'll set you both up a meeting with Ana Romero to work out what systems you think need putting in place to get the ball rolling."

"That would be wonderful, thank you Captain."

Dinner was served and Nina made sure to sit with someone else she hadn't talked to yet. She ended up by Mira Saeed, who would be overseeing the planning and construction of the settlement.

"Good evening, Captain," Mira greeted as Nina sat. She was a small woman, curvy in a soft way and with a friendly smile. She wore a purple hijab and a bright red shirt, which Nina found herself appreciating after weeks of uniform grey.

"Good evening," Nina returned. "How are you adjusting?"

"Not too badly, thank you. It's all been on the cards for so long now, I'm mainly just excited to be here and ready to get cracking!"

Nina smiled at her enthusiasm. "That's great. We haven't got far yet, other than putting up a science station at the spot we've deemed most sensible, but of course we'll need your opinion on that too."

Mira grinned around a mouthful of her stew. Liu had cooked tonight, and he'd gone for a 'throw everything into a pot and hope' style meal as the excitement of the day had cut into his prep time. It wasn't bad, Nina mused as she mopped some up with a bread roll, just not as good as his usual. Everyone else seemed to be tucking in with gusto as they chatted away, the ship's crew glad to see fresh faces and the newly woken keen to get involved. Nina watched without appearing to, keeping an eye out for anyone seeming under the weather, and it wasn't until she caught Sarah's eye, then Liu's, that she realised she wasn't the only one doing so.

The next morning, the shuttle was prepped bright and early for Nina and Fraser to start the guided tour. Liu was staying on the ship in Nina's stead and they were taking Taylor with them to swap back for Pavluhkin at the end of the day. They had decided to visit the bay first, then take Sakamoto with them when they visited the other site. Nina was hoping they were all in agreement about the desirability of their current location, but she couldn't (and didn't want to) decide for everyone.

The first trip consisted of the Johnsons, Jerry, Mira and Nehemiah. This shuttle only seated eight, including the pilot, and

Nina had judged this group to be the people who needed to see both the potential settlements the most urgently. If the others wanted to have a look around, and Nina would be surprised if they didn't, they would be able to go down tomorrow. Mira was the first to arrive, practically bouncing with excitement. She went over to talk to Fraser as they waited for the others, inspecting the shuttle with interest. Jerry arrived last, deep in conversation with Taylor who nodded patiently as he tried to urge him towards the shuttle. When they were eventually all buckled in, Nina leaned over to Taylor.

"What was all that about?" she asked quietly.

Taylor grinned and raised his eyebrows. "Thirty years ago, he used to work at the hospital I did my internship at. He wants to know what's changed."

"Quite a lot, I'd imagine!" Nina replied.

Taylor turned philosophical. "I wonder if it's still there?"

Nina let out a breath and patted him on the shoulder, forcing herself not to push the thought away. She allowed herself to consider the question as well, letting her mind explore the possibilities and found to her surprise that it didn't hurt quite as much as it had the last time she'd thought about Earth.

As the shuttle approached the planet, the noise in the small cabin died. Nina watched as her new colleagues gazed, enraptured, out of the window. Mira gave her a small smile before fixing her eyes back onto the planet. As they entered the atmosphere, the spell seemed to lift, and people looked back around at each other. An excited hubbub rose up again as the shuttle landed and Fraser couldn't get the door open fast enough. Nina gestured for the others to precede her out of the shuttle and they tumbled out, stopping immediately to stare around them. The air felt familiar to Nina as she joined them, and she smiled as her feet found the ground again.

The crew were waiting for them, and Leclerc stepped forward to introduce everybody. There followed a jumble of hand shaking and greetings, then people started to disperse. Mira and the Johnsons went with Leclerc to her lab to view the relevant findings, while Jerry and Nehemiah stood a little uncertainly and surveyed the area. Nina beckoned Sakamoto over to her.

"Nanako. Everything okay?" Sakamoto nodded, and Nina indicated the two men. "They probably want to explore. Go with them?"

"Sure thing, Captain." She nodded, and headed over to them. Nina heard her greet them cheerfully, then all three set off along the shore.

Nina stood for a moment and looked after them, admiring the curve of the bay as it swept out to sea. It was cloudy today, a slight chill on the breeze making her shiver, but even without the clear skies and sparkling waters from her first visit, it was still a view she could get used to waking up to. Fingers crossed the results all turned out okay. Tearing her eyes away from the water, she turned and picked her way over to Leclerc's lab.

Monique was in full stream when she arrived, with her guests nodding enthusiastically at what Nina assumed were appropriate points. She didn't understand all the science herself; that was what she had specialists for, after all, but what she could decipher sounded positive. It was hard to believe the lab had only been there for a few days—the newly added shelves were full of samples, bottles and complicated looking instruments. There were a couple of plants in pots on a windowsill, species that Nina thought she recognised from her planetary explorations. Trays of tiny seedlings covered one work surface, small orange growths poking out from the top of the soil. A long panel hung low above them, with a warm glow emitting from the underside, reminding Nina of the heat lamp her best friend's pet tortoise had had when she was back in primary school. Another tray had plants that looked more familiar; Nina was sure she remembered growing them herself in early science lessons. Turning, she found Monique already at her side, a grin on her face.

"Yes, you're right; that is watercress. We're using samples of the soil here and acceleration lamps to see if it's compatible with plant life from our world."

"It's looking good so far," Nina ventured.

Leclerc nodded. "It is. Soil composition is very similar to what we have at home, although it's actually marginally better here than a lot of places on Earth, probably due to the proximity of those volcanoes we noticed. I can't see a problem with settling here and the Johnsons agree—they're over the moon to find such a good location. They were expecting to have to do a lot of work to get the land ready, so they're really pleased."

Nina cast a look over at the head farmers and had to agree. Lowanna's face was animated, and Jarli was nodding enthusiastically as they discussed whatever was under the microscope on the far side of the lab.

"And how about you, Mira? Initial thoughts?"

Mira had appeared at Nina's other side, also smiling. "Looks good to me too, Captain. Pretty similar from initial results to Southern Europe back in the 1900s. No signs of regular flooding, earthquakes or land subsidence around here, or any other obvious warning signs. I'd say this is as good a place as any to start building a first base, even if we find somewhere better later."

"Excellent. Let's head back out and find the others."

Outside, dark clouds were gathering overhead as they waited for the three explorers to get back. Leclerc frowned up at the sky, but Lowanna was bouncing.

"See that? That's the good kind of rain cloud right there!" At Monique's shudder, she grinned. "Can't grow crops without rain, you know."

"Doesn't mean I have to like getting caught in it," Leclerc retorted.

Lowanna grinned back, unabashed. Before they had a chance to experience the rain first-hand, Sakamoto returned with Jerry and Nehemiah and they crowded back into the shuttle to visit the next site. This was the first time Nina was going to see the other option for home in person and she was secretly hoping it didn't suddenly seem more viable; she had already become quite attached to the idea of a sea view. However, the chatter in the shuttle reassured her—everyone else was also very taken with the bay as the main settlement and this trip was being viewed almost as a formality. The shuttle landed and again, they all climbed out.

Nina blinked around at the almost overwhelmingly orange vista and hoped once more for the other site. Orange scrubland extended as far as the eye could see in every direction, with very little variation save for a bit of gentle undulation to the north, and not as many trees. It was hotter, too, in an unpleasant, muggy way; Nina could already feel sweat starting to prickle on her skin. Having spent the majority of her life on Earth in the UK, she really wasn't keen on the idea of living anywhere too warm. Leclerc went to check on some equipment she had set up and Nina wandered over to Jerry.

"Thoughts?"

"I like the other one better. Sea air does wonders for a patient."

Nina scoffed. "Pull the other one, Doc. That one was debunked a long time ago."

Jerry smiled. "Okay, the actual air itself has no particular medical benefit. But you can't deny that being in pleasant surroundings helps greatly with recovery, and especially with mental wellbeing."

"Very true," Nina agreed. "I like it better too."

"And me," chimed in Mira, joining them. "Sure, here would be fine. The ground composition is suitable for building on and there's nothing wrong with it. But I'd rather live by the sea."

"Definitely better for farming at the first one," said Lowanna. "We could make it work here, if we had to, but the soil is a lot drier and we'd have to work harder. We'll get better results with all that lush land back in the bay."

That seemed to be the general opinion so, after a much shorter visit than the first one, they climbed back into the shuttle and prepared to depart. As they got ready to lift off, Sakamoto held up a hand.

"Wait!"

The urgency of her tone made Nina stop in her tracks. Sakamoto was still standing in the open hatch of the shuttle, looking across the plateau.

"There." She pointed. "Something big. Do you see it?"

Nina squinted, and in seconds Leclerc was there with a long-distance scanner.

"Some kind of animal. I'm picking up heat signals—it's big, whatever it is."

Nina saw a rustle of orange leaves in the distance and then nothing else.

Leclerc frowned. "It's heading away from us." She paused. "Lost it." She looked up. "Good spot, Nanako. That's the first indication we've had of anything bigger than the rat-dog. We'd better keep an eye out."

"Yeah, but does it eat plants or people?" Fraser quipped from the front.

Nina frowned. "Not helpful, Sam."

"Sorry, Cap." Looking less apologetic than Nina would have liked, Fraser swung back around to face her console and began the launch sequence.

The trip back to the ship took place in relative quiet. The newly woken were easily tired and most retired to their cabins for a rest once back on the ship. They had stopped briefly at the existing base on the way back to swap people around, Leclerc practically chomping at the bit to get back into her lab. After Nina had seen everyone on their way, she went to find Liu. He was on the bridge and rose to greet her when she came in.

"Welcome back, Captain. Successful trip?"

"I think so," she nodded. "Got a minute to come see me?"

Liu handed over command to Kjeldsen then followed Nina into her little cubicle off the bridge. She quickly filled him in on the trip to the planet and the opinions of their new companions.

"I'd like you to take the others down tomorrow, as this is the first official decision of the new Union and it doesn't seem right to cut some members out completely. However, it'll need to be a pretty big objection at this stage to change everyone's minds."

Liu nodded. "I agree. We don't want bad feeling if half the Union think they weren't consulted."

"Absolutely. Thanks, Dan. If you can take them down, I'll get started organising everything from up here. If all goes to plan, we can initiate Stage Two the day after."

Chapter Seven

Liu's trip did go according to plan, so two mornings later, Nina found herself in the shuttle bay bright and early. Chaudhary had dragged in anyone without a current job to assist with his preparations the previous day, so Nina not only had the regular shuttle crammed with equipment but also three more transport vehicles. The shuttle they had been using so far was the most convenient as a runabout, but the ship had also been supplied with larger, less comfortable vessels that could be adapted and used for transport of equipment, animals or people. These were also full, mostly with the sturdier, permanent housing units and everything they would need for building them. The droids still on the surface would assist with unloading the shuttle as soon as it landed, and more had been packed into the transports with the housing.

Mira had spent the previous day drawing up plans for the settlement. They were fairly basic at this stage and consisted of three housing areas, grouped around a central area which would contain the communal buildings, and a farming area set back a little between two of the housing quarters. These had been passed around at a swiftly convened general meeting in the evening and agreed on by everybody present. The team was excited, buzzing at the thought of starting construction in earnest. Mira herself was operating at peak efficiency, checking everything and everyone and impressing Nina with her crisp competence. She was accordingly dressed in a more practical work ensemble of jeans and a long-sleeved t-shirt but still with colour in her hijab; today's was a light blue with swirling gold highlights.

Soon, everyone was seated in the shuttle and they were cleared for launch by Kjeldsen, who was staying on the ship to act as mission control. After a quick trip down to the surface, Mira took charge.

"Right," she said, standing as soon as they were cleared to unstrap, "Nobody touches anything until I say so. Got it?"

Nods and murmurs of assent were offered in reply, so Fraser opened the hatch and they trooped out. Liu had parked the first of the transports a short distance away, earning a nod of approval from Fraser, which amused Nina greatly as Liu had at least fifteen years more piloting experience than she did. Once he and his passengers had joined them, Mira started her safety briefing. In addition to the usual wrist units that everyone wore, she had a larger tablet unit with her today, about the size of four of Nina's hands and similar to the military issue notepads used by her crew. She tapped it a couple of times, ran a quick eye over it then let it hang by her side as she addressed the group.

"Okay people. Welcome to the first day of construction. I imagine most of you have very limited experience of building sites, so please pay attention. Rule number one: make sure you wear appropriate personal protection equipment at all times. Number two; make sure you follow instructions accurately. And if at any point you hear me yell 'stop!', then stop exactly where you are as it could be you who's about to do something incredibly dangerous. Understood?"

There was more muttering, slightly warier this time. Mira and Chaudhary conferred, then Mira assigned people into groups, sending a couple of bunches off immediately to start measuring and marking out the ground, while Chaudhary wheeled himself off to set the first batch of droids up. Liu's transport contained purely housing, including a sort of hostel where, from now on, the newly woken would spend their first couple of nights before being allocated their own living quarters. Living space had quickly become the biggest priority.

As everyone took to their assigned work, Nina looked up, instinctively searching the skies for the ship she knew she couldn't see.

Up on the ship, Doctors Caimile and James and Nurse Taylor were at this moment starting on waking up the next batch of colonists, and this group was larger than the previous ones. A large amount of the 'doers' of the colony were in this batch, including builders, other construction workers and farmers. At Mira's suggestion, a number of religious leaders were also being woken today, in case any of the colonists found themselves in need of guidance on waking. Nina wasn't particularly religious herself but Mira, Dr Caimile and a number of the rest of the crew were and she respected the idea that it would be reassuring to some to have those resources available.

Nina dragged her thoughts back to the surface and forced herself to focus. She grabbed a hard hat and pulled on her gloves, pleased that gloves and reinforced boots were part of her standard uniform so she didn't need to try to find some to fit. She smiled at the sight of Patrin who was doing just that, with a fair amount of difficulty from the look of it. Once appropriately attired, she reported to Mira and was sent to join a team shifting smaller items from the shuttle to the site of the first houses. The droids would do the majority of the heavy lifting, but they moved much slower than people and it was a waste of time to set them doing jobs that could easily be done by humans.

As a result, Nina spent a good portion of the morning ferrying tools and small parts from the shuttle to the houses and between partially built structures. By the time Mira called a break several hours later, Nina was sweating and more than ready for a rest. The day had warmed up as they worked and the sun was now hotter than Nina would have liked it to be whilst doing physical labour outside, but at least it wasn't raining. Chaudhary brought out the picnic hampers and everyone sank gratefully to the floor in small groups as they tucked in.

Nina found herself next to Saima Rayat, with whom she hadn't had much contact so far. The head of the arts was fairly tall, with light brown skin and her hair neatly styled in a pixie cut. The two women shared a smile and after throwing back some water, Nina said hello.

"Thank you so much for mucking in and helping out with the building," she said as they ate.

"Of course," the other woman replied. "It's a town for everyone, so it makes sense for everyone to help build it." Nina nodded and Saima continued with a grin. "Also, how do I know which houses are best if I haven't helped to build them?"

Nina laughed. "There is that. Do you have your eye on anywhere in particular?"

Saima swallowed a bite of sandwich and nodded. "Over there," she replied, pointing across the bay to a seemingly random patch of land. "I think the view is especially nice from that point."

Nina stared for a moment, non-plussed, until Saima laughed and she realised she was joking.

"I'm really not that bothered, to be honest. I spent so much of my youth on tour in grotty digs that I'm grateful just to be anywhere without mould."

Nina grimaced. "Sounds like the student barracks when I joined up. Thoroughly unpleasant."

They chatted a while longer and Nina was relieved to find that Dr Caimile's fears about having a 'flouncy artist lady' in their midst were completely unfounded. Sooner than she would have liked, Mira called an end to the break and they all got to their feet, ready to continue work.

The heat intensified as the day wore on and by the time Mira called another break, Nina's back ached and her clothes were drenched with sweat. Most of the crew had unzipped their jumpsuits and wrapped the sleeves around their waist, but even in just her undershirt, she was still uncomfortably warm. She had put her hair up into a ponytail early on, but she could feel the escaping tendrils sticking to her face and neck, and every inch of her undershirt clung to her skin. Stretching with relief, she looked around and noted with satisfaction that they had made quite a lot of progress.

They had started a little way out from the centre of the bay at what was to be one end of the first housing area. Now, several neat rows of cabins stretched out from where Nina stood, all slightly different from one another. She could see a few that looked suitable for one or two people to live in and others that would fit a family or a group of friends. Nina knew that as yet they were all unfurnished and uninhabited, but it was nice to look at them and think that soon they would be the start of a new community. At the end nearest to what would be the town centre, several stories high and much bigger than the rest, stood the hostel that would be housing all the workers that had been woken up today. All around her, people milled around, smiling and chatting about the day's work. Chaudhary brought out a crate of cold drinks and she helped herself to one with a sigh as they waited for the transports back to the ship.

Work continued like this for a few days. The workforce increased as those who had been recently woken were declared fit for duty, although they were advised to take it easy for the first couple of days, and progress ramped up accordingly as the number of workers grew. Those with specialisms were assigned to appropriate jobs and the town was well on the way to becoming a functional settlement. The second of the larger transports that Liu had flown down contained farm buildings and equipment, and a couple of teams had been assigned to help the Johnsons get up and running as soon as possible; the appropriate areas had been marked out before the end of the second day, with the first buildings going up not long after. Jarli and Lowanna had been allocated a residential building right by the farmland, but the rest of the farmers would reside in the main living quarter for now; as Mira pointed out, at the moment it wasn't a particularly unmanageable commute.

Nina felt slightly uncomfortable about the fact that she had already got to the point where she didn't know all the colonists by name. Perhaps naively, she had been expecting to be the first point of contact for all the newly woken for a while, but that was not the case. She supposed that it was a good thing and that the rapid progression of things should be viewed as a positive, but part of her already missed the days where it was just her and her crew and the unknown.

It was the evening of the third day after Stage Two had begun and Nina was sitting in the galley with Sarah and Dan, a bottle of beer in her hand, attempting to explain this feeling to them. To her surprise, they were both sympathetic.

"I know what you mean," Dan agreed. "It almost feels like our part is over now. I know it's not, but it feels a bit like it."

"It's an entirely natural feeling, actually," Sarah cut in. "The initial excitement of getting here is starting to wear off and you're handing some elements of the mission over to other people. It's natural to be feeling a bit down—you've been firing on all cylinders for weeks and now some of the pressure has lifted. I'd be surprised if you weren't starting to feel a bit of a slump."

Nina smiled and leaned back in her chair. "Thanks, Doc. That's a relief to hear. I was starting to worry I was secretly hoping for something to jeopardise the mission or something."

Sarah laughed. "Well, don't shoot the messenger, but you are the sort of person who likes a challenge. Make sure you don't get stuck doing the same thing for too long is my advice and get plenty of variety on your day-to-day activities."

Dan laughed. "I don't think variety is going to be a problem, Doc. Yesterday I helped build a milking parlour. I don't remember seeing that anywhere on the job spec."

Nina and Sarah both laughed too, and Nina drained her beer.

"I'd better get to bed. I've not been keeping as close an eye as I'd like on everything, what with all this manual labour, and I want to make sure I fit everything in tomorrow."

Sarah got to her feet as well. "I'm going to hit the sack too. Three days of waking people up takes its toll."

They said goodnight to Dan, who still had half a beer and a book resting on the table he had been looking longingly at, and headed out into the corridor. As they reached Sarah's quarters, Nina turned to her.

"Thank you for everything, Sarah. I can't think of anyone I'd rather have by my side on this adventure."

Sarah laughed again, properly this time, and a warm glow spread through Nina at the sound. Her stomach fluttered but before she could make up her mind what else she wanted to say, Sarah grinned, her dark eyes sparkling, and shook her head.

"Not tonight, Nina. I'll see you in the morning." She opened her door and entered, and Nina was left trying to figure out what exactly her friend had meant with that cryptic remark.

As Nina had remarked to her crewmates the night before, she had been so busy helping with construction on the surface that she had let a few of her other responsibilities slide. Now that there were enough better qualified people awake to finish the current phase of building, Nina reported to her station on the bridge first thing in the morning. It made her feel slightly better to find everything as she had left it and some of her worries from the day before about being redundant were relieved. There was still an entire planet left to explore, and even after that, her team would be crucial to the operation of the colony. Not to mention the rest of the as-yet-uncharted solar system.

She checked in with Kjeldsen, who seemed pleased to have some company, then began looking through the latest data from the satellites. She was chagrined to realised she had lost track of time again and had missed the weekly information drop by a day, but Kjeldsen didn't say anything on the subject for which Nina was grateful. She knew they were more than capable of sending the update without her input but she preferred to add a personal note. There was nothing in return from Earth, but then she wouldn't expect anything for at least another month and a half. A month and a half, old Earth time, she reminded herself. She needed to start thinking and working in their new time frames if they were going to settle quickly. Come to think of it, it was probably time to start taking suggestions for names for the planet too.

Her first stop of the day—once she had dealt with her admin—was the stores. Chaudhary had been busy the past couple of days prepping large amounts of building products and she was hoping this morning would be quieter. When she arrived, she found him doing what looked like a stock-take.

"Good morning, Captain," he greeted cheerily, wheeling around to meet her. "What can I do for you?"

"It's a bit of a big one, actually, so send me packing if it's not a good time." He nodded and waited for her to continue. "The personal craft… how accessible are they?"

Chaudhary grinned and turned around, and Nina saw a large shipping droid trundling towards them with a small craft on its back. Her jaw dropped.

"I know you're good, Ramin, but how could you have *possibly* known I'd be down here asking for one of these this morning?"

Chaudhary winked. "A good quartermaster never tells."

Still dumbfounded, Nina stepped forward to inspect the ship. It was exactly as she remembered, a small, pointy-nosed craft, designed to carry one or two people at most, good for short hops between planets and ships in orbit or across continents. Anything more exciting and she'd need to use the shuttle, but this would give her a bit more freedom. She had been worrying about using resources and dragging Fraser away from other duties to ferry her around, and had come to the conclusion that having her own vessel would be more of a practicality than a luxury.

"You're a gem, Ramin. Can you get it set up for a trip this afternoon? I'll get Fraser to give me a rundown of anything I need to know but I'm pretty sure I remember how to fly one of these."

"I'm filled with confidence," Chaudhary remarked drily. Nina refrained from sticking her tongue out at him and left.

Once she had checked in with Fraser and reassured herself that yes, she did remember how to pilot a small passenger vehicle, Nina took off by herself for the surface. It was an entirely different feeling being in charge of her own ship, and watching the planet approach through her front screen, she was reminded why she used to enjoy piloting so much. To be in control and feel all that power responding at your fingertips was quite the rush and Nina savoured the feeling as she touched down a short distance from the lab on the planet.

Powering down, she exited the vehicle and breathed the new air as she opened the hatch. Would they ever get used to this view, she wondered? Would there be a time, several years down the road, where the slightly odd colour of the sea and sky looked normal to her and she had forgotten what they looked like on Earth? Shaking herself, she forced herself to stop daydreaming and get back to work.

Her first stop was the science lab. With all the construction over the past couple of days, she hadn't had a chance to stop by and was excited to see what progress Leclerc had made. On stepping inside, however, her Science Officer was nowhere to be seen. Nina headed over to the central workbench and idly looked through the microscope there, only to find that she had absolutely no idea what she was looking at. She had just straightened up when the back door of the cabin opened and Monique stepped in, followed by a young man Nina didn't recognise.

"Ah! Captain!" Leclerc greeted. "I haven't seen you in a couple of days."

Nina grimaced. "I know, I'm sorry. I got caught up in the construction and after a whole day of building things, I didn't really have the brain capacity for science too."

"There is always time for science," Leclerc admonished. "Robert, this is Captain Nina Brooke. Captain, this is Robert, my technician."

The young man extended a hand and Nina took it. He was slight, with light brown skin and dark hair flopping into his equally dark eyes. Nina guessed him to be originally from the Philippines or somewhere similar.

"Nice to meet you, Robert. I bet you're relieved to have some help?" Nina addressed the question to Leclerc, who nodded emphatically.

"Taylor was wonderful. But he wasn't qualified, and I spent a lot of time checking his work. I can trust Robert to get on with things and not need babysitting, it's brilliant!"

Nina grinned as Robert blushed. "Enough embarrassing the poor chap. What have you got?"

Leclerc walked Nina through the progress of the past few days. The plants they had been growing were doing well and some had even been transplanted into the newly created garden out the back, which was where Leclerc had been when Nina had arrived. Leclerc expressed confidence that when the farmers were all set up and ready to go, they would be able to begin production of a number of Earth staples immediately.

"The only thing I'm concerned about is the rice crop—there isn't anywhere suitable around this area, as there's not a large enough water source. The stream that we've been using isn't big enough to supply paddy fields as well as a colony, even with our water recyclers. Robert and I are researching a number of possible options, the most promising being setting up some fields further away."

Nina nodded. "Keep me posted." Rice was still a staple of most people's diets back on Earth, as it was so easy to store and cook. To have to go back to not using it would be a bit of a blow, but Nina knew they'd adapt if they had to. "What else have you found?"

Leclerc crossed to a counter by the window and dialled up some images on a screen. "Very successful results from the marine cameras we dropped the other day. We've catalogued over one hundred species of fish so far, ranging in size from one centimetre long to three metres."

"Three metres?" Nina said, recoiling in horror. "Was that what we saw eating the tit-bit the other day?"

Leclerc shook her head. "I'm not sure. It didn't look like a predator, but then groupers can get to the size of a small shuttle and you wouldn't want to argue with one of those."

"True," Nina agreed. She knew that Monique was an experienced scuba diver, both for work and leisure, and she didn't doubt that this information came from first-hand knowledge. "So no swimming still for a while yet?"

"Well, I've been thinking about that," said Monique, turning around to lean on the edge of the counter. "There are no harmful bacteria in the water, so I see no reason why we couldn't cordon off a fish-free area of the bay as a swimming area. We'd just have to start small and extend out to make a large enough area that we knew was safe."

"That's an excellent idea, Monique," Nina replied, enthused by the thought. "I know people are getting frustrated looking at that beautiful bay and not being able to get in the water. I'll ask for some volunteers to start getting that set up tonight at the meeting."

Tonight was the first time there was to be a mass gathering of all the colonists. The aim was to check in with everybody, introduce key people and make sure everyone was up to date with what was going on. Saima Rayat had suggested it and the rest of the Union had agreed. When the colony was larger it wouldn't be a realistic option, but for now it was the quickest way to disseminate information, rather like the evening meal had been in the first few days on the ship. Nina quashed that thought before she allowed herself to get nostalgic; there would be time again for exploring once they were all a bit more settled.

"Any more results from the land cameras?"

"Not really. The rat-dogs are pretty prolific out at the other site and there a few on the outskirts of this settlement, but other than that, we haven't seen anything."

"No sign of the big thing from the last trip out?"

Leclerc bit her lip. "Nothing. And that concerns me, because if it's that good at hiding itself, there's a strong possibility it's an elite predator."

Nina swallowed. "Let's keep that one to ourselves for now then, shall we? No need to incite panic until we know what we're dealing with."

The other two nodded, Robert with a distinct look of worry on his face. Nina's wrist unit bleeped and she checked it, just as the scientists' units went off as well. It was from Kjeldsen, a mass communication to all the colonists reminding them to submit their suggestions for names for the planet and the settlement before this evening's meeting. The Union were to convene an hour before to go over the agenda and review the submissions, before announcing their decision during the meeting. Nina hadn't chipped in; she felt she had enough decisions to be making without sticking her oar in on things outside her jurisdiction.

Chapter Eight

The meeting took place on the beach, as there weren't yet any indoor spaces large enough to hold everyone. People made themselves at home on the fine black sand, sitting in groups of varying size but all facing the same direction, towards the makeshift podium hastily put together by some of Chaudhary's droids that afternoon. Nina smiled to see people chatting, looking relaxed and comfortable. A hum of conversation floated on the breeze, backed by the low wash of the waves. The evening was warm and balmy, the sky thankfully clear and cloudless and the sun wasn't due to set for another hour. Nina took her place by the podium, smiling her hellos at the other Union members. The remaining presenters joined them, and Nina started the meeting.

"Good evening everyone," she announced loudly, stepping up onto the stage and waving. She waited a moment until all the chatter had died down, then repeated her greeting. "Good evening. For anyone that doesn't know me, I'm Nina Brooke, the Captain of the *Posterity*. It's such a pleasure to welcome you all to this meeting tonight, the first of what I hope to be many such gatherings. I hope everyone is settling in well; if for any reason at all you're not, please do come and find me and I'll do what I can to help. But now, let me introduce you to the rest of the Union." She ran quickly through the names and jobs of the other leaders, who rose and waved when their names were called.

"Now there's a few other people I'd like to introduce you to. Firstly, can I please get all our medics to rise?" Sarah, Jerry, Taylor and a few other newly woken health professionals stood. "Remember their faces; these are the people you need to see in an emergency." There was a smattering of laughter. "Dr Caimile, anything you'd like to say?"

Sarah nodded. "Thanks, Captain. I'd just like to say that this is a new planet and as such, there is no 'normal' for any of us anymore. Please see a medical professional for the slightest thing, and I really do mean the slightest thing. If you find you've got a bit of a rash on your arm, we want to know about it. It might be that you're having a very mild allergic reaction to some of the local wildlife—it might not be bothering you much at all. But if you're having a mild reaction, there's a chance someone else might have a serious reaction. The same goes for anything—local viruses, bacteria, everything is new. So please, don't feel silly for coming to us about anything. You might just save someone's life."

Solemn silence greeted this announcement as Dr Caimile nodded to Nina and sat back down again. Nina took that as a good sign.

"Thank you, Dr Caimile. Now I'd like to ask our counselling team to stand up."

Ana stood, as did about ten other people who had mostly been sitting together. Nina was pleased to note they were of all races, ages and genders and hoped the variety of people available to talk to would mean that the colonists took advantage of the provision.

"Thank you. There is also a list of medical professionals and counsellors on the system, which we'll make sure we update with locations of where you can find them as we proceed." There were various nods and the counsellors sat down again. "One last group of people to introduce you to before we continue; these are our religious leaders. Could you please rise?"

Again, about ten people stood, smiling and waving around at the assembled colonists. Some, like the Sikh Granthi in his turban, had obvious signs of their religion, but others had no outward indicators of what religion they represented.

"Thank you." Nina nodded to the group and they retook their seats. "Again, the list of religious leaders will be updated as we go with where you can find them. There will also be a dedicated prayer room in the community hall as soon as it is built, so please do make use of that." She paused, checking that she had covered everything. "I'm now going to hand you over to Saima Rayat." Nina moved away and sat down, and Saima stepped up to the front of the stage.

"Good evening everybody! Are you all well?" There was a very quiet murmur in response. "I said are you all well?" Saima repeated, louder. Nina bit back a laugh; it was immediately obvious why the arts representative had been chosen to give this announcement. A half-hearted cheer rose up in response to the second question and grins started to appear on faces. Saima tutted and looked towards Ana Romero. "Counsellors, I think you've got your work cut out for you. I said, are you all well?"

This time the audience cheered properly and Saima smiled. "Now that's more like it! Welcome to the official naming of the planet ceremony!" Another cheer. "Excellent! Now, we've had some really good suggestions, and this has been a really difficult decision to make. I'd like to thank everyone that put in an option, even the person that suggested 'Vulcan'." Saima paused to scan the crowd with an eyebrow raised and everyone laughed. Nina leaned back, watching with a smile playing on her lips. This had been a good decision; everyone needed a bit of entertainment after working as hard as they had.

"We'll start with the name of the settlement. After much deliberation, I can tell you that the name of our new hometown is Bayville!" There was a round of applause, and a few cheers. Nina didn't mind it; it was a little unimaginative, but it described the settlement adequately. After a moment of encouraging the clapping, Saima waved to the crowd to calm and continued.

"And now, for the planet herself. I am pleased to announce," she paused to pull what looked like a miniature bottle of champagne out of a pocket, "that this planet is officially called… Demeter!" She threw the bottle hard at the ground, where it exploded. Cheers, laughter and clapping rang out, continuing as Saima bowed and retook her seat. Leclerc grinned as she took her place.

"Thanks, Saima. I'm not sure how I can follow that—this is going to feel very dry after that rousing speech. Sorry, everyone; I'll try to keep it short. There will be drinks afterwards, I promise." There was another laugh then the audience quieted, settling in to listen.

"So, Demeter." There was a single cheer, followed by a ripple of laughter and Leclerc paused and shook her head with a smile. "The year is slightly shorter than on Earth, at around three hundred and twenty days. The day is slightly shorter too, at twenty-two Earth hours instead of twenty-four. We are in the process of coming up with a new calendar, which we will run concurrently with the old Earth calendar for all official communication. However, for day-to-day life, we will use the new system."

Nina watched the crowd as Leclerc continued in the same vein, covering the basics of the scientific discoveries the crew had made including geography, climate and a dire warning not to go in the sea. There was a collective groan at that and Nina sympathised. It was difficult to live on the shores of a bay this beautiful and be told not to go in it. Monique allowed herself a wry grin.

"However," she continued, drawing the word out as she raised an eyebrow, "there are plans afoot to create a safe bathing area in the near future, so I am hopeful that we will soon have an area that we can use for recreation. Please come and see me if you would like to volunteer to help with its creation."

A few people cheered in response and Nina could see Sam Fraser positively wriggling with excitement.

"There is a directory of flora and fauna that have already been discovered on the system; feel free to read it and please do add to it if you find something new. We will be working closely with the farming community to make sure we are making the most of our natural resources as well as planting old Earth staples, but I must stress that if you do find something new, you should bring it to our attention to investigate—under no circumstances should you try eating something unknown yourself. We haven't discovered any species with levels of toxicity that would cause serious harm to humans, but we would rather not discover them the hard way.

"If anyone is interested in any more of the scientific discoveries we have made, please feel free to send me a message and I will answer any questions. Other than that, I think that is most of the basics covered. Thank you."

Mira Saeed was next to speak. Her tone was different yet again from the two previous speakers; brisk and efficient and clearly used to speaking in order to get things done.

"Ok, everybody, I'll make this as brief as possible. As most of you will know as you've been involved in it, construction is coming on a treat. We've built enough permanent units to house everybody currently awake, with several to spare. This means that tomorrow we're going to begin building some of the bigger communal units, starting with the medical centre, the community centre and the canteen. I know you're probably all getting a little bored with the pre-packaged meals you're making do with at the moment, so hopefully once we've got some kitchen space, our wonderful cooks will be able to give us a bit of variety." A couple of ironic cheers rang out, followed by laughter. Mira smiled before she carried on.

"Tomorrow we're also going to start allocating homes. Those of you who have been awake for a while will be able to move into your new houses after that." An excited murmur ran through the crowd, and Mira directed her next comments at those who were looking disappointed. "The rest of you sit tight; it won't be long before you've got your own places too. I think this is a good point to hand over to you, Ramin." She sat down and he propelled himself neatly up a small ramp and onto the stage, braking at the front.

"Evening folks. I'm Ramin Chaudhary, the Quartermaster onboard the *Posterity*. Now I know what you're all thinking. Those of you that are getting housing allocations tomorrow are getting all excited about decorating. And that's great—within reason, we'll be able to accommodate requests. But let me just say this now; I'm not IKEA." There were some laughs and some confusion. "I don't have lots and lots of exciting little trinkets and knick-knacks. I have furniture and you'll be able to choose the design of most things, to a certain extent. Once we're more settled, we'll be able to start opening some of specialist shops and we'll have much more variety then, but for now, we need to work with what we've got.

"When you receive your housing allocation, you'll be able to request what furniture you want. Please don't request more than you need. I don't have time to check up on everyone but if I see sixteen chairs on one person's list, I'm going to have questions. If you're planning on entertaining a lot, tell your friends to bring a chair! And if anyone has any access requests that aren't on your file, please let us know as soon as you can."

Chaudhary nodded to Nina and pushed himself backwards and down the ramp. He executed a neat pivot to bring himself back in line with the others as Nehemiah stood, unfolding himself slowly off the floor to reach his full height. The crowd were starting to fidget, and he smiled reassuringly as he ran an eye over them.

"I'm the last speaker, I promise, but I do need to update you quickly on the plan to introduce children to the colony." The audience stilled, fixing their eyes on him with renewed concentration. "We are aiming to wake the first children up in a week or so. There are, however, a few factors that we need to take into consideration. Children will only be woken when all their carers are awake and have moved into their permanent residence, as they will be discharged immediately into the care of their guardians; we want to make sure that they have a safe place they can go to that they can start to think of as home immediately. We will also be waking children in groups of no less than ten, to ensure they have other children around them while they integrate.

"If you have children and you think you fulfil the criteria, please apply via the form on the database and we will be in touch soon. Thank you."

Nehemiah inclined his head towards the audience, then turned to Nina. She stood, muscles protesting after sitting on the ground at the end of a long day's work. She rolled her shoulders out as she retook the stage.

"I think that's everything, so I suggest we adjourn for this evening. We've brought down some drinks so please do hang around; have a drink, have a chat and come and find us if you have any more questions." She grinned. "Dismissed."

Everyone laughed and conversations started breaking out all over as people stretched and stood. Fraser made her way over to the crate of drinks and snapped the catches open, lifting the lid and playing bartender for a moment until people were comfortable enough to help themselves. Then she wandered over to Nina, two bottles of beer in hand. Condensation ran down the outsides of the bottles invitingly.

"Thought you could use a drink, Cap," she said, handing one over. "Cheers."

"Cheers," replied Nina, lifting her bottle in return. "And thank you."

"Just doing my duty," Sam replied jauntily. "Catch you later." With a little wave, she headed back over to the group she had been sitting with, which included Taylor and Kjeldsen.

Nina was pleased to note relationships developing between the younger members of the crew, though she was still unsure as to the exact nature of those relationships. Probably best not to think too much about it, she mused, turning away. They would let her know if there was anything that was her concern.

There was quite a crowd around Chaudhary and Mira so Nina picked them up some drinks, guessing they might not get away for a while. She slipped in and passed Mira a chilled lemonade, which the other woman took with a grateful smile before turning back to her audience, then Nina fought her way through to Chaudhary and handed him a cold beer. Probably being hounded by people wanting to know exactly what they were entitled to and how they were supposed to personalise their homes with mere essentials, she thought. Nina would have felt sorry for him if she hadn't known exactly how experienced Ramin was with dealing with those sorts of queries, and she knew he was more than capable of handling himself with a few well-placed quips and a no-nonsense tone.

Leclerc also had a few people surrounding her, one of whom she recognised as her lab assistant, Robert. They were all talking eagerly and Nina guessed the others were amateur scientists, keen to know everything she could tell them about the planet. She left them to it and went in search of the rest of her crew. Unexpectedly, she found them all together; Pavluhkin and Sakamoto were talking earnestly, with Dan nodding along. Sarah was also with them, but she didn't appear to be paying much attention to the conversation, instead scanning the crowd as if looking for someone. Liu spotted her first, waving her over to join them and Sarah smiled and relaxed when she did.

"Evening, team," she greeted. "How is everyone?"

"Good, thank you, Captain," replied Pavluhkin formally.

Nina waved a hand. "Please, don't let me interrupt your conversation. I was just looking for familiar faces. I know I said I'd be available for questions but all the public-facing stuff does get a bit draining after a while."

Dan grinned. "Not admitting weakness, are you, Captain?" Dr Caimile elbowed him in the ribs. "Ow! What happened to 'do no harm', Doc?"

Sarah muttered something under her breath in response and Nina relaxed and sipped her beer, savouring the flavour as the cold liquid rolled over her tongue. It was encouraging to see relationships between her crew continuing to grow on the planet's surface, even in these new, unfamiliar circumstances. She knew then that they'd be ok; that even though the mission to get here was over, they were still a crew.

Chapter Nine

The next day, Nina made a trip to see Chaudhary first thing. She knew that the crew and the Union would be the first to be allocated quarters, as they had been awake the longest, and wanted to make sure she didn't get caught in the rush. She found him in the stores, directing droids who were stacking boxes into piles. Despite what he had said at the meeting, it looked very much like Nina's memories of trips to IKEA when she was a little girl, and she smiled at the image.

"Captain! Come to claim your bounty before it's all gone?" Ramin greeted her, and Nina marvelled at the man's constant good humour.

"Something like that," she replied drily. "Did you get my message?"

Chaudhary nodded and pointed to a small pile just to the right of the doors. "First bits I sorted. Captain's privilege." He cocked his head and regarded her quizzically. "Though I must confess, I'm a little surprised. I'd have thought you'd be spending longer on the ship before committing to being a ground dweller."

Nina grimaced. "Oh, you're right. I have no intention of settling permanently on the surface for a while yet. This is purely to make sure I have a base set up for when I'm down there, or when I'm too tired to fly myself back to the ship at the end of the day."

Chaudhary grinned. "Pragmatic as ever, Nina. I'll make sure your stuff is on the first shuttle down."

"Thanks, Ramin. See you later."

With a cheery wave, Chaudhary spun himself round and headed back into the stores. Nina left and started to make her way back up to the bridge. Kjeldsen was up there by themself quite a lot now and Nina had resolved to ask them about that. She didn't want them to be stuck on the ship while the rest of the crew made themselves more and more at home on the ground and was concerned they might be feeling a bit abandoned. Sure enough, they looked up, startled, as Nina entered.

"At ease," she said, as they attempted to get up. "Carry on, I've just got a bit of admin to write up." She fiddled with her screen for a moment, sending a few updates over to Kjeldsen's console and waiting for them to relax again before looking over.

"How are you doing, Bille?"

The Communications Officer looked surprised at the use of their first name. "I'm okay, Captain."

"Did your brother get woken up yet?" Nina asked, remembering.

Kjeldsen's face brightened. "Yes, he woke up at the end of last week. He's just been cleared for duty, so he's excited to start getting stuck in. He was at the meeting last night."

"Oh." Nina's brow furrowed, remembering the group of young people she had seen them with last night. "I'm afraid I didn't register anyone you were with in particular."

"That's okay, Captain. It's nice to know he's awake now, though with him working out on the farming side, I don't know how much I'll see of him. He's hoping to get quarters over that way, too—we talked about living together but we don't think it'll work."

"It must be a bit odd being up here on your own most of the time now."

Kjeldsen half smiled. "It's a little strange, yes, Captain. But it can't be helped."

"I think it can, actually," she said, leaning over towards them. "I'm considering setting up a command station on the surface. Once we've unloaded most of the passengers and separated the ship, we'll probably start using it more again. But for now, I don't want you stuck up here on your own when you can do your job perfectly well remotely on Demeter."

Kjeldsen looked torn. "I wouldn't want you to go to all that trouble just for me, Captain."

"It wouldn't just be for you," Nina countered. "I'd find it very helpful to be able to access the ship's systems from on the surface, too. And Leclerc and Chaudhary would benefit from an interface as well." Mind made up, she nodded decisively. "I'll talk to Mira about it. Sit tight for another couple of days, but let me know if you want to come down to see your new home today and Sam or I will come and get you."

Kjeldsen's face lit up at the thought and Nina left them looking considerably more cheerful than they had done when she had entered.

Nina had lunch on the ship with Pavluhkin, Chaudhary and Kjeldsen, sent a quick memo to Mira regarding the planet-side command centre and headed down to the settlement. The first housing allocations had been released and, despite what she had said to Chaudhary, she was keen to see her new digs. She knew that the crew had mostly been placed in the same area and Nina couldn't contain her amusement at the image of her and Dan growing old as next-door neighbours. How far they'd come from the first missions they'd done together as fresh-faced youths, she mused, never staying still for longer than five minutes in their quest to see as much of the galaxy as possible. Well, they were certainly a long way from home now.

Nina parked her tandem next to the shuttle, on what had unofficially been designated the landing strip. She'd have to have a word with Mira and check if that was going to become the official landing site or if they should switch to using somewhere else if that spot was needed. Nina thought it a good location; at the southern end of the bay, away from the prevailing wind and on a slightly raised section of cliff, out of the way of the rest of the settlement. It was also close to where the crew had been allocated quarters; a short walk took her to her new home. She stopped and looked it over.

It was an H-shaped, greyish building with a shallow sloping roof and a front door in the middle. It was slightly different from the other buildings on her row; Dan's to the right was L shaped and Sakamoto's on the left appeared flat from the front. A space marked out in front of each house (cottage, Nina decided on a whim) delineated the garden, which presumably they could use how they wanted. Taking a breath, she walked up where she decided there needed to be a path and lifted her hand to the keypad by the door. It clicked and swung open a fraction; obviously coding the houses to their new occupants' biochips had been part of the allocation process. Nina pushed the door open the rest of the way and stepped inside.

She found herself in a small open space, as yet unfurnished. There were doors on the left and back walls, two doors on the right and a window next to the door at the back. Underneath the window was a small kitchenette with a sink, two rings, an all-purpose cooker mounted on the wall and a chiller unit under a slim workbench. Crossing first to the window, she looked out. There was another marked up area at the back giving her another, more private space than the front garden that looked out over the road and the bay. Nina chuckled at her mental use of the word 'road'; it was nothing of the sort yet, just a section of ground that had been left clear for people to pass by on. The eventual plan was to finish all the roads with solar paving, but for now it remained untouched. She supposed that was what roads had been like before the invention of tarmac and she certainly preferred it to the mass of grey that Earth had become before she left. She pulled her gaze back from the window and looked again around the empty room.

Making her way to the next door, she pushed it open and began her investigation of the other rooms. The door furthest back on the right was her bathroom; her jaw dropped to find she had a full size one, including a bath with shower attachment as well as a sink and toilet. There was even a small frosted window to allow some natural light in, a huge improvement on the cramped, dingy cubicle she had had in her Earthside digs before this mission. Making a mental note to thank Mira profusely, she left the bathroom and tried the other door in the same wall, then the last door. She found two rooms, each with a large window at the front overlooking the bay. Nina decided the slightly smaller of the two would be her bedroom and the largest her living room. It would be nice to have enough space to entertain in, she mused with a smile.

She crossed to the window at the front of her new bedroom and gazed out at the view. Even on a cloudy day like today, it was still stunning. The wind whipped the sea into ever-changing peaks, thrown into relief by the occasional surge of sunlight that pushed its way through the clouds. She sighed, her smile growing, and decided to put a bench in her front garden so she could sit outside in the evenings and watch the sunset.

As she didn't yet have any furniture to make a start on building, she headed back out with the intention of locating the new homes of her colleagues. All of them, with the exception of Dr Caimile, who now lived on the other side of town closer to the hospital, were in the same area. They were split between the front row and the second row of houses, with half of them backing onto the gardens of the others. All very cosy, and prime locations for everyone. From around the back of the houses, she could see the small generators on the roofs that converted the energy collected from the solar tiling into usable power. The houses were designed to power themselves, with plans for larger sources out of town and solar paving to power the bigger buildings and top up any deficiency in the rest of the settlement. They hadn't known what kind of climate they were going to find, so there was a wide variety of power sources in the stores; Nina knew that they were considering installing a wind farm somewhere close by, but this was all still in the very early stages. Much more exploration needed to be done before they could decide what would work best.

And that, thought Nina as she started heading towards what was fast becoming the centre of town, was the next step. Now that they had a base on the ground, they could start exploring in earnest. Get some ground vehicles shipped down from the stores, start sending out teams to do reconnaissance of the surrounding area and start properly mapping it. She angled her steps towards Leclerc's lab, with the dual intention of asking her opinion on their readiness to start exploring and kicking her out of the lab for ten minutes to go and see her new home.

Both Leclerc and Liu agreed with Nina's plans to start exploring, so a request was sent through to Chaudhary, when he could find time in between digging out tables, chairs and beds, to locate a couple of ground vehicles that would be suitable for exploring locally. He replied that he would be able to get them down sometime the next morning, so Nina headed back to the ship to make preparations. She also took Liu, who was so delighted by his new cottage that Nina had trouble getting him to talk about anything else. He had already put in his furniture order, decided where everything was going and started planning the interior décor. Nina envied him slightly; he had a creative streak she had never been able to tap into. As they exited the shuttle bay, Dan still in full flow about the mural he was going to paint in his bedroom, her wrist unit bleeped with a message.

"It's later than I thought!" she exclaimed, checking it. "I still haven't adapted to this shorter day."

"Of course you haven't," Dan replied, raising his eyebrows. "We've only been here four weeks. It'll take longer than that to reset a lifetime of conditioning and circadian rhythms."

"True," Nina acknowledged. "Still, it feels like we've been here long enough that it should be feeling a bit more natural, at least."

"Nina." Dan stopped, crossing his arms and facing her, his face serious. "You're not a superhero. You're an excellent captain and one of my best friends, but you're still human. You can't put expectations on yourself that you wouldn't put on other people. It doesn't work like that."

Nina sighed. "I know. I just feel like I have to set an example."

"And you do," stressed Dan, "but the example you need to be setting right now is that it's going to take time to adjust. If everyone else sees you losing track of time as well, that's going to make them feel better about doing it!"

Nina laughed, the tension in her shoulders easing slightly. "You're right. Thanks, Dan."

"Any time. Now let's go get dinner before Taylor eats it all."

The galley was pleasantly full tonight, with Fraser, Taylor, Chaudhary, Pavluhkin and Kjeldsen also in attendance. Nina found herself relaxing as she tucked into Taylor's chilli, which he assured them was his mother's secret recipe. It was quite possibly the best thing she'd eaten since she woke up and Taylor grinned proudly when she said as much. Afterwards, she sat down for a rare quiet moment in one of the comfy chairs at the other end of the galley and was about to get stuck into a book when Fraser approached her.

"Sorry to interrupt Cap, but have you got a minute?"

"Of course, Sam, what can I do for you?" she replied, setting the book aside.

"I was wondering about setting up some kind of schedule for shuttle trips," the pilot said, lowering herself into a seat opposite Nina. "I've been doing a lot of running up and down from the ship with just one or two people and it seems kind of wasteful. I was thinking, it would be much more efficient if people knew when to aim to get there for a ride, rather than just going whenever they want to."

"You mean like a timetable? That's an excellent idea, Sam." Nina knew that certain people, like the medical team, were now working on rotas which required them to be planet-side some days and on-board ship others. Doctors, for example, spent two days a week in the cryobay and the rest of their time on the surface. It was imperative that they had a way to get up and down, but Sam was right, it needed to be more structured.

Fraser nodded enthusiastically, buoyed by Nina's praise. "I was thinking, I could run one in the morning and one in the evening, and maybe a couple more in the middle of the day depending on demand, but it would mean that everyone going up and down for a work shift would know what time they needed to be at the landing area to catch their flight."

Nina nodded too. "That's really sensible. Can I leave that with you? Have a look at some work rosters and maybe talk to some people, then send it over to Kjeldsen for release. I'm happy for you to decide, you know best."

Sam grinned widely. "Thanks, Cap." She bounced back over to Taylor and Kjeldsen, glowing from the praise.

Nina studied her for a moment. The young woman had come on a lot in the short time since they had started the mission and Nina was proud of her development. She had never been shy but she had been good at what she did and she had stuck to that, obeying orders with accuracy and precision while staying within her limits. Now, she was constantly looking to better herself, learning new skills and seeking places she could help out. Coming to Nina with ideas for how to improve the efficiency of the colony was another big step for her. Nina knew there were personal benefits too; running to a timetable would allow her a lot more freedom in between those times, but it would also mean she had to stick to it. She made a mental note to wake up another pilot to make sure that Fraser was able to get at least one day off a week.

Leaving the young people to it, Nina picked up her book and headed back to her quarters. Those three were a strange mix, she mused; Fraser was the most exuberant of them, with Kjeldsen's shyness and Taylor's quiet confidence an odd combination at first glance, but they seemed to balance each other out. She was almost entirely convinced that they were romantically attached now; their interactions were full of subtle touches and loaded glances that indicated closeness. She was glad that Fraser and Taylor were currently still lodging on the ship to give Kjeldsen some human contact in the evening, and hoped she'd get the okay from Mira to get them all more planet-based tomorrow.

Once safely in her room, she managed fifteen minutes of her book before her eyelids started to droop and she surrendered to the call of an early night.

The next morning, Nina headed down early with Dan in the tandem. She had sent over a message to the two newly woken cartographers to meet them at the lab at 10.00, Demeter time, for the first planning meeting of the new wave of exploratory missions. Just before 10.00, two people that Nina didn't recognise at all knocked on the door and entered timidly. The man had dark skin and was short and stocky, with a worried expression. The woman had very pale skin covered with freckles and shockingly red hair. She too, had a look of concern on her face and Nina wondered if this was common to cartographers as a breed or if it was just due to the current situation. Introductions were made; the man was called Tumelo and he was originally South African and the woman was Niamh, unsurprisingly from Ireland. Nina made a mental note to add sun cream to the list of supplies that the exploratory teams would need to carry; with skin that pale, Niamh would be burning in minutes. Sakamoto was there too, with her deputy; a tall, slimly built man named Miguel who hailed originally from Columbia. He was military, like Sakamoto, and bore himself in a remarkably similar way for two people with such different builds.

The meeting was brief but thorough. They were to divide into two teams, each team consisting of a cartographer, a security officer and two others. They would follow routes that Leclerc had mapped roughly from their limited intel and stop every five kilometres to conduct the tests that had been devised. The first mission was due to last two days, with the teams camping overnight at the furthest point before returning by a different route the following day. Leclerc made a point of stressing the unknowns of the environment and Nina was glad Dr Caimile wasn't there to further compound the worry on the faces of the cartographers. The teams would leave cameras at the campsites on their return, so that they could continue to monitor the wildlife in the surrounding areas and especially, as Leclerc said, in case there was anything intelligent enough to come and investigate after it was clear there had been unusual activity in the area.

The missions were due to set off first thing the following morning. Due to the shorter day, 10.00 had been decided on as the official starting point for a day's activities to make sure everyone got enough sleep with the two hours missing overnight. Nina dismissed the teams and set about deciding with Liu how to divide people up. He was going with them, she was not; they had agreed that both of them disappearing was a bad idea and that there would be other opportunities for her to explore further down the line. She had started out feeling slight pangs of jealousy but those began to dissipate around the point that Sakamoto started talking about how to take extra care while camping around unknown predators.

It was still too early for lunch, so Nina and Dan headed out to see how the rest of the town was coming along. Construction had begun on the three large communal buildings, with more to be added as the need arose. Things like shops and other more niche premises were a long way down the list; it was generally assumed that the colonists had brought everything they needed to get started with them. Anything extra for now would need to come from the stores, and anything that had outlived its usefulness could be passed on or recycled.

As they rounded the side of the lab, the building sites came into view. Of the three that had been marked up, the furthest one was completed, with the central one looking like it would be nearly done by the end of the day. Nina imagined they would all look fairly similar when they were built; functional looking buildings, two storeys high with flat, nondescript fronts and multiple windows. A mixture of droids and people poured into the finished one, carrying equipment in various states of assembly. Doctors James and Caimile were standing out the front, checking their notepads and pointing as swathes of kit passed them by. Nina breathed a sigh of relief that the medical team would soon have a proper place to treat the patients that were bound to appear. Last week they had been lucky and only had a couple of sprains from the construction crew, but they couldn't bank on luck forever.

The middle building, which was around the same height as the medical bay but as yet without a roof, was to be the canteen. Construction workers still swarmed over this one, working hard to get it completed. Nina looked forward to the wider community being able to have proper meals, though she knew that until the farmers were more established, there was going to be a limit as to what those meals could be. She felt slightly guilty about the facilities they had on board ship to make themselves real dinners while everyone else was still on the pre-packaged rations. Sure, they delivered all the nutrients required for a balanced diet, but they did all start to taste the same after a couple of weeks. A bit of variety would be as good for morale as it was for people's health.

The third building was half built, with a few walls already in place but nothing secured yet. This would be the community centre, a generic building to be used by anyone who needed it for a whole host of purposes. The laundry would also be housed at the back of this one, with options for both self-service and fully serviced laundry. Nina noticed that the entire area in front of the structures had been covered in the same solar paving that the roads between houses were destined for. She supposed it made sense; in high traffic areas it was important to have something underfoot that wouldn't give way and the panels would add a massive boost to the town's energy supply, but she rather missed the feeling of spongy ground under her feet.

Finished with their recce, Nina and Dan had just turned back towards their cottages when they were hailed by a shout. Mira rounded the corner of the middle building, waving her notepad at them. Nina raised a hand in greeting and she jogged over to them, slightly breathless.

"Sorry I haven't got round to replying to your message, Captain. It's been pretty busy."

Nina smiled. "Not a problem. I know it wasn't a high priority, just on the off chance you had a moment."

Mira nodded. "It's a good idea, actually. It makes a lot of sense for you to have mission control on the surface, saves you having to jump back up to the ship every time you have to do something. Would just a normal housing unit work?"

Nina thought about it for a moment. "Yes, I think it would. Could we arrange it so that it had one big room, one for meetings and then another smaller one, in case we need somewhere private?"

Mira tapped at her notepad. "Done. Should by up by end of play tomorrow. Did you want the lab swapping out for something more permanent too while we're over that end of town?"

"Probably. Although check that with Leclerc first, there may be reasons why she doesn't want to that I don't know. I'd imagine we're good to lose the temporary accommodations by the lab, too."

"Great. I'll check in with Leclerc and get that all sorted."

Nina remembered something else she'd been meaning to say to Mira. "Thank you so much for my bathroom, by the way."

Mira grinned. "I thought you'd like it. Got to give you something to tempt you to stay with the rest of us on this planet, instead of running off in search of black holes or whatever it is you military types do these days."

Dan roared with laughter as Nina chuckled. "Very true, Mira. May I add my thanks to Nina's; my house is perfect and I love it."

"You're both very welcome. Now if you'll excuse me, I'd better get back to work. Buildings don't build themselves, even in this day and age."

Chapter Ten

The ground vehicles were due to arrive that afternoon, so after lunch, Nina dropped Dan off at the science lab while she headed back to her tandem. She had got most of the way there when she heard screaming coming from the shoreline. Alarmed, she ran in that direction, thoughts jumping immediately to huge aquatic predators. Her concerns turned out to be unfounded and she stopped, bent double to catch her breath while she took in the scene before her.

Sam Fraser was knee deep in the sea, soaked overalls rolled up to mid-thigh and shrieking with glee as she splashed water at an equally soaking Taylor. They were both in fits of laughter, with Kjeldsen looking on from the shore with a curiously mixed expression on their face.

"I take it the net's up, then," Nina said, smiling as Kjeldsen jumped in surprise at her approach. "Why don't you join them?"

"There's only room for two at the moment," Kjeldsen replied, looking slightly wistfully at the pair in the water. Nina looked closer; sure enough, the top of the security webbing was just visible, poking up over the water and enclosing what looked like about a square metre of safe space.

"Nonsense," Nina remarked. "Plenty of room, it'll just be a bit cosy."

Kjeldsen hesitated a moment, biting their lip, then ran at Fraser and Taylor, yelling and flailing their arms. Nina laughed out loud as Taylor fell over in surprise, pulling the other two down when they laughed as well.

"Well, that's not the medical emergency I was expecting."

Nina turned, startled, to see Dr Caimile panting and clutching a stitch in her side behind her. She grinned.

"Infinitely preferable, though."

"I don't know," muttered Sarah, "those overalls are miserable when they're wet." Nina laughed and the two of them observed the three in the water for a moment. Sarah glanced at Nina. "Is it just me, or is this a fairly apt metaphor for the relationship between that lot?"

"Definitely not just you," Nina replied, and they shared a small smile.

The three gods of chaos squelched out of the water and Fraser attempted a salute, at which all three dissolved into giggles again.

"At ease," Nina grinned. "Nice work on getting the net up."

Fraser beamed. "Thanks, Cap. It's technically my day off, so I thought I'd do something a bit different in between my shuttle trips. The timetable is working out brilliantly, by the way, thank you."

"Glad to hear it," Nina replied. It was hard to keep the smile off her face; Fraser oozed happiness and it was contagious. "Have you been to see your houses?"

The smile on Fraser's face grew even wider. "They're brilliant! Me and Steve are next to each other and Bille's garden backs onto Steve's, so we're all together." She stopped abruptly and flushed bright red, confirming Nina's suspicions. "Er, I mean…"

Nina held up a hand. "Relax, Sam. We're on this planet to start a new life. New relationships are a part of that. As long as you don't bring your private lives to work with you, I don't care what you get up to off duty. Though I am pleased to see you all so happy," she admitted, and the other two flushed as hard as Fraser.

"Thanks, Captain," Taylor mumbled, staring at his feet.

"By the way, Bille," she addressed Kjeldsen, "Mira's okayed the command centre. She estimates it should be up by the end of tomorrow, so you can move down here a bit more permanently if you like."

Kjeldsen beamed and Fraser high-fived them. "Thanks, Captain."

Nina nodded. "Now why don't you see if you can widen that net out a bit more? I bet Dr Caimile here would love a dip before bedtime."

Fraser took one look at Sarah's face and very obviously bit back the retort she had been about to make. "Yes, Captain." She aimed another soggy salute at Nina and the three youngsters spread out to tackle the net again. Nina and the doctor made it around the corner of a nearby building before catching each other's eye and bursting into laughter. Several passers-by shot them curious looks, but it was a few moments before they managed to pull themselves together enough to straighten up.

"Did they think they were being subtle?" Sarah asked, genuine curiosity in her voice. "I've never seen less well-hidden romantic attachment, and that's saying something."

"They're still very young." Nina sighed. "I seem to remember thinking I was a master of everything at that age."

"True." Sarah smiled wistfully. "What are you up to now?"

"I'm headed back up to the ship, if I don't stop getting distracted. I'll be back down tomorrow to set up for the exploratory missions."

Sarah smiled again, this time a little wickedly, and Nina felt a tug in her stomach. "Are you up for a bit more distraction tomorrow evening?"

"I was going to make a start on building my furniture, but if you've got a better idea…" she trailed off, uncertain. Was Sarah implying what she thought she was implying?

"Perfect. I'll come over and give you a hand. Then when we've worked out how to do it, we can go back to mine and build those too."

Nina laughed, both relieved and disappointed. "You've got a mercenary streak in you a mile wide, you know that?"

Sarah just waved and headed off towards town, and Nina set off in the opposite direction towards her shuttle.

After a quiet evening on the ship, Nina found herself back in the science lab the next morning at 10.00. A large amount of the equipment appeared to be missing and she looked around in confusion, trying to locate it.

"Try the garden," Robert quipped, noticing her gaze. "We're switching to the permanent lab later, so we've got to empty this by lunchtime." Nina glanced out of the window and sure enough, there was a large assortment of kit piled on trolleys by one of the planting patches.

"Nice. I bet Monique's happy about that."

Robert grimaced. "She can't decide if she's ecstatic about getting a bigger, better lab or annoyed that she has to take this one apart."

Nina laughed, recognising Leclerc's changeable temperament easily from Robert's description. As they talked, the mission teams assembled in a jumble of people and luggage, gathering for a quick, last-minute briefing. Pavluhkin gave the trucks a final check over before clearing them to leave. Nina followed everyone out and pulled Dan aside quickly before he got into his truck.

"Be careful. I know you will be, but I just wanted to say it."

He nodded. "Thanks, Nina. See you in a couple of days."

She watched him get into the truck, swinging himself up into the front compartment to sit next to Sakamoto. They were headed north, towards the foothills, while the other group went south. Sakamoto saluted as they drove off and Nina returned it, with a mixture of jealousy that she wasn't going and worry for their safety. The truck rolled swiftly out of sight; the standard issue ground vehicles could manage up to 100 kilometres per hour over all but the steepest terrain, and they had a lot of ground to cover.

After a moment, she turned and headed back into the lab.

"Need a hand clearing this?" she asked, gesturing to the still cluttered work surfaces.

"Yes please," Robert replied fervently, so she spent a busy hour pottering in and out of the lab garden. Robert and Monique turned out to be surprisingly restful company; neither of them was the type to chatter so much of the work was done in silence. Nina enjoyed the brief respite from command and was pleased at the end of the hour to look around and see a mostly empty room.

"Thank you, Captain. That was most helpful of you." Leclerc was in the process of removing a rather unwieldy plant, balancing it awkwardly on her hip while she talked to Nina. "Where are you going next?"

"I've got a meeting with some of the specialists after lunch about waking up the kids. We're meeting at the Lovells'."

Robert smiled widely as he held open the garden door. "Excellent. It's not the same without my little bundles of chaos running all over the place."

"You've got kids?" Nina asked, reassessing him. She hadn't taken him for a dad, somehow. "How many?"

"Two. A five-year-old girl and a three-year-old boy. My wife is one of the nurses that woke last week, so we're hoping we'll be able to get the kids joining us as soon as possible."

"I'm sure you will," Nina replied, smiling reassuringly. "I'll let you know how we get on."

"Thanks, Captain."

Nina made her goodbyes and left them to finish the clearing up, munching on some portable rations while she enjoyed the view from her front garden before heading to the Lovells'. The house was bigger than hers, built both higher and wider. Nina knocked on the door and it was opened by a smiling Patrin.

"Captain, come in!"

She entered and was immediately blown away by the difference between the houses. It wasn't just that it was bigger—with an extra room on the ground floor and a sleeping loft above the largest of the rooms—it was the whole feeling of the place. The colonists had been allowed a small crate of personal effects each; these had been located when the individual was woken and were now being sent down to houses with the furniture delivery. Nina hadn't used her crate; having spent most of her life on ships with small quarters, there hadn't been much that she'd wanted to bring. The Lovells, however, had obviously used their allocation fully and wasted no time in making themselves at home.

The room Nina entered into had a rectangular table and four chairs, with a cheerful tablecloth spread over it that nicely disguised the fact it was one of the three dining tables available to choose from. It had a similar, though slightly larger, kitchen area to Nina's, tucked neatly into a corner behind the table. A bookshelf stood against one wall, already half-stacked with books and with several paintings leaned up against the bottom of it. Nina, curious, requested a tour and was shown into the other rooms by a more than willing Patrin.

The next room was the biggest and was clearly going to be the living space, with a large colourful rug in the middle of the floor and a sofa to one side. Two open crates sat half-empty on the rug and more art leaned against the walls, spread around the room in what Nina assumed were approximations of where it would finally hang. A ladder at the back of the room led up to a sleeping loft, which she climbed at Patrin's invitation and poked her head into with interest. Far from being small, it was roughly the same size as her bedroom, with a bed and two matching nightstands already assembled up there. It looked cosy and snug, and Nina had a small moment of irrational jealousy which she quickly squashed; her bedroom was larger than any she had ever had, would house a double bed and had a sea view.

Clambering back down the ladder, she looked into the other two rooms, one of which was empty as yet. The last one contained another crate, a storage unit and a small bed. Toys spilled out of the crate onto the bed and all over the floor, books lay piled on the storage unit and Nina could see lots of very bright clothes in one of the open drawers.

"This will be Kezia's room," said Patrin, smiling at the mess. "Oddly enough, it'll probably look pretty similar to this again within days of her getting in here."

Nina laughed and they went back into the first room, where Ana Romero and a woman Nina didn't know now sat with Nehemiah.

"How old is Kezia?" Nina asked as she sat down. Patrin dragged a crate through from the living room and perched on the edge.

"Seven," Nehemiah replied. "She'll have memories of Earth when she grows up, but I imagine they'll start to feel like a long time ago quite quickly." He indicated the woman sitting across from him. "This is Makena Marangu."

"Back home, they'd have called me a social worker," she explained as she shook Nina's hand. She had dark skin, and hair that bounced around her face in medium length tightly coiled curls. She spoke English with a strong accent. "I'm not sure what I want to call the job here yet but I'm here to look after the children."

Ana nodded, her face serious. "There's going to be a lot of different coping mechanisms from all the children, depending on so many factors. We'll have to be prepared for anything."

Nina nodded too, looking back to Ana. "How are your team faring? Will they be ready if we move forward with waking the children?"

"They are mostly adjusting well. The few that have had difficulties have been talking to those who haven't, and I think are doing better now. We have a team of around twelve people who are ready to start work tomorrow, and five of those have experience or a specialism in working with children."

"That's brilliant news," Nina said. "We'll have to work out where they can see clients until the medical centre is finished—I'd prefer people not to have to use their own homes for that."

Ana frowned. "Back on Earth, many of them practised from home. I would imagine they would have no objection to doing so here. Certainly, some of those who work with children will prefer to, as the children often find a medical environment intimidating."

"That makes sense," Nina replied. "I really know nothing about how any of this works, so I'll need you to guide me through it."

"That's what our extra room will be," added Patrin. "It's mostly my office, but doubles as somewhere I can work with my children until we have a school with dedicated facilities."

"That sounds wonderful," Nina responded. "It's so reassuring to be working with experts." They all laughed and Nina found herself relaxing. She really didn't have anything to worry about. "So, you think we can start introducing children to the colony then?"

All four of her companions nodded.

"Under the conditions that I mentioned the other night, of course," Nehemiah reminded her. "Makena will be checking in with families that apply to have their children woken, to make sure that they meet the conditions before we start."

"That's one reason I'm not sure the job title 'social worker' will fit me here," Makena put in. "Some people will have very negative associations with that term and might resent what they would see as an intrusion."

Nina nodded. "I see. Something like 'Children's Officer' might suit better, perhaps? Something that makes it sound like you're more linked to my team than any agency."

"Children's Officer is good," said Ana, nodding. "Official, without making families feel like you're interfering in their lives."

"I like it," agreed Makena.

"Excellent," said Nina. "Shall we start looking through applications this evening and you can begin to make home visits from tomorrow?"

"Works for me," replied Makena. "Once we have an idea of numbers for this group, we can work out how long it'll take me to visit everyone and get a date set for waking." She looked appraisingly at Nehemiah and Patrin. "I think you two have passed your initial check-up already."

"Aha, so it is a test!" quipped Patrin. Makena waggled her finger at him and everybody laughed.

"This has been really positive everyone, thank you," Nina said, when the laughter had died down. "I'm feeling much more confident about starting this next stage of making this planet feel like home."

Chapter Eleven

Nina took a quick stroll by the shore on the way to her next stop, noticing as she did so that the designated safe area had been enlarged considerably since the day before. From what she could see, it now looked to be about the size of an average sized public swimming bath. About a dozen people lounged on the black sand while a similar number paddled and one or two brave souls actually swam. She briefly considered coming down to join them later but thought she'd wait until the area was a bit bigger again; she had never been one for crowded beaches.

She reached the centre of the village and was again struck by the speed that things seemed to happen around here. Two of the large buildings were now complete, with the remaining one a storey higher than it had been the previous day. Nina knew that the aim had been to get the canteen finished today, but it had still seemed so far off when she had popped by yesterday morning. Now there was activity visible through the windows and people streamed in and out of the doors setting the last bits of furnishings up. The canteen would open for business at breakfast tomorrow morning, and Nina knew it was much anticipated.

Mealtime slots were to be sent out along with work rotas, so people would be able to eat at convenient times whilst not overloading the canteen with everyone all in one go. There would also be several food processing units, programmed to output a wide variety of snacks, treats and luxury items. They had been state of the art when they left Earth, so they only had a few as the technology had had limited availability. They also used a lot of energy, so each colonist was allocated a certain number of credits a month to use with them. How much had things come on since they had left, Nina wondered. Funny to think of technology advancing while they stagnated, or had the fall of the planet stopped any more progression?

She stopped for a cursory inspection of the canteen, which all looked highly sleek and modern, unlike the rusty old canteen at the training barracks she had first lived at. The ground floor had been left as one large room, with a serving area along the back wall where colonists could be supplied with one of the several hot options that would be on offer at each meal. There was also a hot and cold drinks bar and an area for collecting pre-prepared lighter meals from the large chiller cabinet humming away on the wall next to the food processing units. These were currently being installed by engineers; Nina waved at Pavluhkin, but didn't go over to say hello as she looked rather busy.

Upstairs was split into smaller rooms, which would be available to book for private dining or special occasions. After poking her head into a few, she headed next door to look at the partially built community centre. This was to be a multi-purpose space, so the downstairs consisted mostly of a large bright hall, with expansive windows running along all the edges. The laundry was at one end, attached to the main building but with no access from inside to avoid disruption to events in the main hall. Stairs and a partially installed lift led up to the second floor, which was wasn't yet finished but would be split up into lots of smaller rooms of various sizes. The prayer room would be on this floor, as well as a small office where the centre manager would work.

Most of the colonists had been picked due to their expertise in a particular area, and a wide swath of humanity had been chosen to offer as diverse a selection as possible. However, some people had had to leave their old jobs behind to join a partner or family member and would have to look for new employment once here. The centre manager was one such position, and it was hoped that someone with an appropriate skill-set would crawl out of the woodwork soon. Now that the first batches of permanent housing had been built and they could accommodate more colonists, partners were being woken at the same time as people with jobs to do immediately and Nina was optimistic someone would be found before long.

Nina checked the time on her wrist unit and decided it was late enough to head over to the medical centre in search of Dr Caimile. She hadn't wanted to go too early, as she was sure Sarah had plenty to be getting on with in her new building, but she did also want to have a bit of a nose around before she met up with her. She descended the ramp and crossed the open area between the buildings, noting with pleasant surprise how well the new science lab was coming along just a few hours after she had left the temporary one. There was a marked-up area in front of it too—in the place of one of the recently removed sleeper units—that she took to be the spot for the new command centre.

The medical centre already felt like a hospital as she entered, with a clean chemical smell and lots of activity. She indulged her curiosity and did a little snooping, checking out the signs already stuck to doors and marvelling at how quickly something like this could be created. On the top floor at the far end of the corridor, she found a staff lounge and an office with Jerry's name on the door. A murmur of voices sounded from inside. She raised her hand and knocked, and immediately Jerry called for her to enter.

"Captain Brooke! What a pleasure! Please, come in!" Jerry was sitting behind a large desk on the opposite side of the small office, with Dr Caimile perched on the edge. They both cradled mugs and looked as if they'd been there for years, not hours.

"This is very impressive, doctors," Nina commented, taking everything in. Shelves lined one long wall, already stacked with boxes and folders, and more boxes ran under the window on the wall to her left. Only the wall behind the desk was bare and Nina suspected that if there had been more space, then that too would have been used for storage. "Everything going to plan?"

"It's brilliant, Nina," Sarah said, smiling an unusually wide smile. "We've been able to map everything out how we want it, without any interference from smarmy board members and it all just makes so much sense!"

Nina grinned; it was good to see her friend so happy. "A medical centre designed and run by doctors? What will they think of next?"

The doctors both laughed and Sarah checked her wrist unit. "I suppose you've come to extract me from my work to come and build your furniture for you?"

"That is decidedly *not* how I'd have phrased it," Nina informed Jerry, who shook his head.

"Don't worry, Captain. I've spent long enough working with her to know when to not take any notice of what she's saying. Have a nice evening." He waved, then sighed as Sarah got up, leaving her coffee cup on his desk as she left with Nina.

"You get worse when you're happy, you know that?" Nina remarked as they exited the building. All the multi-storey buildings had lifts and access ramps, but Sarah led Nina out down a wide flight of stairs to the right of the office instead.

Sarah snorted. "You've never seen me happy."

"Nonsense. You're ecstatic right now. You've got the centre you always dreamed of, all the staff and equipment you've asked for and a lovely new house with a sea view. If you were a normal person, you'd be singing with joy."

Sarah shot Nina a sideways look. "If you'd ever heard me sing, you'd be counting your blessings that my happiness takes other forms."

Nina chuckled, and they walked in peaceful silence back through town to Nina's cottage. Nina swiped her hand over the sensor, then gestured for Sarah to precede her inside. She scanned the room then turned back to Nina. "Nice. Doesn't feel exactly the same as mine. Impressive, actually, considering they all come from pretty much the same template."

"You should see what the Lovells have done with theirs. It looks like they moved in two weeks ago, not two days. What on Earth is that!"

Sarah had pulled a bottle from her bag, containing what looked like dark blue liquid. "Relax, it's just wine. I ran out of regular bottles; it's the colour of the glass that makes it look weird. I thought we could toast to our new homes, like a proper housewarming."

"Oh!" Nina found herself rather touched, but then blushed. "I, erm, haven't got any glasses yet." In response, Sarah took the cap off the bottle and took a swig.

"Cheers," she said, passing the bottle to Nina, who raised it in return.

"Now I am glad we're building mine first," she quipped. Sarah laughed and they got started on the furniture.

Although Nina hadn't ordered much, it was slow going at first. Sarah suggested some music, so Nina crossed to the room's control module to see what she could find. To her pleasure, all the housing units had come with modern entertainment systems built in, with speakers throughout the house and a main console screen that she decided would go on the wall in her living room. She didn't mind roughing it for a bit while on a mission, but when building a home, it was nice to have all the things one was used to. She imagined people like the Lovells were particularly glad of it too; it would be much harder to get children to settle in on a new planet if they had to leave their favourite programs back on Earth! All the consoles were linked into the central database, so they could be used for music, reading material, entertainment and even education. Nina dialled up some old-fashioned hot club jazz and they got stuck in.

After the first couple of chairs, they started to get the hang of it, and after a few hours, they stood up to survey their handiwork. As well as an empty wine bottle, there was now a decent sized table that could comfortably seat six (or eight if they squeezed), four upright chairs and a pair of matching blue armchairs. They had also hung the console screen, programming it to display a cheerful Cézanne when not in use, and the room felt cosier as a result. The only thing left was Nina's bed, and she wasn't sure if it felt like more effort to build a bed at this point or fly back to the ship to sleep in her quarters there. She exhaled, blowing hair out of her face.

"I'll be honest, Sarah, I'm not sure I've got the energy to do yours as well tonight."

Sarah nodded fervently. "Agreed. Let's get your bed done and call it a night."

Putting aside the questions that statement gave rise to, Nina nodded as well and they set to. After another hour of swearing, giggling, getting tangled in linen and bashing the frame to get the bloody thing to line up, Nina stood with her hands on her hips and let out a happy sigh.

"It actually looks like a bed!" she cried in delight.

After years of sleeping in military issue bunks, Nina had splashed out and ordered herself a king-sized bed, like the one she remembered jumping into with her parents as a child. It had a wooden frame, dark red and glossy, and she had picked cream linen with geometric patterns to go on it. The pillows were plump, the duvet was fluffy, and Nina wanted nothing more than to dive into it and curl up for a week.

"It looks great," Sarah agreed, coming to stand next to her. They stood for a moment, admiring the rare sight of a full-sized bed. Sarah cleared her throat awkwardly. "I know we said we'd call it a night, but would you mind giving me a hand with mine? I'll have missed the last shuttle back to the ship now."

Nina eyed the time, reluctance warring with guilt. "It's pretty late," she hedged.

"I know. I'm sorry; I really can't be bothered either."

Nina sighed. "Fuck it, just stay here tonight, there's more than enough room for both of us."

Sarah's eyebrows shot up. "Did you just swear?"

The tension that had been building in the room evaporated instantly. Nina rolled her eyes and refrained from hitting Sarah with a pillow. Sitting on the side of the bed, she began pulling her boots off.

"I don't think, in thirty years of knowing you, that I've ever heard you swear," Sarah continued from behind her.

Nina twisted to look at her. "Really?"

Sarah swung her legs up on to the bed and leaned against the headboard. "Really."

"Sorry?" Nina offered, smiling.

"Don't be. Good to know you are human, after all."

Nina grinned. "Definitely human. Speaking of which, be back in a minute." She left the room and passed through the entrance hall to the bathroom, smiling at the sight of her newly furnished living room through the open door. When she got back, Sarah took her turn. While Nina waited, she deliberated what to wear; after all, she hadn't been planning on spending the night on the planet so she hadn't brought any sleep wear. Stripping almost to her underwear, she decided the t-shirt she wore under her uniform would have to do.

When she got back, Sarah said nothing but climbed out of her overalls, too. To avoid staring while she undressed, Nina wriggled under the covers and accidentally moaned out loud.

"It's so comfy!" she exclaimed in protest when Sarah shot her a look. Sarah turned out the lights and joined her, snuggling under the covers and rolling to face Nina.

"It is pretty damn comfy," she agreed, smiling. A faint glow from the stars still shone in through the un-curtained windows and Nina could just about make out Sarah's face across from her, her dark skin contrasting sharply with the cream of the pillow. Demeter had no moon, so the stars shone brighter than Nina had ever seen them on Earth and they painted the bed with dappled pinpricks of light.

"Thanks for helping me with all this," she said. "I'm sorry we didn't get to yours tonight."

"It was my pleasure." For once, Sarah's tone was completely genuine, her walls down and her expression unguarded.

Nina found her hand under the covers and squeezed it. "Thank you for everything, actually. I don't know what I'd do without you."

Emotions flickered across Sarah's face and Nina felt her stomach flutter. "Thank you, Nina. I feel the same. You keep me grounded." Nina's heart sped up as Sarah's hand slid to Nina's waist and she pulled her close. They held each other for a moment, Nina's pounding heartbeat gradually slowing, before Sarah pressed a kiss to Nina's head. "Let's get some rest."

Nina reluctantly untangled herself, and the two rolled over to sleep.

Chapter Twelve

Nina was woken early the next morning by Sarah's wrist unit bleeping in an irritatingly chirpy way.

"Sorry, sorry!" whispered Sarah frantically, shushing it.

"What the hell is that?!" Nina groaned, pulling the duvet back around her.

"It's the only tone I've found that wakes me up," Sarah apologised. "Go back to sleep, it's only 07.00."

Nina squinted out of the window. "That explains the lack of light. Why on Earth are you up so early?"

"Lots to do," Sarah replied simply, sitting up.

Nina stretched and sat up too, shaking her head. "I'm awake now."

Sarah eyed her, and Nina flushed as she remembered her state of undress.

"Fancy getting some breakfast? I've heard there's a new place just opened up downtown."

Nina laughed out loud and got out of bed, trying not to stare too overtly as Sarah started to get dressed.

"Breakfast sounds great." She grimaced as she pulled on yesterday's socks. "Remind me to leave some clothes down here."

"And maybe get yourself a chest of drawers to keep them in."

The early morning sun was just peeking over the treetops as they walked to the centre of town, painting the settlement in pale yellow strokes. The canteen had just opened, the double doors thrown wide and a pleasant bustle of activity about the place. They joined the small queue, made up mostly of farmers, and after a short wait, they reached the servery. A cheerful catering assistant with long braids greeted them with a toothy smile.

"Any dietary requirements?" he asked. When they both replied in the negative, he presented them with two matching bowls and a spoon each. They found seats and helped themselves to coffee from the bar at the side. All in all, it reminded Nina of some of the more salubrious places that she had stayed on leave. She said as much to Sarah, who nodded.

"Like that motel in Southend?" she said, through a mouthful of what looked and tasted mostly like porridge.

"*Not* like that motel in Southend," Nina corrected firmly. She sometimes regretted sharing information with Sarah, who had a knack for remembering things that she herself would much rather forget.

After breakfast, which was a treat more for the fact that it was something different rather than the actual quality of the food, they said their goodbyes and headed off in opposite directions. Nina was headed to the farming quarter, where she felt she was long overdue a visit, and Sarah to work in the medical centre. As she turned to go, Sarah caught her hand and pulled her in, then planted a quick kiss on her cheek.

"What was that for?" Nina asked, startled.

"Because I like you." Sarah grinned, before walking away.

Nina shook her head, a smile easing onto her face as she walked slowly in the opposite direction. Sarah continued to surprise her, even after thirty years of friendship. Was now really the moment to find out if it could be something more?

A longer walk took her to the farming quarter, which was slightly out of town due to the space it took up. Her eyes bulged as she took in all the changes that had taken place; buildings stood scattered across the landscape, farmland was already being worked and people thronged everywhere. She hailed a passing farmhand and asked where she might find the Johnsons; the girl pointed out a large building and Nina headed over, finding them in a garden at the back of what she assumed was their farmhouse. They were sitting at a table strewn with various bits and bobs, including seeds, papers and the remains of their breakfast. Lowanna waved her over and they both greeted her with enthusiasm.

"The soil here is so good!" Lowanna exclaimed, after the pleasantries had been exchanged. "I've already planted loads out, and we've had to start expanding the fields already!"

She took Nina for a walk, pointing out the various areas that had been marked out.

"This is our cornfield over here," she explained, waving a hand at a large area to Nina's right. "We've just planted out the first batch of seed, so we hope to be able to start harvesting in a couple of months. Leclerc thinks we should have a nice long summer, so we'll keep planting every couple of weeks to keep it coming as long as we can." She then took Nina past more freshly-planted fields towards some greenhouses, where row upon row of seed trays waited. "We're trying to accelerate the growth of some of our vegetables by keeping them in here, while growing others out in the fields. A few varieties won't be ready until next year, but the root vegetables are doing nicely and some of the fruit is really taking off too."

Jarli was equally voluble, and offered to show Nina around all his sheds. They were large sturdy buildings, well-ventilated and with partially retractable roofs to give plenty of natural light. Nina smiled to herself as he showed her the clean modern-looking milking parlour that she remembered Liu had had a hand in building.

"We'll be ready for animals soon," he said proudly. "We're going to be starting with goats and chickens, then we'll get some cows, sheep and pigs once the others have settled in. Goats are pretty adaptable, so they're a good bunch to test the new environment on before we go forward with any of the more temperamental creatures. Your head scientist has done all the tests and we've got plenty for them to eat that grows naturally, so we're just going to rope off some areas for grazing and see how they get on! We'll supplement if needed, but we're hopeful we'll just be able to use what nature's given us instead of trying to grow old-fashioned Earth grass."

"Where will the windmills be going?" Nina asked, looking around her.

"Over there," Lowanna replied, pointing inland to a spot where there were as yet no fields. "We've got solar roofing on all the barns, so we shouldn't need too many, but once things like the milking parlour are up and running, we're going to need a fair bit of energy."

"Can we send surplus back into the main settlement?" Nina queried.

Jarli shook his head. "Not at the moment, no. This area is completely separate so we haven't got the lines plumbed in yet. We can store it in the batteries, or if it turns out we're producing way more than we can use, we can always run lines in later."

"That makes sense," Nina agreed. She had originally been an engineer before training for her captaincy, so she took a particular interest in the parts of the colony that she knew a bit more about. Of course, she trusted all her experts completely, but it was nice to be able to join in a conversation and understand more than she didn't.

Just then, a young man walked over to them. He was tall, thin and blond and Nina had an inkling who he might be even before he spoke with a Danish accent. He smiled shyly at her.

"Captain Brooke?" he asked.

"That's me," Nina affirmed. "You must be Bille's brother."

His smile grew wider. "How did you guess?"

"The family resemblance is striking." Nina grinned back. "How are you settling in?"

"Good, thank you. I've been assigned housing over here so I haven't seen as much of Bille yet as I had hoped, but they've told me they're going to be around more when they're based in the centre on the surface."

He smiled a little wistfully. "I hope they can find time to fit me in."

"I'm sure they will," Nina reassured him. "They were talking about you before you woke; they were really looking forward to you being here."

Looking brighter, the other Kjeldsen smiled properly. "That's good to hear. I'd better get back to work, but it was nice to meet you."

The afternoon passed quickly and Nina soon found herself back at the lab, waiting for the explorers to return. The new, permanent lab was slightly bigger, much slicker than the old one and offered a number of features that they hadn't bothered with in the temporary one. Leclerc had also moved some of her more specialised and expensive kit down from the lab on the ship, and was vastly relieved by not having to spread her work between the two quite so much. The garden had been tidied and Leclerc was working on a permanent layout, with neat paths running between rows of experimental plants. While they waited, Nina got the grand tour and Robert spent fifteen minutes giving her an increasingly confusing explanation of all the meteorology equipment now attached to the roof. She was saved from the awkwardness of having to make her excuses by the return of the first truck. They heard it before they saw it, and not long afterwards, it drew to a halt outside the lab. A jubilant — if slightly sunburnt—Liu swung down from the cab.

"Evening Captain," he greeted, throwing a salute.

Nina returned it, grinning as his enthusiasm infected her, too. "Welcome back," she replied. "How did you get on?"

"With all due respect, Captain, we need to unload before I can do a proper debrief. Some of these specimens need to get into refrigeration as soon as possible; we ran out of space in our storage units."

At that, Leclerc bustled forward and took charge, and the truck was unloaded with alarming speed. Nina joined in and found herself carrying a variety of things, including several species of plants she hadn't yet seen and a couple of small animal carcasses.

"Really, Dan?" she sighed, as he handed her a dead rat-dog.

"They might be good for eating!" he reprimanded with a grin, waving her towards the lab. Leclerc took the animal from her promptly with a pleased nod and opened up a refrigeration unit that already had several other animals and a few fish in it. Nina supposed that farming the local wildlife would, if viable, actually be a very sensible option, and they couldn't do that if they didn't take a look at it first, but it still felt strange to be collecting dead animals on an exploratory mission. The next one Liu handed her, however, wasn't dead at all.

"*Really*, Dan?" She took a small cage with something squawking in it. "How on earth did you even trap it?"

"These ones are ground dwellers," said Sakamoto, coming up behind her. "I basically put a box over its head while it was eating."

Nina laughed as she took it inside. Leclerc was ecstatic to have a live specimen to study and immediately started rearranging the garden to fit a small pen in.

"Successful mission, then," Nina remarked to Dan, once the truck was empty.

"Very," he agreed. "Even she," he tilted his head at Niamh, the team's cartographer, "couldn't find much to complain about after the first couple of hours."

Nina walked them slowly away from the others. "Tricky customer?" she asked quietly.

Liu scrunched his face. "Not tricky. Just grumpy. The truck wasn't comfy enough, we were going too slowly, she didn't have the right equipment. Still, she calmed down after a bit." He grinned wickedly. "Until we stopped for the night and started to set up camp. Apparently camping isn't her bag."

Nina was saved from having to ask why he was grinning by the return of the second truck. They repeated the same unloading ritual, this time with more plants and fewer animals. Once Leclerc was happy that everything was safely away, they sat down in the lab. Nina noticed that the cartographers stayed at the back of the room, muttering to each other as everyone took their seats.

"I'm not going to ask for a full debrief now," she said, to the relief of the teams, "as I know you're all exhausted from two days' hard work and I don't want to keep you. Put everything you've found in your reports and submit them over the next couple of days, please. The next mission will be leaving in three days' time, so I'd like to be able to go over everything before we send you out again. Is there anything urgent that anyone would like to raise now?"

Sakamoto cleared her throat. "One thing. We saw traces of what I think might have been something similar to the predator on the other continent. We'll put details in the report, but just wanted to make people aware. Until we know what they are, I don't want anyone leaving the village without a security escort."

Nina nodded. "Noted. I'll get Kjeldsen to word something non-alarmist for the morning bulletin to make sure people are being cautious. Anything else?" The teams shook their heads, tiredness starting to show now that the adrenaline was wearing off. "Okay. Go get some dinner and an early night; the canteen's open now, so you can all get a hot meal in you. Dismissed."

A couple of days after the return of the first exploratory missions, Nina once again found herself with Dr Caimile and Nurse Taylor in the cryobay at 10.00, preparing to wake the first batch of children. This time, they were not alone with the sleepers. Makena, Ana Romero and another, younger woman with bouncy curls who Ana had introduced as Maria Gonzalez, were standing a little apart from them, going over notes. Nina understood that Maria was a specialist in children's mental health and was to be the first point of contact for families with any concerns. There was also another doctor, a paediatrician that Nina didn't know, with olive skin and sleek, well-coiffed hair that Sarah had introduced as Dr Gerard Abdul.

About forty parents dotted the waiting area, mostly in pairs, others grouped into larger clusters or waiting on their own. The room hummed with an odd mixture of nerves and excitement. A large amount of people clutched teddy bears, dolls and other stuffed companions. Nina noticed a pale, nervous-looking man with a multi-coloured knitted octopus standing by himself and moved to talk to him.

"Hi," she greeted, holding out her hand. "Captain Nina Brooke."

"Pete Stafford," he returned, shaking her hand with a firm grip. "This is Octy," he added, noticing her gaze and indicating the creature in his arms. "Sophia named him."

"How old is she?" Nina asked.

"She's six now. She's had Octy since she was in hospital after she was born—she was premature, and we were all worried she wouldn't make it. It's bringing back a few bad memories being here, to be honest."

Nina squeezed his arm. "She'll be up and bouncing around before you know it." Pete smiled and nodded, but the smile didn't quite reach his eyes. "Do you have anyone else awake yet who you know from before?"

Pete shook his head. "No. It's always been just the two of us; my partner and I split before Sophia was even born and she never had any interest in being part of her life. My family were great back on Earth, but they're not awake yet. I'm part of the construction team but my brother Davy is a singer and Mum used to do odd jobs before she retired, so I imagine they're still a while off waking."

"I'll bump them up the queue," Nina promised, making a note on her wrist unit. "And make sure you talk to Makena about getting any support you need." She caught Nehemiah's eye across the room and waved him over. "Let me also introduce you to Nehemiah Lovell. His daughter, Kezia, is waking today too, and Nehemiah will be running the school once we have enough children, so he's a good person to know."

She left the two men chatting, Pete looking marginally more relaxed than before, and crossed to where Dr Caimile was standing by the wall unit containing all the information about today's sleepers. "How are we doing, Doctor?"

Sarah gave a decisive nod. "Good. I've staggered them so that if there's a problem we aren't inundated, so they'll be waking every five minutes. First one's just about to wake up, so let's get started." She gave another nod to Taylor, who consulted the list on his notepad and stepped forward.

"Ella Rosenberg?"

Two very tall blond people, one cradling a cuddly elephant, stepped forward with anxious looks on their faces. Taylor smiled reassuringly as he guided them to the cryopod nearest Dr Caimile. He continued through the list of names, explaining to each set of parents that there would still be a small wait but that they were welcome to wait by the pod and watch as their child woke up.

By the time that each pod had at least one adult next to it, the first cycle was complete. Nina kept her distance and watched as Ella, who looked to be about ten, held her elephant tight and gazed up in wonder as Dr Caimile talked. The parents looked down at her, one on either side of the bed and both with an arm around her. The girl was nodding, smiling, laughing and her parents laughed too. Taylor arrived to escort her to the med unit and she hopped down willingly, her parents following close behind. Sarah caught Nina's eye and crossed over.

"Not bad," Nina commented.

Sarah grimaced. "Ten's old enough to understand the theory. Logically, she knows everything has changed, but right now she just feels like she's been asleep. That age group shouldn't be too much trouble to wake up, but might have more difficulty later, Ana says. Unlike the younger ones, who might struggle with this first bit but should adjust a lot quicker."

Ella emerged from the med unit and went to sit with her parents in the waiting area, eyes rapt as she listened to everything they said. Dr Caimile moved to the third pod, skipping number two where Dr Abdul was talking to another newly woken youngster. This one was older, a boy that Nina guessed to be about fourteen, who nodded along with the doctor's explanations with a serious expression. His father had a hand on his shoulder and his mother sat next to him holding his hand. As Nina watched, he turned to his mother and squeezed her hand, smiling reassuringly at her, before following Taylor to the med unit for his scan.

Nina watched the routine repeat another twenty odd times, with the youngest child being only two. He clung to his mother immediately on waking and refused to get in the med unit, leaving Taylor to get out a portable scanner and do the best he could.

"Not much reasoning you can do with a two-year-old," commented Dr Abdul to Nina, with an indulgent smile.

"You sound like you're speaking from experience," Nina replied. "Personal or professional?"

"Both. My sister had twins. Grown up now, but I remember the tantrums like it was yesterday."

Nina wondered if he meant the twins had been grown up before he left, or if he was thinking of the time difference. She decided not to ask.

A couple of hours later, everyone had been successfully woken and the room felt much fuller. Some parents had been waking two or three children in one go, so there were now nearly thirty youngsters scattered amongst the adults. There weren't enough chairs for everybody, so children sat on knees and parents stood or sat on the floor with some of the smaller ones. Nina could see Pete with a little girl she knew must be Sophia, giggling as she bounced on his lap. Pete was making Octy dance just out of her reach and her laughter echoed through the room as she made wild grabs for the toy. Nina smiled as she stood to greet them all.

"Good morning everyone, it's a pleasure to meet you all. My name is Nina Brooke and I'm the Captain of the *Posterity*. My apologies for keeping you all here, I promise this won't take long; I just need to introduce you to a few people and let you know some important rules before you can go and explore your new homes."

She introduced Ana, Maria, Makena and the doctors to the families that hadn't met them on waking and explained what they all did. She also introduced Nehemiah and Patrin, who weren't officially there in their capacity as educators but had said they were happy to be pointed out. She then explained a few of the rules that she thought worth reiterating, just in case the parents were so overwhelmed that they hadn't got round to mentioning everything.

"And are we really living right on the beach?" piped a little boy of about nine, putting his hand up and bouncing. His parents shushed him and pulled his hand down, but Nina waved a hand.

"We are. Depending on what jobs your parents do, you might be a bit further away, but most people are about two minutes' walk from the beach." Nina eyed the leg length of her audience. "Maybe ten minutes for some of you."

The earnest teenage boy who had woken second put his hand up. "What are we going to do about schooling?"

"Good question. It might be a little haphazard to start with compared to what you're used to, and we don't even have a school building yet. The plan is to give everyone a month or so to adjust to their new homes before we start official schooling, but of course, if you're eager to learn and getting bored then we can provide plenty of resources to keep you busy, or even set up some lessons to do at home," Nina improvised, hoping that was okay with the educators.

"There's also plenty to do around the colony," Nehemiah added, from where he was standing at the side of the seating area. "It's equally important to focus on things outside the curriculum, so you can always approach one of us for some extra credit projects if there's something you're particularly interested in. Don't forget, certain things that you used to do back on Earth, like Geography, are going to be different now."

The boy nodded eagerly. He looked with excitement at his mother, who smiled back at him. Nina wondered at the different ways people reacted to things; as a teenager, the only things she had been interested in were flying and taking machinery apart. Nina looked at Dr Caimile to see if she had anything to add and she nodded minutely and stepped forward.

"I just have a few words to add to what the captain has already mentioned. I'd like you all to remember that you've been asleep for a very long time, even if it doesn't feel like it, so try to take it easy for a few days. I know that's going to be difficult, because everything is so exciting. Just remember to listen to your parents, because they've all been through this too and they know what they're talking about.

"I also need you to remember that this is a new planet and everything is different. So please, tell your parents if anything feels strange. If you're itchy or sore, you get a tummy ache or you feel sick, please let us know. We don't know what all the plants and insects are yet, so you might have met a new one that's bad for us. Don't worry about making a fuss, we want to know. And I've said the same thing to the grown-ups too, so if your grown-up is getting very itchy and not telling anyone, make sure you tell them to go to the doctor too." Sarah paused to glare sternly at the adults in the room, eliciting a giggle from some of the children. "That's everything from me. Have fun, and I hope not to see you again too soon."

Nina stepped forward again, marvelling at how good Sarah was with the children compared to her prickly demeanour with her adult patients. "I think that's everything. There's a transport waiting to take you down to the surface; I'll hand you over to our pilot, Sam Fraser, who will take you from here."

165

Fraser had snuck into the room during Nina's speech, and now she stood, waving at the assembled families.

"Hi everyone! Get yourselves sorted, and when you're all ready, follow me. There's too many of us to use the regular shuttle, so I'm afraid we're in the transport which is a bit slower. But don't worry, that means you get extra time to look out of the windows at the planet!" There was lots of noise and scuffling as everyone grabbed their bags, children and cuddly animals, but after a few minutes they all trooped out of the door towards the shuttle bay, leaving Nina and Dr Caimile alone in the cryobay. Nina exhaled in relief.

"That seemed to go well." She slumped into one of newly vacated chairs.

Sarah took her hand and squeezed it. "Really well. You did good."

Nina sat up straighter and turned to Sarah. "You, too. Who knew, you do have a bedside manner after all!"

Sarah averted her gaze, not quite meeting Nina's eyes. "I've always been good with children." She shook herself, turning back to Nina with a wry grin. "It's the adults I have problems with."

Nina laughed, wondering what that had been about, but decided not to ask. Sarah would tell her if there was something she wanted to share when she was ready. "Lunch?"

"Lunch," agreed Sarah.

Chapter Thirteen

The evening after the first set of children had been woken up, Nina made her way to the science lab at 18.00. She had been surprised to receive a message from Leclerc asking her to get there promptly at the allotted time and to bring a chair. She was even more surprised when on arrival, she found she was not the only one there. The whole of the ship's crew sat in the front garden of the lab, on mismatched chairs that had clearly come from their respective homes. Lowanna and Jarli Johnson were also present, and Nina was completely stumped as to what was going on. She put down her chair and sat between Sarah and Sakamoto, neither of whom were any the wiser. After a short wait, Leclerc stepped out of the lab to greet them.

"Good evening, everyone. Thank you for joining us on such short notice and I promise to explain everything in a moment. Please, relax and talk amongst yourselves and I will be back soon."

She turned and headed back into the lab and Nina raised her eyebrows. Leclerc loved a bit of mystique, but this was extreme even for her. Someone giggled nervously and people exchanged glances.

"I suggest we do as she says," she said, raising her voice to be heard. "Whatever this is, and believe me I'm as confused as you are, you're not on duty."

The crew smiled at that and a few of them relaxed, slouching into their seats. Fraser unzipped the top of her uniform and shrugged out of the sleeves, wrapping them around her waist. The chatter grew up again as people checked in with colleagues they hadn't seen for a few days and caught up on the latest gossip.

Nina had at first been confused by the presence of the Johnsons, but as she eyed them discreetly, she realised they knew what was going on. They had a different aura surrounding them, watching everyone else, and when Jarli caught her watching him, he grinned.

"I don't suppose you'd like to fill me in?" she asked, leaning towards him.

He laughed and shook his head. "And steal Monique's thunder? Not a chance."

Nina didn't have long to wonder before the door opened again and Leclerc came back out carrying a small table, followed by Robert with a tray. She put the table on the ground between everyone, then stood facing them.

"Thank you again for being my guests this evening. I hope you're all hungry!"

Robert moved forward and placed the tray down. On it was a variety of food of which Nina recognised nothing. She frowned and looked back up at Leclerc.

"Monique, what is going on?"

"This is a selection of the finest delicacies found on Demeter. Maybe. We don't know yet, and that is where you all come in. All of these products are native to Demeter and might be worth cultivating. None of them are toxic, let me assure you of that first. We have run every test possible to make sure they are all safe. However, as yet we have no idea what they taste like. So the Johnsons and I decided we needed a group of people to do taste tests for us; just one person would not be enough, as everyone has different likings. Et voila! Here you all are!"

Taylor leant forward in his seat. "Let me get this straight. This is a bunch of stuff that nobody has eaten yet, and you want us to try it?"

Lowanna laughed. "You're all explorers; who better than to launch our new menu on?"

"Of course, they could all be disgusting." Leclerc shrugged. "We shall have to find out."

"Gee, thanks for the reassurance," Pavluhkin replied, narrowing her eyes at Leclerc. Everyone laughed.

"They're right, though," chimed in Kjeldsen. "We *are* explorers." They reached out a hand and plucked a small green shoot off a plate close to them before putting it straight in their mouth. Nina was impressed; she had always considered Kjeldsen to be one of the more cautious members of the team. They chewed for a moment and then smiled. "Kind of nutty. Nice, actually."

"Excellent!" Leclerc beamed, sitting down and jotting something down on her notepad. "Would anyone else like to try this plant?"

Emboldened by Kjeldsen's success, several others sampled the same shoot.

"Pretty bland," Chaudhary gave his unimpressed verdict. "I might add it to dishes, but wouldn't want it on its own."

Leclerc nodded. "All the samples have been lightly steamed or boiled, so we can recognise their natural flavour. Obviously, one can do many other things with them should we choose to cultivate them."

"I think they're pretty good," Fraser countered. "I'd eat that. What's next?"

"Whatever you like," smiled Robert, hovering behind them. Fraser considered for a moment, then selected another green item, ball shaped this time, from the plate next to the now empty first one. After eyeing it dubiously, she sniffed it, popped it in her mouth and crunched down.

"Yeuch!" she cried immediately, spitting it out. "That is revolting. Like aniseed, only ten times as strong." She reached for the cup of water Robert handed her and swilled her mouth out, spitting it on the floor behind her. "Thanks," she gasped, returning the cup to him and wiping her mouth with the back of her hand. "Really acrid. Not nice at all. But, maybe if you liked aniseed?" she added hopefully.

Nina laughed and reached out her hand. "I do like aniseed. I'll give it a try, though I'm not holding out much hope." Robert brought the plate and another cup of water over and Nina chose her ball. Wary after Fraser's reaction, she nibbled cautiously at the side of it. It wasn't as bad as she'd feared, but it was very strong. She could see why Fraser had spat it out; she managed not to copy her but swallowed the tiny bite after a few chews. Robert handed her the water and she downed it immediately. After a moment, she managed to speak.

"I'd suggest that be used as an additive, rather than an actual ingredient?" she rasped, and everyone laughed. "A few shavings or something might add a nice kick to food. I don't think anyone will be wanting to eat it, though."

Leclerc nodded earnestly, writing everything down as they went. They sampled a few more greenish things, several orange ones and some blue fruit, none of which were as bad as Fraser's choice. One of the orange shoots turned out to be surprisingly tasty, and everyone except Sakamoto agreed they would happily eat it.

"Shall I be brave and try one of these?" Liu asked, indicating several plates that held what looked like meat and fish.

"Definitely," stated Sarah, and Nina wondered privately which one was rat-dog. Dan's hand hovered over the plates for a moment, probably deliberating the same question, until he selected a chunk of a whitish meat from a plate in the middle. He chewed it slowly, then nodded.

"Not bad. Add a few herbs and spices, and that'd be quite tasty."

Jarli looked overjoyed and leaned over for a sample, which he shared with Lowanna. They both nodded too. "Absolutely. Very nice."

The rest of the crew joined in, and before long, all of the meat and fish samples had disappeared. They were all definitely edible and Nina found one of the fish varieties incredibly tasty.

"Like sea bass, back on Earth," she told Leclerc. "One of my favourites."

"Fish is very good for you," Sarah commented. "If we've got edible varieties available, that'll be a real asset in trying to get a balanced diet."

"And it could be available almost immediately, too," added Jarli. "It would help keep us going until everything we've brought with us is ready."

When all the plates had been emptied, Robert cleared the tray inside and everyone sat back, recovering after the most exciting meal Nina had ever eaten.

"Thank you so much, everyone," Lowanna said. "This has been a real help."

"It was our pleasure," Nina replied.

"Speak for yourself!" Fraser retorted, but the wide grin on her face belied her words. "I'm still reeling."

"Maybe we should name all the plants after the first person to try them," Robert suggested, to general laughter. "I'm serious! We've got to name them something, after all."

"I'm up for that," Fraser nodded, her face lighting up. "From now on, anyone wanting their stew to taste a bit aniseedy is going to have to add a touch of frasicum."

Jarli roared with laughter and the next few moments were taken up with people claiming their vegetables. Nina, who hadn't tried anything first, was happy to sit back and watch, until Sarah started to suggest they name a fish after her.

"Absolutely not," she said, vehemently, unable to keep the smile off her face.

"Oh come on, Captain!" wheedled Sarah. "Don't you want people tucking into battered Nina and chips?"

"The really important question," Dan interrupted, much to Nina's relief, "is which one was rat-dog?"

Leclerc hesitated a moment, fighting a smile, then pointed out the first dish Dan had tried. Dan groaned and fell back in his chair.

"But it was so tasty!" he wailed in despair.

"Which is great, because they're so prolific!" laughed Jarli. "They can become a staple of the Demetrian diet! What shall we call them, Liu's Rat-dog?"

The laughter continued into the evening, the team enjoying a rare moment of downtime, until the temperature started to drop and they separated. Dr Caimile loitered close to where Nina was saying goodbye to the Johnsons.

"Everything ok, Sarah?" she asked, as the Johnsons left in the direction of their farmhouse.

The doctor grimaced. "I hate to ask, but could I stay at yours again? I still haven't got around to building my furniture."

Nina laughed and they fell into step. "Why do you hate to ask? Was I that bad a companion?"

Sarah shoved her gently. "Quite the opposite, and you know it. I just feel like I'm imposing."

Nina stopped, forcing Sarah to stop too. "You are many things, Sarah Caimile, but you are never an imposition."

She stepped forward decisively, meeting Sarah's lips with her own. Part of her thrilled at the thought of making a move and being the one in charge for a change, while another part shrieked in terror at upsetting the status quo. Sarah's hand came up to rest on her hip and Nina slid an arm round Sarah's waist, her body soft and warm against her. When they pulled apart a moment later, Sarah's eyes were gleaming. Nina smiled back, slightly flushed, and they turned to continue on in silence. Sarah caught Nina's hand in the darkness and they twined their fingers together as they walked.

When they reached Nina's cottage, Nina wordlessly changed her security settings to recognise Sarah as well as her. Sarah raised her eyebrows but didn't comment. Nina pulled her in.

"You know you're always welcome here. Now you don't need to ask."

"Thanks, Nina." Sarah rested her head against Nina's, before pulling back. "Are we crazy?"

Nina knew what she meant. "I don't think so. I think it's just never been the right time before. But now, we're both here on this planet for the rest of our lives, so maybe it is the right time."

Sarah regarded her for a moment, then snorted. "There's no way you're going to be on this planet for the rest of your life. I give it less than six months before you're back on that ship, itching to explore the rest of the system."

Nina laughed. "Okay, fair point. But I have a home to come back to now. And I know you won't be off on another ship at the other end of the galaxy when I do."

Sarah acknowledged this with a tilt of her head. "True." There was a pause. "Plus your bathroom is nicer than mine."

Nina shook her head, still smiling. "You're awful. But yes, it is pretty nice. I keep meaning to have a bath in the evening and then I get summoned to eat rat-dog or something instead. We really should build your furniture tomorrow night, though. Happy as I am to have you here, you should have your own space too."

"I'd like that. Thanks, Nina." Sarah tried and failed to hold back a yawn. "I'm bushed. Bed?"

"Yes, please," agreed Nina, and Sarah grinned at her tone.

"Something tells me I'm not getting much sleep tonight, am I?"

Chapter Fourteen

The next morning, Nina was sitting in the new command centre, personalising her console and enjoying the fact she could do almost everything she needed to from down here, when she noticed Kjeldsen scratching. It wasn't obvious to start with but once she had become aware of it, it started to become distracting, then worrying.

"Is everything alright, Kjeldsen?" she asked eventually, after an hour had passed.

Kjeldsen grimaced. "Just a bit itchy this morning, Captain," they replied, and Nina frowned.

"Do you normally have skin problems?" she asked, and they shook their head.

"No, I don't know where it's come from," they replied with frustration, reaching down the neck of their uniform to get to their back.

"I've got an idea," replied Nina grimly. "Medical centre, now."

Less than five minutes later, Nina marched Kjeldsen in through the door of the medical centre. There was a new receptionist on duty, a short, plump woman with blonde hair that stood out starkly against her dark skin and she greeted Nina as they arrived.

"Good morning, can I help you?" the woman asked in a polite yet eager voice.

Thrown, Nina paused. "Er, yes. We need to see Dr Caimile. My officer is having a reaction to something they ate."

The receptionist pulled something up on her display. "Do you have an appointment?"

Nina tried hard not to sigh, aware of Kjeldsen scratching away next to her. "No, but I'm her captain. She usually manages to see me."

The receptionist frowned. "I'm afraid Dr Caimile is in another appointment at the moment. Please take a seat and I'll let you know when she's free, unless you'd like to see another doctor?"

Nina glanced at Kjeldsen, weighing up the seriousness of their reaction with the thought of seeing another doctor. Before she could make up her mind, Dr Caimile's voice rang through the corridor and they both turned towards it. She was standing in an open doorway partway down the corridor, smiling at a young boy who was just leaving the room.

"I'll see you next month, Frank," she said clearly, moving her hands in time with her words, "but come back anytime if the implants cause you any problems." The boy nodded, touching his hand to his chin and pulling it down and away before leaving with his mother, moving his hands in a complicated sequence as they left. Sign language had been standardised globally in the mid-21st Century, though most people who signed used the local dialect as well; Nina caught a few words, but she hadn't signed regularly since school and was rather rusty. It was still very popular despite technological advances in hearing aids, with over fifty percent of children choosing to learn it as a language in primary school, and it was compulsory for all teachers to be fluent. Most children with hearing problems opted for implants these days, of course, but it was reassuring for them to know they wouldn't be isolated if something went wrong. Dr Caimile spotted them and waved them in.

"Thanks Tina, I'll take these ones now," she called to the receptionist over Nina's shoulder.

"I thought Dr Abdul was looking after the children," Nina commented. Memories of last night's activities popped into her mind as Sarah smiled at her, and her stomach wriggled pleasantly.

"He is, mostly, but he doesn't have any experience in audiology, so Frank's cochlear implants fall to me. Now, what can I do for you two?"

Nina forced herself to focus, pushing Kjeldsen towards her.

"I think Kjeldsen's having an allergic reaction to something they ate yesterday evening. They've been scratching all morning."

"And last night," added Kjeldsen apologetically. "I'm sorry, I should have said something earlier, I just didn't put two and two together."

"Not to worry, you're here now, and it's obviously not too serious or you'd already be dead." Nina stifled a laugh at Sarah's bedside manner, and Sarah looked over at her. "Thank you for bringing them over, Captain. I'll take it from here."

Nina nodded, recognising the dismissal. "Thanks, Doctor. I hope you feel better soon, Bille."

Kjeldsen nodded and Nina was ushered unceremoniously from the room. She headed back to the command centre and continued working at her console, until Kjeldsen returned several hours later with a long-suffering expression and explained that Dr Caimile had checked the list of foods they'd eaten last night and subjected them to a skin prick test for every single item. On the bright side, the doctor had discovered that it was one of the greens that had caused the problem. She had given them an antihistamine that almost completely soothed the itching, and the greens had been added to the ever-growing allergens list. With a slightly sheepish air that Nina tried hard not to be amused by, they got back to work.

The next day Nina had another unusual appointment. The first of the colony's livestock were being woken and transported down to the surface, marking the next phase of the farmers' progress. Nina was hugely relieved that she didn't need to be present for the actual waking up part; she had left that to the specialists, but she wanted to check in with the Johnsons to make sure everything was going according to plan later on in the day. The animals had their own section of the cryobay, with units adapted to fit smaller or larger bodies, and for some reason, Nina couldn't contain her amusement every time she looked into a cryopod and saw a goat.

"Probably best you're sitting this one out," Dr Caimile had agreed, when Nina confided this to her. Dr Caimile, as the resident cryogenics expert, the freshly woken colony veterinarian, the Johnsons and a small group of farmhands would be today's team, and Nina trusted them to get on with it without her dubious supervision.

Chaudhary had had great fun fitting out one of the transports for the occasion. They were waking chickens and goats today, so the ship had been divided into two sections: one with pens for the goats and one marked up with areas for the chicken coops. The chickens were to be placed in transportation pens as soon as they began waking; these could then be moved around by shipping droids. Nina arrived at the transport as one trundled past, six squawking denizens flapping around inside the small frame. She grinned and followed it into the ship. Inside, it was a mass of bleating and clucking, noises and smells mingling in the enclosed space.

"Everything going okay?" she called to Jarli, who stood on the other side of the ship. He finished directing the droid, which carefully placed the pen down in the allocated spot and purred off to get the next.

"It's going great!" he laughed, peering through the wire at the chickens. He poured some seed into a dish in the middle and they descended, pecking at the food with heads jerking. Jarli straightened up, scratching his chin as he looked around. "All the chickens are awake, and we're nearly done with the goats. Just need to get them all in here now. Watch out!"

Jarli grabbed at Nina's arm and she stepped back, out of the way of another droid. This one carried two goats in a small metal frame and was aiming for the other end of the ship. Nina caught a strong whiff of goat musk as it passed, and she followed it with interest. It stopped by a small enclosure, a farmhand leaping forward to open the gate, and edged forwards until its nose was inside. The front wall of the frame dropped and turned into a ramp, which the goats eyed with suspicion. The farmhand came round the back and gave one of them a light tap on the rump. With a bleat of protest, the goat and her companion both trotted down the ramp and into the pen, joining several others already munching on some pellets. The droid reversed, the farmhand closed the pen and the droid disappeared again.

"Smooth," Nina commented.

Chaudhary appeared from behind a stack of feed sacks. "Thanks," he grinned. "It's giving the old brain cells a workout this, I'll tell you that."

"Well, we wouldn't want you to stagnate," Nina said, biting back a smile. Another batch of chickens announced their arrival, and Nina took that as her cue to leave. "It looks like you've got everything under control, as always. I'll leave you to it, but comm me if you need me."

"Will do, Captain!" Jarli waved her off, his attention already back on his charges.

The next few weeks passed swiftly. The colony expanded rapidly as more and more people were woken and housing was built more or less continuously. The first group of children had settled in so well that another two groups had been woken since, and there were now enough young people that Nehemiah was starting to move forward with the next steps. More teachers had been woken and small, informal gatherings were being held at the now finished community centre to make sure the children had some interaction with their peers while longer term plans were made.

Nina spent more and more of her time on the surface in the newly kitted out command centre and often went for days at a time without visiting the ship. She was surprised at how little this bothered her; there was more than enough to do on the surface to keep her busy, but she suspected that it wouldn't be long before she felt the need to get back out and do some exploring of her own. The exploratory missions were going well; there were currently two teams out investigating the area immediately surrounding the settlement and the cartographers were making real progress. They now had detailed maps reaching ten kilometres out in all directions from the settlement and trips were being planned to investigate points of interest further away. Nina hoped to lead one of these, as her responsibilities had become more devolved the more the community developed, and she was no longer needed with such immediacy at all times.

Or so she had thought, she grumbled to herself as she raced across the settlement early one morning. The sun was not yet up, and she squinted through the half-light at familiar shapes rendered unfamiliar by the gloom. She arrived at the medical centre, panting, and Tina the receptionist directed her to a room halfway down the corridor. On arrival, she knocked on the door. The worried face of Dr Caimile greeted her, then moved aside. Nina caught sight of Liu lying prone on the bed, his face pale and his body covered by a sheet. All her irritation at the early summons vanished.

"What happened?" she asked, blood draining from her face.

"He was attacked." The answer came not from Dr Caimile, but from Sakamoto, who Nina belatedly realised was sitting on the other bed in the room. Nina scanned her frantically, but saw no obvious signs of injury on her. She smiled briefly, realising where Nina's thoughts had gone. "I'm fine."

"Commander Liu, on the other hand, is lucky to be alive," Caimile said gravely. "He's lost a lot of blood and if it weren't for Sakamoto here's quick actions, we might have lost him."

Nina stared desperately at her friend on the bed. "Do you have any idea what it was?"

"My best guess is that predator we still haven't identified. It was quick, too quick for us to see; the first we knew of it was a shout from Liu and by the time I got there, it had gone."

Nina could tell Sakamoto blamed herself and shook her head. "You couldn't have done anything different, Nanako. You heard what the doctor said; you saved his life."

"Have a look at the injuries, Nina," Dr Caimile said. Nina braced herself but came around the bed. Dr Caimile lifted the sheet and Nina sucked in a breath. There were long, deep marks all down his left side, starting at chest level and continuing all the way down to his feet; Nina could see them disappearing under the edges of the towel that had been placed to protect his modesty. They had already been cleaned and stitched up, but she could tell how bad it would have been before the medics got to him. They didn't all look like claw marks, either; some were more like gouges, overlaid with long scratches that looked like they came from something extremely sharp.

"What the hell could have caused that?" she asked, baffled. Sakamoto shrugged, looking more helpless than Nina had ever seen her.

"We'll send some images over to Leclerc, see if it matches anything in her experience." Sarah was at her most reassuring, which worried Nina in itself. Sarah didn't do reassuring for small things. "And maybe, when he wakes up, he'll be able to tell us something."

Nina asked the question she had been dreading. "How bad is it?"

The doctor shook her head, her expression sombre. "I can't tell yet. Some of those wounds were deep. He's lost a fair bit of muscle; he may not ever be quite back to the way he was." She looked down at his still form. "I'm keeping him sedated for now so I can pump him full of drugs. Muscle therapy medicine came on a long way in the decade before we set off and there's a good chance he'll make a full recovery if these early stages go well. But I just can't say yet whether it'll work or not."

Nina nodded, swallowing the lump in her throat. "I understand. Thank you. Please keep me updated."

"You know I will."

Nina reluctantly left Liu in the hands of the doctors and walked slowly back out of the medical centre with Sakamoto. "When did it happen?"

"About 04.00. We were all sleeping in the truck; I guess Dan had got up to go to the toilet or something. We drove straight back, but he was bleeding all the way. He lost consciousness about an hour from here; I didn't think we were going to make it."

"You did well. I'm sure Dan will want to thank you too, when he's awake."

Sakamoto smiled, looking a little more like herself. "Just doing my job, Captain."

They reached the command centre and Nina sent Sakamoto home to get some rest. She then dialled up the information on the rest of Liu's team and sent them all messages to let them know he was okay and suggested they try to get some rest too. She debated for a moment whether to recall the other exploratory team but decided against it; they were on the last day of a four-day mission and were unlikely to put themselves in any danger on the drive home, even if they did stop to complete their planned assignments. By the time she had finished, it was late enough for breakfast and she headed over to the canteen to try to focus her mind on something else.

The day passed slowly. Nina met with Leclerc in the morning and the rest of Liu's team after lunch when they had all managed a bit of rest. They all looked pale and shaky but determined. Everyone agreed that more precautions needed to be taken by the exploratory teams but that the missions themselves needed to continue.

"We always knew something like this was a possibility," Sakamoto pointed out, "That's why I was there. We can't stop exploring just because we've hit one hurdle."

The sun had moved right across the sky by the time the other team arrived back, the baking heat of midday reduced to a more bearable temperature. Nina let them unload and have their moment of excitement at returning to town before breaking the news about the attack. They were all badly shaken and Nina promised that the expeditions would come under serious review before they went out again.

Once everyone had been updated and sent to the canteen for some dinner, it was late evening and Nina set out to visit the medical centre again. The orange glow of the setting sun reflected off the crests of small waves in the bay, making it look more alien than ever. Birds chattered and screeched as they put themselves to bed and Nina could see the flurry of activity around the top of one of the trees in the town centre as they swooped and dived in and out of the branches. Where possible, the buildings had been put up around existing foliage to minimise the impact on the environment, and Nina appreciated it after years on drab, grey ships with only humans for company.

She was completely unsurprised to find Dr Caimile in Liu's room when she arrived, accompanied now by Nurse Taylor. She realised this wasn't personal just for her; Sarah had known Dan even longer than she had and she knew Sarah would be just as worried about her friend as Dr Caimile was about her patient. The doctor didn't appear to notice Nina's arrival, so preoccupied was she with staring fixedly at the machines showing Liu's readings.

"Has she left the room at all?" Nina asked Taylor quietly. He replied with a mute shake of the head. Casting a glance at Dan on the bed and at the machines which appeared to show no change, Nina took Sarah lightly by the elbow. "Come on," she said, gently tugging her out of the room. "Let's get some dinner. You can't look after him if you're passed out on the floor."

When Sarah made to protest, Taylor blocked her way back.

"I'll let you know the second there's the slightest change," he promised, and the doctor acquiesced silently.

Nina led her to a quiet corner of the canteen, which was dimly lit and practically empty at this time of night. She sat her down and returned a few minutes later with two bowls of soup that had large chunks of bread on the side. Sarah started to eat without seeming to notice what it was, but once she tasted the soup, she perked up a bit.

"This is good," she commented in surprise.

"Probably because it's the first food you've eaten all day," Nina reprimanded gently. Sarah sighed, but didn't respond, the life gradually returning to her as she finished her bowl and used the bread to mop up the dregs.

"Thanks, Nina." She stretched and shook her head with a self-deprecating smile. "I know you're right, and I really shouldn't let it get to that point. But it's just so difficult to leave when it's your oldest friend lying on the bed."

"Believe me, I know," Nina agreed, reaching across the table to take her hand. "And you wouldn't be you if you didn't feel like that."

"At least I've got you to look after me." Sarah squeezed Nina's hand. "There hasn't actually been any change all day," she admitted. "I should probably get some rest while I can, then check in first thing in the morning."

"That sounds like an excellent idea," Nina agreed, pleasantly surprised by the pragmatic suggestion. She'd expected more argument. "Want me to walk you back to yours?"

Sarah nodded and they stood, clearing their plates to the recycling area at the side on the way out. They walked in silence through the now dark settlement, the reflection of the stars on the sea and the occasional glow from a curtained window the only sources of light. For a moment, as they passed the shadowy medical centre, Nina thought Sarah was going to insist on popping in and her body tightened with tension. The moment passed, Sarah relaxed once more, and a minute later, she let them into her house.

They had all been spending more time on the surface than anyone had anticipated at this point and their houses were accordingly homey. Nina had finally got around to helping Sarah build her furniture, which was mostly very similar to hers. Sarah, however, loved colour, and had brought a number of items from home to decorate, so the two rooms were pleasantly full.

A patterned rug warmed up the larger room, which served as an all-purpose day room, and the chairs all had different coloured throws made by various members of Sarah's extended family. The table had a large stripy tablecloth and on the wall hung a few formal family photographs and a couple of large bright paintings. Nina had been surprised to learn that Sarah had painted them herself back on Earth. They pulled their shoes off, then crossed straight through the living room to the bedroom, where Sarah made immediately for her bed. In here was equally vibrant; a colourful handmade cross dominated one wall, the bed linen was bright yellow and orange, and another rug lay on the floor. Nina hovered in the doorway until Sarah looked up at her.

"Stay tonight?" she asked, and Nina could only see how much she wanted her to because she knew her so well.

"Of course," she nodded, closing the door and crossing the room to join her. Sarah wriggled into her arms wordlessly and they fell asleep almost immediately.

The next few days passed in odd bursts of quick and slow, with speedy visits to Liu in the medical centre squeezed in around other parts of Nina's day. Her main task was to continue with the planning of the next exploratory mission, which would explore the foothills of the mountains. There were a number of things they wanted to investigate there; suitability for farming, what the forests were like, and whether there was a good site for a wind farm. They would need to visit a number of spots in the area to fulfil all these agendas and the original plan had been to fly over and then separate out in trucks.

However, since the incident involving Liu and the predator, they needed to be more cautious and would conduct the whole mission out of the transport, which was to be adapted to be lived in by a small group for a couple of days. Nina was still optimistic that this mission, which was currently planned for the end of the week, would include her; she knew Kjeldsen was more than capable of handling the weekly information drop by themself and the crew were now so integrated in planetary life that there was very little that needed her immediate attention. Sarah was also encouraging Nina to go, and Nina thought she knew why; after Nina's intervention that first night, they both appeared to be doing their utmost to look after the other and keep them from brooding over Liu during his recovery. Both Doctors Caimile and James had insisted however that from now on, all exploratory missions must include a medic as part of the team, a request that Nina was more than happy to accommodate.

The rest of the planning involved lots of liaising with various specialists. Nina had several lengthy sessions in the meeting room at the command centre, which was now fitted out with a large central console table and a selection of almost matching office chairs. These sessions introduced Nina to a few new faces, an occurrence which was becoming more and more common as the colony grew. First were Owain Roberts and Heidi Gomshaw, the forestry experts that came from Wales and Canada respectively. Both had ruddy, weather beaten faces and cheery dispositions, and Nina wondered if these came from spending so much time outside or if that was the cause of their vocation rather than the effect. Dao Van Khiem was a rice farmer, a gentleman in his sixties who had been the head of his family business back in Vietnam. He was keen to locate somewhere that he and his daughters could set up before he retired and left them to run the business. The last person Nina had met briefly before; Adana Okonkwo, the settlement's energy expert, a tall, serious-faced woman with short hair and intelligent eyes who hailed originally from Nigeria. They had crossed paths early on in the construction phase, but Nina had never spent longer than five minutes in a room with her.

The sessions were pleasantly constructive, with all parties agreeing about the importance of other people's needs as well as their own. In fact, Nina thought with amusement, they might get along a lot faster if everyone stopped being so considerate and stated what they actually needed without deferring to everyone else first. Eventually, though, a plan was agreed on and the route mapped out.

Nina popped into the hospital early on the morning they were due to leave, sighing as she looked down at the motionless form of her First Officer and friend. She couldn't help but feel guilty, gallivanting off to explore while he was still ill.

"You know he'd be telling you to knock it off, stop feeling sorry for him and have fun out there."

Nina looked up, startled; she hadn't heard Sarah come in. She leaned on the doorjamb, a grin on her face and an eyebrow raised.

"You're in good spirits," she replied, ignoring Sarah's barb.

Sarah nodded and came over, pointing at the readouts on a machine to Nina's left. "He's responding very well to the medication I'm giving him. Muscle re-growth is really taking off; the rate has almost doubled overnight. If it carries on at this rate he should be completely back to normal with just a bit of physio once he's up and about."

Nina beamed. "That's excellent news. Thank you so much for telling me."

"I thought you were more likely to enjoy your trip if you knew." Sarah kissed her. "Look after yourself. Try not to worry. I'll let you know if there are any major changes, but just focus on doing what you're doing. And try not to miss me too much."

The rest of the team was already assembled when Nina made it to the landing pad, and she uttered her apologies as she hurried to join them.

"Not to worry, Captain, you've still got five minutes," Fraser said, chipper as ever and Nina appreciated the reassurance. She stowed her bag under the last bunk in the sleeping quarters, then headed back up front to join the others.

"All set?" she asked. There was general agreement all round. "Then let's get going, Fraser."

"Aye, Captain."

.

Chapter Fifteen

The transport touched down in a small break in the trees that couldn't quite be called a clearing. Nina marvelled again at Fraser's piloting skill; it hadn't looked to Nina like the ship would even fit, let alone be able to land safely.

"Nicely done, Fraser," she complimented, as they released their safeties.

They all got to their feet and Fraser slid open the side hatch. It was a short climb down to ground level from this point, but the repurposing of the ship into somewhere they could all live and sleep for a few days meant that this was the only entrance currently usable. Chaudhary had had to use droids to do most of the refit, as once he'd blocked off the rear hatch, he hadn't been able to get inside himself. Nina felt her way down the short ladder, stepped onto the slightly springy ground and looked around her.

Extremely tall trees surrounded them. She tried to work out if they were evergreen or deciduous, then remembered that on this planet, trees might not work like that. Their leaves ranged from orange to plum, with a just few greens dotted in amongst the rest. Plants rambled across the floor, including some of the orange bushy ones she remembered from the first landing site and some more she recognised from around the settlement. The air felt warm, though a slight breeze stopped it from being unpleasant, and she could hear the sounds of birds and maybe other creatures playing in the treetops above.

"Odd mixture of colours," Heidi commented from behind her. She heard Owain agree and wasn't sure if she was relieved or worried that the experts found it strange, too. "Kind of pretty, eh?"

Nina hid a smile. She hadn't realised the stereotype of the Canadian vocal tic was actually true; she had never heard Jerry do it but then, he had travelled a lot more than Heidi.

The two forestry experts got to work immediately, taking out kit Nina didn't recognise and jumping straight in. Leclerc followed with her, more familiar, equipment and Nina left them to it, crossing to Adana and Van Khiem.

"Probably not much for either of you here, is there?" she asked, noting the looks of concentration on both faces as they looked around.

"There is a good breeze," Adana replied with a shrug, pointing up into the high canopy where branches waved enthusiastically. "If we could get windmills up there we could generate energy, if we had to. But they would need to be very tall. It would be better if we can find something else."

Van Khiem nodded solemnly. "I need much more space than this clearing, with a good water supply. Hopefully we find somewhere further on. After all, this was not our stop."

After several hours of mostly waiting around and a bit of being coerced into gathering samples, they all climbed back into the transport. More timber had been loaded into the cargo hold than Nina thought possible from such a short stop; the tree people (as Nina tried hard not to call them to their faces) had found several varieties that they thought would be good for carpentry and were taking them back to the settlement for further testing. Leclerc had got plenty of samples and set up several more cameras. She was particularly excited about the one she had hidden fifteen metres up in one of the trees, hoping it would give her some more insights into avian life on the planet, which although noisy, was still rather elusive. She had also done a few scans on behalf of the cartographers, who were both otherwise engaged and unable to come on this trip. Nina thought of their sullen faces at the first briefing and hid a smile of relief.

The transport lifted off again and, flying much slower this time, proceeded further west towards the mountains. Leclerc scanned the ground from a portable science station Pavluhkin had hooked up for her and the rest of the party gazed out of the windows with interest. The land got less flat as they progressed, with gradual inclines starting to steepen, but the forest continued uninterrupted. After almost an hour of very little except trees, Leclerc suddenly spoke up.

"Here!"

Fraser slowed the craft immediately and turned to Leclerc. "You want me to land?"

"A moment…" Leclerc frowned, tapping at her monitor. "Turn ninety degrees to the north and proceed slowly. I think I'm picking up some wide, open spaces at the bottom of the mountains. The ground should be about five hundred metres above sea level now."

The transport glided slowly over the low hills, with all eyes on Leclerc's screen or trained out of a window.

"Got it!" said Fraser gleefully a few minutes later. "Looks good. I'm bringing us down." The transport landed and the team climbed out, the ground crunching under Nina's feet as she stepped off the ladder and turned. A line of trees stopped about a hundred metres downhill of where they stood, with the same multicoloured canopy as at the last stop. Where they stood, however, felt more like heath land. Small, scrubby, grey-brown plants grew in scattered clumps with a tough, wiry covering on the ground. To Nina's left a river carved a path through a shallow valley sunk into the scrubland. It followed the gentle incline, meandering away from them to enter the trees five hundred metres from their current position.

"Good. This is good." Van Khiem nodded vehemently. "Let us have a look around." He left with Leclerc and Sakamoto in the direction of the river, leaving the others close to the transport. Nina checked she still had her gun; she didn't think anything was likely to attack such a large number of them but she didn't want to take any chances. She grinned at Fraser when they caught each other's eye and realised the pilot had been doing the same thing. A moment after the others had disappeared down the slight slope to the river, Heidi wandered over.

"Do you hear that?"

Nina strained her ears, but couldn't hear anything unusual. "What am I listening for?"

"There's a low rumble in the background, coming from that way." Heidi pointed to where the river appeared, snakelike, over a small summit above them. "Could be a waterfall."

"A waterfall?" Adana appeared, instantly alert. They listened again, and this time Nina thought she might be able to make something out.

"I hear it too," Fraser agreed. "Can't tell what it is, but it's unlikely to be a motorway."

"We hope!" Owain waggled his eyebrows. "Could be about to meet our first extra-terrestrials, on their version of the M25."

Nina laughed out loud. "Of all the things I hoped to never see again." The ten-lane wide motorway that looped around London was something Nina had hated navigating every time she had to return to Earth.

"I would like to investigate," Adana announced.

"Of course," assured Nina, becoming serious again. "We'd better take a few of us. Heidi, Owain; you stay here. Doctor, you'd better stay too. If the other team gets into trouble, they'll need to know where they can find you, and the same for us."

The serious-faced Dr Ibragimov nodded. The tall stern-looking woman had said little so far on the trip, simply watching and observing the rest of the company. Nina knew little about her, other than that she had asked for a doctor and Jerry had assigned her to the mission, but she knew Jerry was an excellent judge of both skill and character. Besides which, she knew she had a strong bias in her personal opinions of what a doctor should be.

Nina debated whether or not Fraser should come with them; she was reluctant to leave as a team of two, but Fraser was the currently the only other member of the team with a gun. Heidi settled it for them by announcing she had weapons training; Nina took a moment to confirm on her wrist unit and found that she had indeed completed an advanced firearms course, so Fraser dug another gun out of the store for her.

"We won't be long." Adana looked like she was about to interrupt and Nina hastened to reassure her. "If we're walking for an hour and we haven't found anything, we'll get back in the transport and investigate from above." She turned to the others. "Feel free to wait in the transport if you'd feel more comfortable in there. We'll see you in a bit."

The three of them set off, walking uphill towards the source of the river. They soon reached the summit, which turned out to be one of many false summits. The river wound around boulders and trees started to appear again. These trees differed from those in the forest below; more like a pine or a fir, stretching tall and thin into the sky. The forestation got denser as they walked; where at first there had been just one or two, soon there were clumps. The noise they had heard got steadily louder as they walked and Adana nodded in satisfaction.

"I think we were right. It sounds like water. Only question is, is it a big waterfall a long way away, or a little one close by?"

They laughed and continued their trek, soon finding themselves once again surrounded by forest.

"It's completely different from down below," Fraser said in bemusement, looking around her at the tall spiny trees. They were almost all the same colour, with a bluish tinge that became more evident the more of them there were. "Think we should take a stick back for the tree huggers?"

Nina laughed and immediately regretted it. "I don't think they'd appreciate being called that," she remarked, raising her eyebrows at Sam, who grinned cheekily back. "Let's just tell them what we've found, and we can move the transport a bit closer for them to investigate tomorrow." She took a picture with the camera on her wrist unit for good measure and they kept walking.

They rounded a large boulder and the noise suddenly grew louder; Nina thought she could have identified it as a waterfall by herself now. Adana looked pleased.

"It sounds big. It could be very good indeed."

Five more minutes walking and their suspicions were confirmed. The river took an abrupt turn and they found themselves on the opposite side of a large pool of water from an enormous waterfall. Nina couldn't even begin to guess the size of it; it reached higher than the trees, and the clouds of spray it made formed a mist that rolled over the pool towards them. Nina's breath caught as she gazed across the water, unable to take her eyes off it.

"Shall we take a closer look?" Fraser asked, raising her voice to be heard. The other two nodded and they set off round the edge of the pool. By the time they reached the falls a few minutes later, the noise was thunderous. The spray covered Nina's face with miniscule droplets and soaked into her clothes, a not entirely unpleasant sensation after walking uphill in the afternoon heat. They craned their necks to see the top and a myriad of tiny rainbows caught Nina's eye as she looked up.

"It's beautiful," she yelled, far more loudly than felt natural.

"And powerful," shouted Adana over the roar of the water. "If we can use this, we won't need any wind farms until the colony is much larger."

Regret twanged at Nina. Part of her wanted to walk away, to leave the waterfall untouched and undisturbed forever. Adana caught her look and her expression softened. "It will not be like on Earth. We will not damage it. I want to care for our new planet, just like you do."

Nina nodded, and after a moment they turned to trek back down the hills to tell the others what they had seen. It didn't take nearly as long going downhill and the other team was waiting for them when they returned. They had also had a successful trip, and Van Khiem was optimistic that they could use the river to make more than enough paddy fields to feed the existing colony. Heidi and Owain made excited noises over the pictures of the not-pines. It was agreed that they would remain where they were for the evening, as it was getting towards sunset, and all head back up the mountain in the transport towards the higher forest in the morning. They all clambered back into the transport for the evening meal, Nina thinking longingly of marshmallows and campfires. They turned in early, tired from the exercise and still not used yet to the shorter days and nights.

Nina woke early the next morning, unsure what had woken her until she realised the door to the transport was open. Sitting up, she looked around and noticed all the beds were still occupied, apart from Sam Fraser's. She slipped quietly out of bed, fastened her gun-belt around her waist and let herself down the steps to the ground, Dan's injury horribly present in the front of her mind. To her enormous relief, however, she caught sight of her as soon as she turned around, dressed in a pair of non-regulation green shorts and a yellow vest top.

"Captain!" Fraser exclaimed, alerted to Nina's presence by the crunch of foliage underfoot. "I'm sorry, I didn't mean to wake you. I was just going for a run."

Nina's eyebrows shot up. "A run? Have you any idea how bad an idea that is?"

Fraser looked confused, then a look of horror spread across her face as realisation dawned. "God, I didn't think!"

Nina restrained herself from retorting with 'That much is clear' or something similar; she had no desire to become a caricature of herself. "I've got into the habit of going out for a run around the settlement first thing—it's nice to keep my fitness up when I'm spending so much time sitting down during the day. But I've been walking around with a gun strapped to my belt for the last day, you'd think that would have got far enough into my brain to make me stop and think this morning. God, what an ass!"

"I wouldn't say that." Nina smiled. "But I'm glad I caught you."

"Yeah," agreed Fraser, nodding fervently. "Thanks, Captain. Guess I'll give it a miss today then." She looked so crestfallen that Nina felt sorry for her.

"You could always jog on the spot here, or something?" she suggested. "I don't mind keeping watch for a bit."

Fraser looked thoughtful. "I guess I could do a few exercises instead. Would you mind?"

"Not at all," replied Nina, looking around her to find something to sit on and selecting a small boulder. She made sure her gun was easily accessible and turned back to Fraser. "Exercise away."

Fraser grinned and, not looking nearly as self-conscious as Nina would have felt in her place, launched into a series of lunges, squats and other exercises Nina didn't recognise. She tried not to stare, so gazed off into the distance instead, letting her mind wander as the sun rose higher over the tops of the oddly coloured trees, painting them in streaks as the rays broke through the clouds.

"You're allowed to look, you know."

Nina turned to face her and grinned at the sight of Fraser in a perfect plank, balancing on her well-muscled arms. She could see her tattoos running over her shoulders and down her back from this angle, remarkably detailed patterns of swirls and intricate detailing. Nina knew Fraser had tattoos, of course; distinguishing features were recorded on everyone's military file, but she had never seen them before.

"I don't want you to feel like a goldfish," she remarked, and Fraser laughed.

"You should see the way the kids in the settlement gawk when I run past. It's like they've never seen anyone exercise before." Only the slightest bit of tension slipped into her voice, and Nina was impressed.

"They probably haven't, not to this extent anyway. I've never known someone who can hold a conversation while in a plank before."

Fraser dropped from her pose and wiped the sweat from her forehead. "Commander Liu can." Her expression faltered. "Or could, I suppose."

Nina felt her face fall to match. "Dr Caimile is hopeful he'll make a full recovery. It just might be a while until he's back to planking with you."

Fraser nodded, her usually cheerful face still downturned. Nina lowered herself gently down from the rock and sat cross-legged on the ground in front of her.

"I'm incredibly proud of how far you've come already on this mission, Sam. The bonds you've formed with everyone in the crew and the additional responsibilities you're taking on are exceptional. Every day you're growing, and you're constantly striving to better yourself. Commander Liu is lucky to have you as a friend to help him out while he recuperates. I'm honoured to get to witness your development, and extremely privileged to be your Captain." She paused and smiled at the girl. "If you carry on like this, you'll be doing my job before I realise!"

Fraser huffed a laugh, and Nina realised with a start she was holding back tears. "Keeping busy is good. I don't like not having anything to do; it gives me too much time to think."

"Thinking isn't always bad, you know. Sometimes it helps," Nina said gently.

Fraser sighed and looked at her hands, twisted together in her lap. After a moment, she spoke. "When I was twelve, my dad got injured at work. We didn't think it was anything serious, but then it got infected. He got sepsis." She looked at Nina. "He didn't make it."

Nina's throat choked up at the look on Fraser's face, and she leaned forward to clasp her hand. "Oh, Sam. I'm so sorry."

"I've just always looked up to Commander Liu, and he's been so good to me." Sam swallowed. "I'm not sure I can go through losing someone like that again."

Nina didn't know what to say. "Have you talked to anyone else about this?"

Fraser nodded. "Steve and Bille know." She smiled weakly. "They're looking after me."

Nina smiled too. "I'm sure they are."

Sam wiped her eyes roughly. "I feel stupid now."

Nina shook her head. "Never feel stupid for having emotions. It's good to let things out; if you bottle them up it only gets worse. Trust me."

Fraser smiled at her, stronger this time, and Nina let go of her hand. Sam rose off the ground and began a series of cooling down exercises, before pausing and turning back to Nina. "Thank you though, Captain. It means a lot to me to hear you say those things."

Nina smiled. "You're very welcome." There was a moment's pause as Fraser finished her routine, and when she spoke again, she was back to her usual chirpy self.

"All done. Breakfast?"

The second day of the mission went swiftly. They took off as soon as they had finished breakfast and followed the river upstream, landing as close to the waterfall as they could. Heidi and Owain repeated their investigations from the previous day regarding the forestation. Leclerc took an interest too, noting similarities and differences in how vegetation correlated to terrain here versus on Earth. Nina listened for as long as she could before the technicalities started to escape her and she excused herself to give the others a hand. They finished in less time than they had taken the day before and Leclerc proposed a trip to the waterfall; she was keen to find out what secrets the lake might be hiding. They all agreed; the original group had spoken so effusively about the beauty of the spot that they were eager to visit and see it for themselves.

The walk was less than fifteen minutes from where they had parked the transport, so they walked at a much slower pace. The gentle exercise refreshed Nina and when they arrived, her heart soared again; the waterfall was just as spectacular as she had remembered. The rest of the group were equally in awe; even Leclerc stood and watched for several moments before opening up her kit and starting her analysis. Nina helped her set up a camera for installation in the lake to register differences between freshwater versus saltwater life-forms, then watched as she got it into position. When they were nearly done, Leclerc crossed to where the river exited downstream from the lake, took one last item out of her bag and Nina, not recognising it, moved closer to have a look.

"It's an aquatic droid—a mapping device," Leclerc explained, holding it out. It was slightly larger than her hand and roughly fish-shaped, which was what had caught Nina's attention. When Leclerc pressed a few buttons, it activated, lights blinking on the top and robotics starting to move. "Cartography use them; they gave me a couple in case I got a chance to map some of the rivers for them. It'll swim downstream, mapping the river as it goes and sending the data back. When it reaches the sea or if it gets into trouble, it sends out another signal and one of the aerial droids will be dispatched to go and retrieve it."

"Clever," Nina approved, and watched as Leclerc carefully placed the device in the water. It righted itself, then slowly moved off towards the sea. They re-joined the rest of the group and headed back to the transport.

Everyone agreed that they had enough information for now and Leclerc was itching to get back to her lab, so after a quick lunch they all climbed back into the transport and set off back towards the main settlement. It was odd, Nina mused, looking out of the window as they approached, how quickly somewhere could become 'home'. They had only been gone just over twenty-four hours, but the sight of the even rows of mismatched houses warmed her in a way she hadn't thought she would ever feel about a place.

Nina helped unload all the cargo, taking most of it to the lab for analysis, and then said goodbye to the rest of the team. It was still only mid-afternoon, so she made up her mind to head next door to the command centre to check in with Kjeldsen and then visit Liu in the medical centre.

Kjeldsen welcomed her back enthusiastically, as they had been de-facto in command while Nina was off-site, but had very little to report. They had sent through the weekly drop as usual the previous day and Nina's eyebrows shot up as she realised that nine weeks had gone by without her marking it.

"We could be hearing back from Earth next week, if nothing has gone wrong," Kjeldsen pointed out, and Nina's stomach flipped. She hadn't been keeping count, but Kjeldsen, in their role as Communications Officer, obviously had been.

"Wow," she replied, then immediately felt foolish for doing so. Kjeldsen only grinned, though. "It doesn't feel that long already," she elaborated, and they nodded.

"I know. I only know because I'm tracking the days, but our first message should have reached Earth four weeks ago, and if they replied immediately, we could be hearing something next week. It'll be strange, starting communications properly after so long on our own."

"It's possible, of course, that they have technology that sends messages faster than we do, now. They are fifty-three years ahead of us, in some ways," Nina mused.

"I'm not sure how much technological advancement will have been happening with the planet in such decline," Kjeldsen replied delicately, and Nina mirrored their grimace.

"True. Ah well, no point theorising; we'll know soon enough." She clapped them on the shoulder and headed out of the lab.

"Send my best to Commander Liu," Kjeldsen called after her, and she waved in acknowledgment.

On her way across the Plasa, as some people had taken to calling it, a commotion further across the bay distracted her. After a moment's deliberation, she realised that Liu would very likely not mind if she waited another half hour to see him and redirected her steps towards it.

The site buzzed with activity. Dozens of droids and even more people flitted around at the water's edge, but there also seemed to be barriers holding some people back. Concerned, Nina pressed forwards past the onlookers and saw Mira and a number of assistants, all of whom seemed to be running around while she stood still.

"What's going on?" she asked the person next to her, who turned out to be Patrin. "Oh! Hello, Patrin," she greeted, embarrassed. "My apologies, I've just got back from a trip to the mountains and I'm not quite all here yet."

"Not to worry. They're making plans for the jetty that they're going to build soon. They've got divers in the water measuring how deep it is at all the points they'll need supports—the kids are fascinated."

Nina belatedly realised that most of the people on the other side of Patrin were rather small. Most of them still gazed intently at the activity over the barrier, but a couple now goggled at her. She gave them a smile and turned to look back at the not-quite-a-building site. Her eyes fell on Chaudhary, who she hadn't noticed before. He waved her over, so she muttered apologies to Patrin and jumped the fence, grinning back at the children who had whooped at her.

"Hey, Ramin. Patrin says there's a jetty going up?"

"Not yet there isn't," Chaudhary corrected. "This is some pretty serious engineering; it wasn't anticipated so we haven't got anything prepared. I'm going to need exact measurements so we can construct something site-specific, otherwise it'll be rusting into the sea before we get a year's use out of it."

"Were we not expecting to be able to fish?" Nina wondered aloud.

"We were, we've got nets, rods and boats," Chaudhary said. "We just couldn't know where we'd be doing it. There's some kit we can adapt that'll do fine, but we need to know how deep we're going first." He paused and looked up at her. "Everything okay, Nina? You look kind of odd."

"Yeah, fine," she replied generically. Truth be told, she did feel a little irritated, but without being able to identify the cause, she wasn't going to take it out on Chaudhary. His expression told her he wasn't convinced but he let it go, for which she was grateful. "Well, good luck," she said as a farewell, before heading out in the direction of the medical centre.

Chapter Sixteen

It was Sarah who put her finger on what was wrong with Nina later that night, as they sat on the newly installed bench in Nina's front garden, looking out over the sea. They were sharing a small bottle of whiskey that Sarah had produced from somewhere, but Nina found she couldn't relax.

"You're pissed because they didn't ask you first," Sarah stated, and Nina was initially outraged.

"I'm not! Am I?"

"You're the Captain. You like to be in control, and this is the first time a major decision has been made on this colony without your input."

"You're right," Nina mused, running her finger around the rim of her glass. "Maybe I am kind of irked about that."

"Well, you'd better get used to it," Sarah replied, bluntly. "You may be one of the Union, but we're not on a ship anymore. Not everything is your responsibility."

"Christ, I wouldn't want it to be. I'm glad other people are taking charge of other bits. It's just a bit weird, coming back and finding a whole new project started in the less than two days I was away."

"I get it," Sarah sympathised. "It's weird, watching the colony grow. To start with, we knew everyone here and now I get patients I've never even seen before. I had two separate people with bad reactions to insect bites today and I had no idea who they were. It's like a real town."

Nina chuckled. "It really is. And I'm glad it's growing—that's the whole point. It just feels fast."

Sarah nodded and took Nina's hand in hers. "Fast doesn't have to be bad."

"True," Nina agreed. Sarah leaned in closer, and Nina wrapped an arm around her.

The next morning at breakfast, they followed a gaggle of giggling children into the canteen, taking seats on the opposite side so as to hear their own voices over the chatter. Nina watched them speculatively from across the room.

"Does it ever make you regret not having children, seeing them like this?" she asked.

Sarah put down her spoon and eyed Nina seriously.

"About that," she started, "There's something I've been meaning to tell you."

"Oh?"

"Yeah. It's kind of a big thing, and I think you're going to be upset that I didn't tell you before. Can you promise that you'll listen to everything I have to say before getting angry?"

Nina felt her heart stutter. "You're scaring me Sarah, just come out with whatever it is before I think you've killed someone."

Sarah laughed hollowly. "Not quite." She took a deep breath and looked Nina in the eye. "I have a daughter."

Nina's head spun. "Okay," she hedged, unsure. "How do you have a daughter that I don't know about?"

Sarah relaxed a little, seemingly relieved by Nina's willingness to talk about it, though her expression became sad. "It happened while you were off planet. She wasn't planned; I'd been dating someone, a guy from Exploration, for a few weeks, and I discovered I was pregnant while he was on a mission. We weren't serious, but I called him and told him about the baby and he was so happy; he came from a big family and he'd always wanted kids. We said we'd give it a proper go—when he got back he'd ask for a transfer, take a desk job and we could be a proper family." Sarah paused, fiddling with her spoon to avoid Nina's eyes. "He never made it back."

Sympathy welled up in Nina, stronger than any of the other emotions warring inside her at the moment. "Oh, Sarah," she breathed, reaching out to hold her hand across the table.

"He never got to meet her, and Serena never got to know her father."

"Why didn't you tell me?" Nina asked, unable to hold the question back any longer. "You know I would have helped."

"You were on the Mars trip at the time. By the time you got back, we'd settled into a routine." Sarah averted her eyes again. "I couldn't bear to let anyone else in only to lose them again. I was so scared of disappointing myself, or giving her another person to love, if there was a chance we might both suffer that way again." Nina exhaled slowly. Sarah finally looked up at her. "Are you angry?"

"I don't know," said Nina honestly. "I can understand you being hurt and not wanting to feel that way again. But the Mars mission, Sarah? That was nearly twenty years ago! How have you not found a moment in all that time to tell me?"

Sarah hung her head. "I know. But the more time that passed, the harder it was to do. I thought for sure you'd cut me off if you knew I'd kept something that big from you."

Nina shook her head and Sarah slumped in relief. "I'm not going to do that. I think I might be a bit pissed off, but I'll have to let you know. Right now I'm a mixture of a bit sad and quite hungry." Sarah half chuckled, picking up her spoon to start on her now cold porridge and grimacing at the taste. "So, Serena? She must be, eighteen, nineteen?"

"Nineteen," said Sarah, and the proud smile on her face that couldn't be held back even by the other emotions confirmed what Nina realised she had been half-hoping was some kind of joke. "She's a trainee midwife." She paused and a faint red hue appeared on her cheeks. "She's due to be woken up soon with the rest of the midwifery team."

"Oh," and now Nina was angry. "So that's why you've finally decided to tell me. Because you were going to get caught out next week, not because you've decided that this relationship is serious enough that you want to tell me the truth for its own sake."

"Is that what this is then, a relationship?"

Thrown, Nina paused, a mouthful of porridge halfway to her mouth. "Um, yes? I thought so?"

"Because we haven't actually talked about it, you know. We've just slipped into something."

Nina groaned, dragging a hand down her face. "I can't talk about this right now. You've just told me you have a secret daughter and now you're questioning me about exact relationship parameters? I haven't even finished my coffee, Sarah. Can you just give me a chance to absorb this all?"

Sarah nodded mutely and Nina stood, clearing the plates and making her way over to the command centre. Her head whirled with new information, different emotions pushing themselves to the surface every second. At the door to the command centre she paused, taking a deep breath. She had just reached her hand out to the sensor when Kjeldsen leapt through the door, excitement visible on their face.

"I've got it!" they cried, brandishing a notepad in Nina's face. "Come with me, I can show you and Leclerc at the same time!"

Completely stumped but at least distracted, Nina followed the bouncing young Dane into the lab. Leclerc greeted them with a similar expression to the one Nina thought she must be wearing.

"I've got it!" Kjeldsen repeated, and placed the notepad down on one of Leclerc's consoles, tapping at it to link into the display. "The predator! I found it on last night's feed, sniffing around near where Liu was hurt."

"Brilliant!"

Nina and Leclerc shared a look, then rushed around to see. The display flickered on, showing a large shadowy shape moving across the screen. Leclerc gave another shout and held a hand up to Kjeldsen for a high five that they seemed just as surprised by as Nina. Somehow, she hadn't marked the serious Frenchwoman down as the high-fiving type. The pair worked for a minute, zooming, highlighting and otherwise enhancing the image until they were left with a remarkably high definition still that filled the whole screen.

"It's a turtle?" Kjeldsen asked, looking between Nina and Leclerc, confusion etched onto their face.

"I was not expecting a turtle," Nina agreed, closing in for a better look. Turtle, or tortoise maybe, did seem to be the closest word Nina could find; it had a large armoured body with powerful looking legs that ended in clawed feet. The face was distinctly turtle-like, with a sharp looking beak, beady eyes and a long neck that looked like it could dart out and back again with great speed. Unlike a turtle, however, the legs and tail were quite long, and Nina could see the sinews under what looked like scales. It was leaner than a turtle, too, with no actual shell to speak of, just hard scales that overlapped across its back. A horrible thought occurred to Nina.

"If this is our top predator, why does it have such serious armour? What is it trying to defend itself from? Is it possible that there's something even bigger that preys on this one?"

Leclerc, tapping away at her console, didn't answer immediately. When she did, she looked up at Nina with a furrowed brow, as though she wasn't fully concentrating on her.

"I would guess that this animal has stayed at this stage of evolution for a long time, like turtles and crocodiles back on Earth, and so it perhaps developed these defences against a predator that is no longer around. Certainly the evolutionary progress of it is not as advanced as the rest of the planet—the rat-dogs for example are a far more complex form of life. This one has simply found a form it likes and has had no need to change over the last several million years."

"Well, that's reassuring," Nina replied, sharing a look of relief with Kjeldsen. "I was not looking forward to meeting whatever the next stage in the food chain was."

Leclerc shook her head. "No, I am pretty sure that this is our predator and that it is also the top of the food chain in this area. Possibly across the whole planet, although that would be unusual, however, if it can swim…" she trailed off, then turned to Kjeldsen. "Let's get more cameras set up along the coast, in the quieter points away from the settlement. If it's amphibious, it'll probably be entering the water somewhere along there and we can get more information. I would guess that it's a reptile, not an amphibian, from these images, but it is hard to confirm until we know more." Kjeldsen nodded and Nina voiced another unpleasant thought that had occurred to her.

"Could it have been one of these we saw in the water when we took that trip out to sea? How many do you think there might be?"

"I don't think so," Leclerc mused, "But it's possible. If it's an elite predator, there probably aren't many of them, and we haven't seen evidence of lots, but if it is amphibious, perhaps they mostly live in the water. But then would that mean that the one on the other continent was a different species? That was a long way from the sea, unless they live in the rivers as well and have species differentiation across the continents according to habitat..."

Nina shared another look with Kjeldsen as Leclerc resumed her tapping at the keypad, her brow furrowed. She took them lightly by the elbow and tugged them gently towards the lab door.

"We'll leave you to your research, Monique," she said as they left. "Let us know if you find anything of interest." Leclerc nodded and waved a hand vaguely and Nina chuckled as the lab door shut behind them. "Best leave her to it; she won't come out again for a while, I wouldn't imagine. Really stellar work on identifying that, Bille, well done."

Kjeldsen blushed at the praise and they headed to their respective stations, Kjeldsen to get started on sending out more cameras (Nina wondered if they had an unlimited supply, or if not, if they had the facilities to produce more) and Nina to begin the more mundane tasks of the day's work.

Mundane tasks weren't as good at keeping Nina's focus, however, so after a few hours of catching up, including reading a very lengthy report from Pavluhkin regarding servicing and maintenance, she was ready to take a break and stretch her legs. She decided to have another look at the jetty and pop in on Liu again while she was over that way. She sighed as she arrived, knowing that visiting Liu would doubtless mean seeing Sarah, who she wasn't sure she was ready to face yet, and turned to head into the medical centre. Tina nodded her through without question.

Liu was alone in his room, his monitors beeping reassuringly and the rise and fall of his chest surer every day. He looked better, she decided, noting the colour of his cheeks, but still frail. She heard movement as the door opened and she turned, bracing herself, but it was Nurse Taylor, who smiled when he recognised her.

"Captain. How was the mission to the hills?"

"Good, thank you," replied Nina. "It feels like ages since I've seen you, what have you been up to?"

"Mostly keeping an eye on the Commander; I've been exempt from duties in the cryobay so I can care for him. Other nurses take the night shifts but with a patient this serious, it's good to keep the care as consistent as possible."

Nina nodded, appreciating what he didn't say about taking the man's care into his own hands. "Thank you. How is he doing?"

"Much better. We're going to wake him up tomorrow, I don't know if Dr Caimile told you?"

"She hasn't updated me recently," Nina hedged, not wanting to reveal details of Sarah's personal life to her colleagues without checking with her first. Taylor nodded as if he understood, which he probably did, Nina mused; the young nurse had a knack for seeing things other people didn't.

"Right. Well, his recovery has been really good," Taylor moved to show Nina the charts, pointing to a line showing a sharp upwards slant, "and he's responded really well to the medication, so we feel there's no use in keeping him in a coma any longer. Best to get him awake and working to build those muscles back himself."

"That's excellent news, Taylor, thank you. What time will you be waking him tomorrow? I'd like to come along and see him afterwards."

"Probably around 11.00, but I can drop you a comm to confirm tomorrow morning. Obviously if we have any emergencies, we'll have to push him down the list."

Nina nodded in understanding. "Of course. Thanks again." She cast a last look at the sleeping form of her friend and left the room, hoping that the next time he saw him he would at least be conscious.

Nina ate alone in the canteen that evening, working through her thoughts. She considered heading back up to the ship for a night, having not been back in over a week, but didn't want to risk getting stuck up there and not being able to be there for Dan when he woke up. She was about to go and sit on the bench in her front garden with a book when the door chimed. It opened to reveal Dr Caimile, wearing a curious expression and holding something that almost resembled a bunch of flowers. Nina stepped back wordlessly to let her in and waited until the door had closed behind her.

"Hi," she started, but Sarah thrust her hands forward and offered the mixed bunch of mostly orange foliage to Nina.

"These are for you. To say sorry," she added when Nina took them wonderingly. They were a little prickly.

"Thank you," she began tentatively, and then couldn't hold back the snort that escaped her. "Sarah. This is hilarious. Where on Earth did you get these from?"

Sarah visibly relaxed, smiling cautiously. "I went for a stroll around the back of the medical bay and picked them from there. I realised I owed you a massive apology. Not only for hiding things from you, but for lashing out at you when you were trying to understand. It wasn't right for me to make that dig about our relationship, and I apologise."

"You were right, though. I hadn't tried to discuss anything with you."

"Neither did I," Sarah pointed out. "The changes were so new, I was caught up in enjoying them rather than defining anything, and I shouldn't have tried to put the blame on you for not doing so either."

"Well, thank you," replied Nina. "For apologising and for the flowers. What shall I do with them?" She looked around the room, as if expecting to see a vase waiting for her on a shelf.

"Oh! I thought about that!" Sarah rummaged in her bag, proudly producing a beaker that looked as if it had been stolen from the hospital. At the sight of the jar and the triumphant expression on Sarah's face, Nina's restraint broke and she burst into laughter, leaning on the back of a chair for support as she shook with hilarity. After a moment, Sarah joined in and relief washed through them both as the tension eased. When they sobered, Nina took the proffered beaker to the sink to fill it with water, then placed the dubious bunch of flowers in it. Laughter overwhelmed her again as she looked at the most bizarre peace offering she had ever received, and she drew Sarah to her.

"It's the most 'you' thing I've ever seen. It's perfect. I love it." She paused, her heart surging hotly into her throat. "I love you."

Sarah looked up at her, an uncharacteristically nervous expression on her face. "I love you too, Nina." Nina kissed her softly, gently, and when they pulled back, they both had smiles on their faces. "I really am sorry I didn't tell you about Serena," Sarah said, still anxious.

Nina shook her head. "It's in the past. Let's go and sit down and you can tell me all about her."

Chapter Seventeen

The next morning, Taylor sent Nina a message almost as soon as his shift started to confirm Liu's waking time was scheduled for 11.00. Nina spent the time until then in the command centre, after having breakfast with Sarah, who promised to let her know if there were any developments before that. Nina was relieved to find things back to normal; they had spent the majority of the previous night talking and she was pleased to learn they could weather an argument and still come out of it wanting to spend time with each other. Her previous experience of serious relationships had been very different from this; they had either been long distance or serving on the same ship, and none of them had been based on the strong bond of friendship that Nina knew she shared with Sarah. It filled her with hope, and she kissed her goodbye after breakfast with a warm feeling that had nothing to do with the hearty bowl of porridge she had just eaten.

Nina asked Kjeldsen to send out a communication to the rest of the crew to let them know that Liu would be waking up today, as she knew they were all worried about him as well. The tight bond that had grown up quickly between the crew continued to grow even now that they had more choice of people to socialise with. Aside from the romantic relationships sprouting, Nina knew that Leclerc and Pavluhkin had struck up a firm friendship and often saw the two women in animated discussion or serious conversation when she went to take her meals.

Shortly after 11.30, a message from Taylor popped up on Nina's console informing her that Liu was awake, in good spirits and more than happy for a visit. She briefly passed the information on to Kjeldsen to share, though warned them not to invite the whole crew over immediately, and headed over to the medical centre as fast as she could. Nodding to Tina on duty at the desk, who she was starting to get quite friendly with owing to her frequent visits, she turned down the familiar corridor and entered her friend's room. A huge smile broke onto her face at the sight before her. Liu was sitting up, dressed in a hospital gown and with the blanket still up to his waist, but awake, smiling and chatting away to Nurse Taylor.

"Captain!" he greeted cheerily when he saw her. "My apologies for spending so much time sleeping on the job."

"Nonsense," Nina dismissed, enveloping him a huge hug and feeling him vibrate under her as he chuckled. "You have no idea how glad I am to hear you making stupid comments like that," she added as she pulled back. "You gave us all quite a scare."

Liu turned serious. "Me too. I remember being attacked and some of the ride back to camp—I thought I was going to die."

Nina took a seat next to him and squeezed his hand. "I am very glad you didn't."

"Me too. I don't think I was that scared, just irritated I wouldn't get to carry on building the colony. I remember being pretty pissed off I'd never know what attacked me, either."

Nina shook her head. "You wouldn't believe me if I told you."

Liu tried to sit up a bit straighter, then winced.

"Be careful," Taylor intervened, stepping forward from his silent observation spot. "You're still recovering from some very serious injuries."

"I know, I know," Liu grumbled, but allowed himself to be repositioned on the pillows by Taylor's steady hands. "I'm just not good at staying still."

"You'll need to be, if you want to get better," Nina reprimanded.

"Jesus, Nina, not you, too!" Liu exploded. "I know! I got the full doom and gloom speech from Dr Caimile the second I woke up!" He rubbed his hand down his face, exhaling loudly. "Sorry. I know you're just trying to help."

Nina squeezed his hand again. "It's fine." He smiled weakly at her and she started to rise from her seat. "I should leave you to rest."

"No, all I've done is rest! Talking won't hurt me. Tell me about the creature. Was it the predator we saw on the other continent?"

Nina caught Taylor's eye and he nodded minutely. Nina retook her chair. "We think so, but we've only caught one glimpse of it so far. We don't know much really, just what it looks like."

"Well?" said Liu, his face eager. "I couldn't see anything except a large shadow; it was too dark to see anything else."

"It was big," Nina confirmed. "And sort of scaly. We think it might be reptilian."

Liu frowned. "A reptile? Weird."

"Weird was definitely one word for it," Nina agreed. "It looked a bit like a giant tortoise."

Nina heard a snort from behind her and turned to see Taylor muffling his laughter. She turned back to Dan, who had a look of horror dawning on his face.

"Hang on. Are you telling me I was hospitalised by a turtle?" The outrage in his voice broke both Nina and Taylor's resolve, and the latter burst into uncontrollable laughter.

"Not a turtle, a tortoise," he wheezed through loud guffaws. Nina couldn't help but smile and Liu started to grin too.

"Sorry, my mistake. Next time I go to the aquarium, I'll be sure to keep my guard up."

Liu's recovery progressed well over the next couple of weeks, though not as fast as he would have liked. His physiotherapist was very pleased with his progress and chided him frequently for expecting too much of himself. Nina and the rest of the crew made sure to visit him often, and after a week more in the hospital, he was allowed to head home to recuperate in his new cottage, provided he wore a tracker that would alert the medical team to any emergencies. Sam Fraser in particular made a point of visiting several times a day, bringing him food and keeping him up to date on colony gossip, and Nina noted a direct correlation between Liu's recovery and Fraser's spirits.

For the first couple of weeks or so he was unable to walk more than a few steps at a time, so used a wheelchair. Chaudhary was told firmly that on no account was he allowed to goad Liu into racing, in case he pulled his stitches, but was otherwise very helpful in showing him exercises that he could do whilst sitting and letting him know other useful tips for navigating with his chair. The two were often seen taking a trip along the new boardwalk that led to the nearly finished jetty in the evenings after work finished.

The rest of the colony proceeded apace, too. The jetty would soon be complete, and a call had been put out for anyone with relevant experience to sign up to be part of Demeter's new fishing team. Pete Stafford, Sophia and Octy trailing behind him, came over for a chat one morning at breakfast and said that his dad had been a fisherman back in their hometown in Cornwall and that he thought his mother and brother would both be more than willing to join up when they were woken. Nina cursed under her breath, remembering her vow to him to make sure they were up soon, and promised to check when they were due to be woken as soon as she got back to her console.

To her pleasant surprise, they had indeed been bumped up the order and their names were on the list for waking in three days' time. She sent Pete a quick message to let him know, although the system would automatically alert him two days before they were due to wake anyway. She hoped he would find it reassuring to know that she hadn't forgotten him, and it would be good for Sophia to have something to look forward to as well. He had seemed a bit low still and had confided that he was struggling to adjust to his new rabbi; before this journey, he had had the same rabbi since he was a child and missed him a lot.

Around a quarter of the colonists on the ship had been woken now, with more waking every other day, and the town had started expanding beyond its initial borders. The farming quarter now had a number of dwellings closer to the fields for farm workers, more housing was being built north of the bay past the jetty, and construction had just begun on a third block slightly further inland behind the community buildings. The space in the middle had officially been named 'the Plasa'; it was a pleasant spot, bordered by the communal buildings and paved with the same solar paving that all the roads in the settlement had finally acquired. There were plenty of plants, with most of the trees and shrubs that had been there when they arrived now snugly surrounded by newly built planters for protection. Benches and other outdoor seating dotted the area, with a canopied area between two large trees to offer some shelter from both the sun and the rain. Tall lampposts had also been put up, with lengths of festoon lights strung between them, and Nina loved the atmosphere they gave the area in the evening. It made it stand out from the rest of the settlement, where outdoor lighting had so far been kept to a minimum, and Nina knew Saima and Mira still were working on other ways to mark the location as the official centre of town.

Sakamoto and her second, Miguel, had taken over the policing of the colony and so far had had pleasingly little to do. There had been minor disputes between neighbours and two suspected incidents of theft, which had turned out to be one misplacement and one curious toddler. Nina was hopeful that in such a small community crime would remain low but knew that Sakamoto and Miguel had a good team to back them up, should they be needed. There was a room in the community building that could be used to hold any law-breakers, should the need arise, and as the colony currently fell under the jurisdiction of the military, she would have her regulations to back her up if there were any requirement for it.

Although a disproportionate number of those still sleeping were youngsters, enough children were now awake for the school to start operating. Parents were given time off work to look after their children when they were woken, but childcare was starting to become a problem and the few childminders that were operating were beginning to reach capacity. Nina had been in talks with the rest of the Union and the relevant experts about all the logistics; building the school, waking the rest of the teachers, providing equipment and ensuring that everything was ready to run as smoothly as possible when the school officially opened its doors the next week.

They had decided to continue with the days of the week as used on Earth, to lessen disruption and give the children (and the adults) a sense of continuity that would hopefully be beneficial to them. Therefore, the school was due to open its doors next Monday morning at 09.30, to give parents enough time to drop off their children and get to work for the official start of the Demetrian working day at 10.00. Out of hours childcare provision was already being provided for those few, like doctors and nurses, whose work shifts didn't allow them to work normal hours like the majority of the colony, and the childminders would be able to continue looking after children in conjunction with the school.

On the Friday afternoon after Liu had woken, Nina had a final meeting with the appropriate people to make sure everything was all set for the school opening on Monday morning. She swung by the Lovells on her way to the newly finished school building; Patrin opened the door and ushered her in, apologising for Nehemiah who wasn't quite ready. The house had come on since she had visited last, with pictures mounted on walls, bookshelves filled with books and no sign of the half-empty crates. Toys were scattered all over the rugs, accompanied by yet more books. It looked from the debris as if Kezia had been having a maths lesson at some point this morning.

As she waited, Kezia bounced over, clutching a small toy. She had the same hair- and skin-tone as Nehemiah and was wearing well-worn red cut-off dungarees, with her long hair escaping from a plait.

"Hi, Kezia," she greeted the small girl with a smile. "It's nice to properly meet you at last."

"Hi, Captain. Are you really in charge of a whole spaceship?" The girl gazed at her with wide eyes.

"I am, yes. Do you like spaceships?"

Kezia nodded enthusiastically. "Yeah. I wanna be a pilot one day."

"Oh really? I can introduce you to the ship's pilot, if you like. Her name is Sam, and she's a very good pilot."

"Really?" Kezia's face lit up with glee. "That'd be so cool!"

"That's a lesson plan right there," laughed Nehemiah, coming over as Kezia ran off, too excited to stay still, making what Nina now saw was a toy spacecraft zoom around the room with appropriate noises. "Not on the furniture, Kezzy!" Nina turned and saw the spacecraft making its way across one of the wooden tables and an unabashed Kezia turning to continue its flight elsewhere. "Right, shoes on, time to go!"

After what Nina considered to be an inordinately long time, having had very little previous experience with trying to get small people ready to leave the house, the three of them had shoes on and they headed out the door. It was long past the point where they would have needed coats; Leclerc guessed they had arrived in spring, which was very convenient for the farmers, and thought this must be the peak of summer.

Nina had relaxed uniform rules for the military personnel, as their full jumpsuits would be uncomfortably hot and possibly even dangerous for those doing physical activity at this time of year. Most of them had taken to wearing combat shorts paired with their undershirts, but Nina chose to wear an adaptation of her dress uniform on days when she knew she wasn't going to be too active; her dress jacket open over the regulation undershirt, accompanied by lightweight grey trousers. Oddly, she quite liked the combination; it had felt strange at first, but it signalled her out as the ship's captain easily so the colonists could recognise her if needed. Still, she was slightly envious of the shorts that her three companions wore as they crossed the Plasa and made their way to the school, dropping Kezia off at the childminder on the way.

It was a big building, three stories high and both long and wide, built to accommodate all the children currently asleep on the ship, although less than a hundred students would be starting on Monday. There were separate entrances for the primary and secondary students, with the younger ones entering at one end of the long building and the older at the other. The three floors were divided to accommodate infant, junior and secondary level students, with age-appropriate classrooms on each level. They also had three separate playgrounds: two with some climbing equipment and one with more open space. All three had reading areas, shady spots and water fountains and Nina was impressed at the detail that had gone in to creating such a pleasant space in such a short space of time.

They met the rest of the Union, Makena, Ana and Maria and, to Nina's surprise, Sakamoto, at the front of the building. At Nina's raised eyebrow, the latter shrugged.

"Someone has to make sure it's safe and secure," she explained.

A quick tour ensued, starting with the infant classrooms on the ground floor. They were lovely spaces, with bright colours, toys and books everywhere. The walls currently held a lot of empty space, waiting for the work that the children would put up there. They had direct access into their play area, with an area aside from the main playground cordoned off for learning and a rain shelter so they could go out in all weather. There was also a large hall, suitable for school plays, assemblies or sports lessons. The next level up was for the junior children, and the third level held the eleven to eighteen-year-olds. The rooms got steadily more serious as they progressed, with the main classrooms for the oldest students containing consoles not dissimilar from Nina's own in the command centre.

"Of course, we will still have extra-curricular learning for all students," Nehemiah explained, seeing the look on some of the Union's faces at the sight of the rows of desks. "Music, drama, cooking and physical education will all be offered, and the farmers are working on providing us with an allotment so the children learn how to grow their own food. As the children reach their last years of school, we will work with their individual specialisms and interests to aim to provide them with the education that they need to follow their chosen career."

"Saima, are you involved in the non-STEM aspects of the curriculum?" Nina asked.

"Absolutely," Saima nodded emphatically. "I've been working with Nehemiah and they've got a couple of really great music and drama teachers, so we've all planned a programme together that should get kids of all ages involved in the arts."

"How about sports?" asked Sakamoto.

"We've got a brilliant sports teacher who'll be working with them, twice a week for the secondary students and once for the primary. He's also really enthusiastic about setting up clubs and willing to learn new things himself, so if there's anything the students particularly want to try out after school, he's more than happy to give that a go."

"It all sounds great, Nehemiah," Nina said. "I can't believe what an amazingly thorough job you've done in such a short space of time." There were murmurs of agreement from the rest of the tour group and Patrin jumped in to save Nehemiah the embarrassment of replying.

"Let me show you the SEN provision we've got in place currently. As far as I know we only have two children needing regular assistance at the moment, but we have facilities available for any children that might be struggling with the change of environment or any other factors. This is the sensory room."

He showed them into a small room on the first floor littered with beanbags, floor cushions and other soft, squishy furnishings. He tapped a console near the door and the main light went out, leaving dim coloured lights glowing around the walls and making soothing patterns. Another tap at the console and low music started playing, the gentle, calming strains seeming to emanate from everywhere in the room. Nina felt the tension drain from her shoulders and the group looked around, smiling lazily at each other.

"Can I come here when I'm feeling stressed, too?" joked Jarli. Patrin grinned and reset everything on the console as they all filed back out. They crammed into the lift and headed back to Nehemiah's office to go through some more details; timetables, lesson plans, achievement targets and more—more information than Nina, who had never needed to be aware of anything like this before, could wrap her head around. After glancing at a few lesson plans, she retreated to the back of the office while the others, some of whom had children of their own and were more qualified to inspect than she was, looked through it in more detail. After a moment, Patrin came to join her.

"Happy, Captain?" he asked.

"Very," she responded with a smile. "It's things like this that remind me how glad I am to have a team of experts around me, so I don't have to attempt to worry about all the little details myself. It's wonderful to sit back and know that you and Nehemiah have everything under control and that the children of the colony are in good hands."

Nehemiah's amused rumble came from behind Patrin. "Thank you very much, Captain. We hope not to disappoint."

Chapter Eighteen

The evening before the school was due to open, Nina was sitting in her front garden with a book, enjoying what was technically her day off when a breathless Kjeldsen came running up the path.

"There's a message for you," they panted. "Encrypted. I can't open it. Came in via the satellite."

Nina sat up, putting her book aside. "From Earth?"

"Must be. Nobody else would bother sending a message via the satellite and encrypting it, and I can't trace the source."

Nina nodded and stood up, her heart racing. They walked quickly together back towards the command centre. When they entered, Nina saw a light blinking on her console to indicate a new message. She pressed her palm to the scanner and it unlocked, words flashing up across the top of the screen. She held her breath as she tapped the message to open it, entered her security code and an unknown smiling face appeared on her screen.

"Captain Brooke. Such a pleasure to hear from you and your crew, and congratulations on your safe awakening." Nina exhaled with relief. The speaker was a tall black man, with greying hair and the air of a man who had been powerful in his younger years, gone slightly soft after too much time behind a desk. His face was heavily lined, and Nina wondered what he had seen in his lifetime to give him such an appearance. However, his expression was one of joy and his smile was echoed in his eyes, which sparkled with excitement. "I'm Admiral Barron and I'm currently the head of the Interplanetary Exploration Department. I know it must be strange for you to see a different face from the one that saw you off.

"I'm sure you're up to date with our situation here on Earth and how bad things got for a while. You'll be pleased to know that it's all evened out a bit and we're starting to rebuild, although we don't have much left to build with." The sparkle in his eyes dulled a bit for a moment, before lifting again. "You'll also be pleased to know that one of your sister ships has been in touch; the *Relativity* reached her destination approximately four years ago and has had great success with the colony they've established on the planet that they've named Camelot. I'm sending over all the information they've sent us with this message so you can update your database, and I'm sure your scientists will be interested to learn about what they've discovered."

"Too right she will," murmured Nina.

"I'm also attaching some more detailed information about Earth and personal updates for colonists that have relatives on

Earth or on Camelot. Camelot have started a practise of letting their colonists add letters and personal information to one communication a month, which you are welcome to also do, and we will make sure that they reach their intended recipients.

"We will update our schedule to be in touch every week now that we have heard from you, as I presume you have been doing, and we look forward to establishing regular communications, albeit with a slight lag!" Barron chuckled, and Nina marvelled at how the action lifted his entire face. "Let me close by saying once again that we are overjoyed to have heard from you and we wish you every success in your continued endeavours. Barron out."

The video cut out and Nina saw an enormous information dump in progress in the bottom corner of her screen. Elation filled her and she turned to Kjeldsen with a huge smile on her face.

"Brilliant!" She grinned, and Kjeldsen grinned back. "Let's keep this to ourselves tonight and wait for the info dump to complete—it looks like it might take all night with the amount that's coming through. Can you call a crew meeting for everyone tomorrow at 10.30 and we'll share the news then?"

Kjeldsen nodded and Nina returned home, checking the console was set to continue the download overnight before she did so.

The next morning, Nina popped by the school before heading over to the command centre. The urge to head straight there to check out the new information was almost overwhelming, but she knew it would keep for another half hour or so and she wanted to be present for another big Demetrian first. She arrived at 09.15, dressed in her regular uniform as the day was overcast and not too muggy, and found Nehemiah standing by one of the entrances. About fifteen other people, who Nina took to be the teachers and teaching assistants, stood with him. Around ninety children were starting school today, split into class sizes of roughly ten depending on how many there were in each age group, which gave plenty of space for children to join the classes as they became ready before they had to start splitting groups up and moving them around.

A small trickle of children started to arrive and the teachers separated, moving to stand a few metres apart from each other in a line along the front of the building. Nina smiled and nodded lots as the trickle turned into a stream, and some of the children waved at her. A few of the little ones stared and pointed with wide eyes and expressions of awe and had to be tugged away by an apologetic parent. She spotted Kezia, bouncing enthusiastically as she arrived with Patrin, and recognised some of the other children who had been woken in the first batch. She also saw Robert from the lab, holding the hand of a small girl of about five who was wearing a backpack far too big for her as he led her gently towards the school.

Nina knew that the students had all had a home visit from their teachers prior to today's official start date, so most of the older ones simply spotted their teacher, gave their parents a farewell hug and kiss, and crossed to join the appropriate group. Once a teacher had all their students, they headed inside to give their class an induction tour and get them settled in their new classroom with their peers. The younger children were more complicated and some of them needed a bit more persuasion before they could be convinced to join their classmates.

The very youngest group, some of whom had never been to school before, were only doing half a day for the first week and their parents were allowed to join them for the first part of the day to help the children acclimatise. These were the last ones left at 09.45 when the teacher, a plump smiling lady and her assistant, an energetic young man, finally managed to herd the entire gaggle into the room on the end with promises of stories and toys.

Nina arrived at the command centre a few minutes later, anticipation pumping through her veins. She still relished how the nearness of everything on Demeter meant she wasted very little time travelling, although she did wonder how soon it would all start to seem stiflingly small. After all, travelling had always been a big part of her job and it was a bit odd not to be doing any of it. She settled at her console with a nod to Kjeldsen, who seemed unable to control their grin. Nina smiled back.

"Did you manage to keep the news to yourself last night?" she asked, aware of how persuasive Fraser and Taylor would have been if they thought Kjeldsen was hiding something from them.

Their grin widened. "I didn't tell them a thing. They're so annoyed with me."

Nina laughed; Kjeldsen had a devious streak that didn't come out often but was very entertaining on the rare occasions it surfaced. She barely had time to register that the information had all come through and that although there was a seriously large amount, it had been helpfully pre-sorted into folders, before the door to the command centre opened and the crew started to arrive. Liu was first, propelling himself inside with ease, a wide smile on his face.

"Look at you, back at work already!" she quipped, marvelling at how quickly he had adapted to his chair.

"I wasn't going to miss this one. Rumours are flying."

"Are they?" Nina asked, whipping round to look at Kjeldsen, who looked equally surprised.

"Well, no, but Fraser called to ask if I knew what was going on because she couldn't get it out of Kjeldsen. I told her she'd have to wait until this morning to find out, same as everyone else."

Nina felt a twinge of guilt at leaving her First Officer in the dark, but it hadn't occurred to her at the time to burden him with something else on top of his recovery. She told him as much and he waved her apology aside. "Believe me, Nina, I have no problem finding out with everyone else. I can always question you afterwards if I want to."

"True." She grinned.

Fraser and Taylor arrived next, Fraser almost falling through the door in her haste. Fraser kept shooting dark looks at Kjeldsen to which they returned a smug grin, which only served to infuriate her further. Taylor seemed amused by the whole situation; out of the three of them, he seemed by far the most laid back. Soon the whole crew had assembled, and Nina smiled to see them all around the table in the meeting room. Sarah had provided coffee for everyone, for which Nina nearly kissed her, and she waited until everyone had a cup and was seated before she began.

"Good morning, everyone. May I say what a pleasure it is to see everyone in the same room again, and in our new meeting room in our new command centre." She smiled around at everyone, feeling a great surge of fondness for them all. "As I'm sure you've all guessed, we're here because we've finally heard back from Earth." Fraser whooped and high-fived Taylor, and Nina grinned. "I'd like you all to see the video message we received from the Admiral back at base, because I think you'll all enjoy it as much as we did."

She dialled up the video to play on the large screen attached to the wall at the end of the room and watched again as Admiral Barron spoke. She let her eyes flick to the faces of the crew too, enjoying watching their reactions as much as listening to his words, and was unsurprised to see beaming smiles on nearly all the faces in the room when the video finished. Before they could all start talking at once, she held up a hand to cut them off.

"Now I know you're all going to have questions. But right now I know about as much as you do. We received a massive information dump last night, which took eight hours to download, so we're going to spend the rest of today sorting through that and adding it to databases as appropriate. We will of course forward on anything that we think will be of particular interest to individuals, and we'll let you know anything major."

"Can we start putting together information packages to send to people back on Earth?" Pavluhkin asked.

"Yes, I think so," Nina mused. "Make sure they're not too large, though—Kjeldsen and I will work out if we need to set limits to the size of packages people can send, but keep it brief for now."

Pavluhkin nodded and Nina wondered who she wanted to send messages to. The engineer was quiet by nature and never talked much about her family, though Nina thought she recalled her mentioning visiting some siblings on leave several years ago when they had worked together on another mission. Perhaps she had nieces and nephews that would be grown up now and wanted to get in touch. The thought gave Nina an odd sensation in her tummy, as it always did.

"Can we tell other people about this?" asked Chaudhary, pulling Nina's thoughts back to the present.

"I'd rather you keep it quiet for now. I want to make sure the information is disseminated correctly and wait until we have a bit more of an idea about what we've received before we tell the rest of the colony. I'm sure there will be questions, and I want us to be ready to answer them."

Everyone nodded and she dismissed them, though most lingered to chat as she headed back into the main room and sat down at her console. She didn't begrudge them the chance to gossip; she thought it was probably sensible they all had a chat about it without her there, so she put her efforts into concentrating on the information dump that had arrived with the message. There were a lot of files and she was vaguely aware of the crew drifting back out of the meeting room as she worked her way through them, skimming the ones she was interested in and passing the others on to the appropriate people.

She forwarded the enormous number of personal messages to Kjeldsen to disseminate, as well as updated information regarding communications and the satellite networks. There were also a lot of scientific files for Leclerc, which Nina didn't look into apart from a brief curious glance at the data from Camelot. Sorting through it all took most of the day, apart from a quick break for lunch (Liu dropped by with a sandwich for her, for which she was grateful) and she was startled when Kjeldsen interrupted her focus by bidding her goodnight. Checking the time, she realised it was 18.15 and she swore under her breath.

Tonight was the first time she was due to meet Sarah's daughter and Sarah had threatened her with experimental medical procedures if she was late. She pondered briefly, then decided it was worth a quick shower and a change of clothes. Less than ten minutes later, she emerged from her cottage, freshly showered and dressed in a light blue sleeveless summer shirt and long white cotton shorts with sandals. It felt odd to be out of uniform, but she enjoyed both the coolness of the outfit and the anonymity it afforded her.

Breathing another sigh of relief at how close everything around the settlement was, Nina rang the bell of Sarah's house a few minutes later. Sarah answered the door wearing a bright red form-fitting dress which Nina admired very much and greeted her with a kiss.

"Come on through, we're in the garden," she said over her shoulder, leading Nina through the room and out through the door in the opposite wall.

Sarah's garden was compact but tidy, with a bench backed up to the wall of the house and festoons draped from the roof to a small tree at the end. Sarah had moved her kitchen table outside for the evening and it was already laid for dinner, reflections of the lights twinkling in the cutlery. A young woman stood up as she entered, a smile on her face and her hand held out for Nina to shake. She had lighter skin than her mother and high cheekbones and Nina wondered briefly where her father had been from.

"You must be Nina," she greeted, shaking Nina's hand firmly. "You have no idea how much I've heard about you over the years. I'm over the moon you two are finally dating; it's been coming long enough."

Bemused, Nina turned to Sarah, who managed to look both amused and abashed at the same time.

"Thank you, I think?" replied Nina, and Serena laughed.

"I understand you didn't find out about my existence until fairly recently, though," Serena continued, retaking her seat on the bench.

Nina sat opposite her on a kitchen chair. "No, it was a little bit of a surprise, to be honest," she confessed, smiling to keep the sting out of it.

Serena laughed again. "I don't doubt it! Well, I'm very glad we get to meet now."

"Me too," Nina replied, genuinely. Sarah handed her a chilled glass of something that looked like white wine and she raised her eyebrows. "Where did this come from?"

"I used some of my credits to get a nice bottle for tonight," Sarah said, handing Serena a glass and settling next to her on the bench with her own. "Fingers crossed the farmers make good progress with the vines soon; I'm not sure how long I can keep going with wine rationing."

"I've got a visit later this week to check in with them, so I'll let you know." Nina smirked, taking a sip. It was crisp and refreshing, with moisture beading on the side of the glass. "This is very nice, thank you."

"You're welcome. Cheers."

The three of them clinked glasses and they made small talk for a bit while they drank. After a bit of easy chatter, Sarah got up and returned with a tray holding three plates and a large dish in the middle. As the settlement had grown and people became more settled in their own homes, the canteen had started offering takeaway food as an option. Despite the fact that all the accommodation came equipped with small kitchens, there wasn't yet enough food available for people to be able to cook at home, so this was an attempt to make things both more homey and more convenient.

Near the quick bites booth and the food processing units now stood a set of heated shelves holding a variety of hot dishes in portable containers that could be taken home to eat in privacy, or taken outside to the new outdoor seating area. Nina liked the outdoor seating; there was an array of tables so one could eat alone or in a group, and lampposts with more festoons had been added to the area to link it to the rest of the Plasa and liven the place up. This was the first time she had used the take-home option, though she knew families like the Lovells preferred to eat at home every evening, and she watched Sarah serving up with eager anticipation.

"When do you start work, Serena?" Nina asked as they tucked into a lightly spiced casserole. "Sarah said you're a midwife?"

"Next week," Serena replied, after swallowing a large mouthful. "The rest of the team are set up and ready to go, but I'm still in training so I won't be doing anything by myself for a long time yet. At the moment I'm in the following-people-around-watching-them phase."

"That must be quite an odd phase in midwifery," Nina commented, and Serena gave a wry smile.

"Some people don't like it, but less object than you'd think. But there's a lot of midwifery that's not just giving birth, you know. I get to weigh a lot of babies and take a lot of blood pressure readings too. I'll be allowed to do those bits soon," she stated proudly, and Sarah beamed with maternal pride. It was a little disconcerting, Nina found, discovering a whole new side to her girlfriend that she hadn't known existed, but nice all the same.

"I bet you'll have your work cut out for you soon enough." Nina grinned, and both the other women nodded fervently.

"Oh yes," said Sarah. "There are loads of people who were holding off on extending or starting their families because they knew it wasn't advisable to travel while pregnant, so I'm sure they'll be getting stuck in as soon as they've settled. There'll be babies born before a year's passed, you mark my words."

"You needn't make it sound so threatening, Mum." Serena laughed. "Surely expanding the colony is a good thing?"

"Well, there is that," Sarah conceded, gesturing expansively with her wine glass.

Before Nina knew it, the evening had slipped past and the stars were fully out, sparkling above them in a bold attempt to outshine Sarah's festoons. Serena lived in a shared house with two other trainee midwives, so she bade them farewell just after nine and kissed them both goodbye. A warm glow spread through Nina at the unexpected acceptance into the family. She smiled and looped her arm around Sarah's waist as they waved her down the path, giving her an affectionate squeeze. When the door had shut, Sarah exhaled and looked at her nervously.

"Well?"

Nina laughed and took her hands. "Well what? She's a wonderful young woman, just like her mother. You've done an excellent job raising her."

Sarah squeezed her hands, looking unusually emotional. "It's strange, having you both together after so long. I like it, though. It feels right." Nina leaned in to kiss her. "You'll stay tonight?"

"Absolutely," Nina murmured against her lips.

Chapter Nineteen

The crew had so far been successful in keeping the message from Earth to themselves, but Nina knew it wouldn't take long before the news spread through the settlement, with or without their help. She also wanted to get the messages to those who had received them sooner rather than later so, after talking with the rest of the Union, she arranged another mass meeting. There were now considerably more people awake than there had been the first time they gathered, so Chaudhary set up a large screen in the Plasa so that the message from Earth could be shown to everyone. They hung it in front of the community centre, and the canteen arranged to stop serving meals slightly earlier than usual. Chaudhary reassembled the stage from the previous meeting and Pavluhkin and Kjeldsen turned a portable console into a makeshift lectern with a microphone, this time adding speakers around the Plasa.

Nina arrived slightly before the appointed time of 20.00 and smiled to find the Plasa already packed with people. All the benches and the tables outside the canteen were occupied and the centre of the Plasa was full of people sitting spread out across the ground, with groups standing towards the edges. Nina nodded to the other Union members as they appeared, and chatted until the appointed hour arrived. At 20.00 on the dot, Nina cast her eye over the other Union members, who nodded, stood up and moved to the lectern.

"Good evening everyone," she opened, and the excited chatter died down. Her voice echoed back to her from all over the Plasa. "It's good to see so many of you here; thank you all for coming. I'm going to start by passing on the latest news from us and then we'll have general updates from the rest of the Union. If you have any questions, please send them to Kjeldsen, my Communications Officer, who is acting as moderator for this meeting. We won't answer all of them as we go, but we will address some of the more general ones at the end of the meeting.

"The big update from me, as I'm sure some of you are expecting, is that we have finally heard back from Earth." The audience cheered and Nina grinned. "I'll start by playing you the message I've received from Admiral Barron and I'll go through everything in more detail once you've seen that."

Nina dialled up the video from her console and stepped to the side as Barron's face appeared on the large screen behind her, eliciting a few whoops from the crowd. When the video finished, there was a round of applause, and Nina stepped back to the lectern with a wide smile.

"I'm sure the first thing you all want to know after that is, when do you get your personal communications? Kjeldsen has been working tirelessly to sort all the information out and anyone with a personal missive should receive it by tomorrow evening at the latest. We are going to take up the Admiral's suggestion of sending personal communications once a month, so if there's anything you'd like to send, please feel free to start getting it together and we'll let you know once we have a date. At the moment there's no size restrictions, but please be sensible about what you're sending or we will have to implement one."

"The rest of the information has been downloaded onto the databases and is available for anyone to access. Please do feel free to look up anything you'd like to—I know I'm curious about how our sister colony on Camelot is getting on, especially considering they're a few years ahead of us." Nina paused. "I think that's all from me today; the Admiral has said most of it for me. So now I'll pass you on to the rest of the Union to give updates on how they've been getting on. Lowanna, would you like to go first?"

The farmers stood in unison and Nina retreated to her seat as they moved to the podium. The Johnsons were concise and succinct in their delivery; Lowanna explained about the various crops that would be ready for harvest, the earliest probably starting in a few weeks, and Jarli talked enthusiastically about how well the animals were adapting to their new home.

"We're also investigating a lot of the local flora and fauna. We've started cultivating a few of the plant species that went down well in taste tests (Nina caught Fraser's eye and grinned, remembering) and we're having a go at domesticating some of the local animals."

Jarli chipped in. "So far, it's not going great, but it's giving my folks some very beneficial exercise." There was a roar of laughter from the crowd and Jarli stepped back again.

"We're pleased to say initial tests on setting up for rice growing are looking good, and we're hoping that Mr Van Khiem and his team will be able to start growing up by the river very soon."

Nina breathed a sigh of relief; rice was just so easy when feeding large groups.

"I'm also branching out, and seem to have ended up with the fishing team under my heading." Jarli shrugged with an expression of confusion and continued. "Though luckily most of the people doing the actual fishing have a lot more experience than I do. We're still looking for more people to get involved though, so if you've always wanted to have a go, now's your chance!"

The Johnsons started wrapping up, pausing for questions and laughing when Kjeldsen sent one through.

"Very good question," Jarli chuckled, "Someone has asked, 'What about beer?'" Everyone else laughed too, and Lowanna stepped back to the microphone. Nina grinned; maybe she wouldn't need to make a special trip over to find out how the wine prospects were looking after all.

"You'll be pleased to know we've planted a variety of hops, which are doing well, and our brewers are due to start setting up shop very soon, so we'll be working closely with them. We're also growing grapes, which we we'll eventually use to make wine, and looking into what else might make nice drinks. We're hoping some of the local produce might ferment well, so again, if anyone has any experience of any of this, please do come and talk to us."

The audience gave a round of applause and the Johnsons went and sat down again to be replaced by Mira, for an update on the various construction work around the colony. She had prepared some images and Nina sat up straighter, just as interested as everyone else to see her drawings of what she imagined Bayville would look like after all the current work was completed. Mira then swapped to a different image of another, smaller settlement that would be located at the bottom of the foothills, with accommodation for the rice farmers and forestry workers. This settlement also housed the processing buildings for these, as well as a basic canteen, temporary accommodations and an energy distribution centre. Nina couldn't believe they'd already progressed far enough that they needed to break out from the original settlement to build another one.

At this point, Adana stood up briefly to explain her plan to harness power from the waterfalls along the river, which would be easy to link up with the irrigation for the rice fields, and to install a number of wind turbines in the area. It was possible there would be some disruption as the power lines were run under the ground back towards the colony, but as the lodgings had all had power and water connections put in as they were being built, she predicted minimal disruption inside the settlement itself. The distribution centre would be built on the outskirts of town, and once that was in, everything should run smoothly.

After Mira and Adana, Nehemiah gave a brief update on the settlement's provision for childcare and schooling, adding that all the children currently attending the school seemed to be settling in well after their first couple of days. It had been decided that children would start in groups every month, to avoid disrupting the existing classes and so that the new children would have others in the same situation as them as they joined. It all sounded very sensible and Nina could see many faces in the audience looking reassured as Nehemiah spoke.

Jerry got to his feet next for a quick medical update. As he was taking on more of the administrative duties of running the health service, it made sense for him to do the announcement, but Nina missed seeing Sarah there. Although, even she had to admit he might possibly be a bit more reassuring as the face of the hospital, with his friendly demeanour and natural tact. He spoke briefly about the insect bites that had caused a few reactions, reminding people to use insect repellent if they were heading into 'less built-up areas'. The phrase caused a ripple of laughter and Jerry smiled.

"I'm also pleased to announce that our new midwifery team is now up and running!" he enthused, eliciting a round of applause, more for the sheer enthusiasm of his announcement than the content, Nina thought. "We have a team of specialists who are fully qualified as well as some wonderful trainees, who are all ready to look after you. So please come and talk to us as soon as you discover a pregnancy, and we'll make sure you're set up to receive the best possible care for you and your baby the whole way through. I'd also like to remind you that pregnancies will appear to last longer here on Demeter, as both the year and the day are shorter, so that's something to bear in mind when planning your families."

Saima spoke last and Nina smiled to herself when the energy in the Plasa changed as she took the stage. Those who had been at the last meeting remembered her, sitting up eagerly, and those who hadn't were obviously intrigued. She looked comfortable and authoritative in front of the microphone, and despite being considerably less dramatic than at the last meeting, she still held everyone's attention.

"People of Bayville," she began, then trailed off, and turned to the rest of the Union with a grin. "That's the first time I've been able to say that. I like it." Everyone laughed and she turned back to the crowd. "Anyway. People of Bayville! Fellow colonists! The time has come for you to tell us what you want! You've all been working hard and some of you have probably started to settle into a routine. What we need now is a bit of entertainment, and that's where you come in. I'd like to know what kind of entertainment you would like to see us producing. After all, there's no point in us putting on a beautiful ballet if you're all more fans of the circus, is there?"

"Do we have a ballet troupe in the cryobay?" Nina murmured to Mira beside her, who giggled.

"I'll be sending out a survey in the next few days, asking about the sort of thing you like to do. You can fill it out however— let me know anything and everything! If you're a faithful follower of musical theatre and are dying for some jazz hands, tell me that. If you've only ever been to pub quizzes but would love to try opera, I want to know that too. I also want to know about sports. They're not really my bag," there were a few laughs at the delicate grimace that accompanied this statement, "but my colleague André, who some of you may know from your children raving about him after school, knows all about them and between us, we want to set up a social calendar that gets everyone involved." Saima swivelled a little to catch Nina's eye. Nina nodded and gave her a thumbs up. "I believe that's everything for this evening, thank you so much for coming and we look forward to seeing you all again soon."

There was another round of applause interspersed with cheering and whooping, then the noise faded to a rumble again as the crowd began to disperse. Nina mingled for a while, chatting to people she hadn't seen recently, before making her way back to her cottage for the night.

The morning after the general meeting, Nina was sitting at her console when Liu wheeled himself up to her, still looking a bit peaky but determined to be back at work doing what he could.

"Have you got a moment, Captain? There's something I'd like to discuss with you."

"Of course," Nina answered, standing and preceding him into the small meeting room off the main command centre. She had a brief pang thinking of her little room off the bridge of the *Posterity*, sitting unused after such a short space of time. "What's up, Dan?"

"I'm getting a bit worried about some of the crew. I don't think we're checking in often enough with each other. I know we've all got different responsibilities here on the planet, but that would be true on a ship, too, and we'd still make time for each other."

Nina slipped into a chair at the end of the table, frowning. "You're right. I don't think we've done anything social since that evening tasting all the food Leclerc organised, and that was weeks ago."

"Precisely." Liu nodded, looking troubled. "We'd never have let this happen on a ship, but time's run away with us here and I'm worried we're losing touch."

"It's not your fault; you spent a week of it in a coma," Nina reminded him sternly, and he made a face.

"I know, but even before that, I should have noticed."

"We both should have. God, I can't even remember the last time I had a conversation with Pavluhkin that wasn't about work," Nina said guiltily.

"I have a suggestion, if you're open to it?" Dan offered.

"Shoot."

"How about a weekly crew dinner? Like we used to back on the ship."

"That's an excellent idea, Dan," Nina said, exhaling with relief. "Why on Earth didn't we think of that before? It makes so much sense!"

Dan nodded. "We can take turns hosting to make sure there's no pressure on one person all the time, but it'd be a great way to keep in touch with everyone. I'm particularly thinking about people like Pavluhkin and Kjeldsen, who spend so much time working by themselves. Even though I know they've both got connections outside of work, I think it'd be really good for them to make sure they've still got that crew bond."

"I agree. Thank you for bringing this up Dan, and thanks for coming up with the solution, too. Shall we do the first one tomorrow and I'll host? I'll get Kjeldsen to send out invites."

"Perfect." Dan nodded.

"While I've got you, how are you getting on?" Nina asked, before he could leave. "You're looking much better."

Liu grimaced, but shrugged. "Slowly, but I'm getting there. My physio has the patience of a saint; I know I couldn't deal with me. Ramin's been great too—who knew, under all that banter, he's got a heart of gold?"

Nina laughed. "Make sure you don't overdo it."

"My physio says I should be able to do without the chair in another week, provided I don't push myself too far before that and set myself back. That's enough incentive for me to be sensible."

"Glad to hear it." Nina nodded approvingly. "And please do let me know if there's anything I can do to help."

Liu smiled a genuine smile at her. "Just keep treating me like me, like you always do. That's help enough."

Nina squeezed his shoulder and they headed back into the main room. Liu wheeled himself over to his station, and Nina asked Kjeldsen to send out invitations for the crew dinner the following day. Their face lit up as she explained, and Nina shared a smile with Dan; this was definitely a good idea. Now that she thought about it, it was obvious that Kjeldsen had been missing that contact, and she hadn't even seen Pavluhkin enough to notice! How could she have been so blind?

The following evening came around quickly and joy bubbled inside Nina as her crew arrived, in small groups or by themselves, at her door. They were mostly out of uniform, as she had asked Kjeldsen to stress that this was a social occasion rather than a work one, although as she had implied attendance was compulsory, she intended to count the hours as time worked in their logs. She had chosen to host in her back garden; it didn't have as good a view as the front one, but it was bigger and they'd all be more comfortable with the extra space. The crew settled quickly, sitting on the floor or on the few chairs Nina had brought out and she was pleased to see everyone mingling outside their normal social groups. After a few minutes, Nina brought out dinner—a mild, creamy curry with various sides to accompany it—and everyone helped themselves.

"It's so nice to see everyone," Kjeldsen admitted, as they all tucked in. "It feels like an age since we were all on the *Posterity* together, taking turns to cook every night."

"I bet you're all glad you don't have to put up with my concoctions anymore." Fraser grinned, and everyone laughed.

"I can safely say that was the worst pizza I have ever eaten," Liu agreed. Nina remembered the soggy mess of tomato and rehydrated cheese that they had all attempted to swallow to spare Fraser's feelings and winced; Fraser had many skills, but cooking was definitely not one of them.

"I still can't believe you all ate it. You're true friends." Fraser sighed dramatically, her hand on her heart and her eyes sparkling with mischief.

The evening passed pleasantly, and Nina kept an eye on the crew as they socialised. She could almost see the tension leaving some of them and shared a smile with Liu as they watched the rest of the team interact.

"This was a good idea," she murmured to him, leaning over as they sat quietly watching the others. "Thank you."

"I think we all needed it," he responded, "just some of us more obviously than others."

Nina raised her voice so she could be heard by everyone. "I'd like to make this a weekly event, if that works for everyone. Or we can go for fortnightly, if weekly is too often?"

"No, weekly sounds good," replied Pavluhkin, nodding from where she sat on the floor with Sakamoto. "It's so good to catch up with everyone. I feel like part of a proper crew again." The rest of the team murmured their agreement.

"Great, let's do weekly then. If anyone knows in advance they can't make one, let us know and we'll work out whether to reschedule or skip it for that week."

"Excellent," agreed Leclerc.

The crew gradually dispersed, some excusing themselves on account of early starts in the morning, others drifting away. Eventually, just Sarah and Dan remained. It was still warm, even this late in the evening, the balmy air smelling faintly of alien flowers. The sun had nearly gone down and the garden was dimly lit by the amber glow of the last rays sneaking over the horizon.

"Care for a nightcap?" Nina asked, and they both agreed. She popped inside briefly, returning with three tumblers and a bottle of whiskey. They clinked glasses and sipped appreciatively in silence for a moment; Nina had followed Sarah's example and used some of her credits for the food processing units, treating herself to a bottle of nice whiskey and some chocolate.

"So, are you two going to tell me that you're dating now or is it a secret?" Dan asked with a twinkle in his eye.

"Oh!" Nina caught Sarah's eye. Sarah shrugged. "It's not a secret as such; we just didn't think it warranted a big announcement."

Dan shook his head. "You spend a week in a medically induced coma and when you wake up, your best friends are an item."

Both women laughed and Sarah smacked his leg. "Actually, we've been dating for over a month now."

Liu's eyebrows shot up. "Really?" Nina smiled and took Sarah's hand, both of them uncharacteristically short for words. "Well, I'm happy for you both. Just don't go breaking up, or I won't know which of you I need to chase down and have a go at."

Nina laughed, then sobered as she sensed the real worry behind Dan's words. "We would never put you in that position, Dan. You're a good friend to both of us, and we'd never let anything jeopardise that. Anything that happened between us would stay between us."

"Besides," added Sarah, "we still have to work together, so it's in everyone's interests to keep things sweet."

They all laughed. Nina topped their drinks up.

"Do you think we'll hear from Earth again this weekend?" Sarah asked, as they watched the first stars come out. Nina still hadn't got used to the brightness of them, nor the fact that she didn't recognise a single constellation.

"If not this weekend, then early next week," Nina answered. "They said they'd aim to keep in contact once a week, but I don't know what they'll have to say!"

"I've been reading up on this, actually," said Liu, sitting up straighter in his chair. "I've had a lot of time on my hands, so I

265

spent some of this week brushing up on the protocols they talked about putting in place back when we set off. The idea back then was that we'd be assigned a Planetary Liaison Officer, who we'd hear from every week and who would handle any communications sent by us."

"That does sound vaguely familiar, now that you mention it," Nina said.

"It makes a lot of sense," added Sarah. "The Admiral has probably got plenty on his hands already without having to keep an eye on our problems as well."

Nina snorted. "True. I guess we'll wait and see then. Though do pass on anything you think I should know, Dan."

"Always do, Captain."

Chapter Twenty

Nina was right, and the next message from Earth arrived bright and early on Monday morning. So early, in fact, that none of them were at work yet, and Nina arrived at her console at the start of her shift to find it blinking with a new message light and the notification that a communication had arrived at 03.00 their time. She approved the security protocols and opened it up. It was much smaller than the previous communication, and she started with the video.

"Greetings!" began the woman onscreen, bowling Nina over with her enthusiasm. She was fairly young, Nina judged, maybe mid-twenties, and her dark hair stuck up erratically from its pixie cut in a way that made Nina think she had been running her hands through it before sending the message. "I'm Officer Park and I've been assigned as your Planetary Liaison Officer. May I start by saying how excited I am to be in this role and how much I'm looking forward to working with you."

Nina smiled at the unconventional greeting, remembering how much of a big deal this must be for those back on Earth who had been waiting fifty-three years to hear from them. People of Park's age particularly would have grown up hearing stories about the ships that were sent out, and to be designated PLO for one of them must be quite something. Park drew in a breath and continued.

"Admiral Barron has passed all the information from your first communication over to me and we're pleased to say that we received your second drop yesterday. We're so pleased that you've arrived at the planet, and hope the initial explorations went well." Park paused, and frowned. "I'm aware that with the message lag, this was all probably quite a while ago for you now, but I'll be responding to information as I receive it so apologies if anything comes across a bit strange." She grinned slightly self-consciously, then continued. "I don't actually have much to update you on this week; this is mainly just a message to introduce myself. I've also attached an updated list of military regulations and protocols so that we make sure we're operating in unison across the board, as it were, so please do take a look at that when you get a chance."

Nina groaned, aware of how long and dull a job that was likely to be, and wondered if she could get away with delegating it.

"The Admiralty are in talks about what your arrival at your planet means for us here and in the wider universe, so I'm sure I'll have more news next time. For now, Park out."

She smiled brightly at the screen, then the image flickered out. Nina took a look at the rest of the package and sure enough, it consisted of just one document, which Nina had no desire to look at. The door to the command centre opened and Liu walked stiffly in.

"Dan!" Nina exclaimed, leaping up. "What are you doing?"

"It's okay, Captain," said Kjeldsen, following him through the door with the wheelchair and replying to the question that Dan was too focused to answer. "His physio has okayed him to be taking longer walks as long as he doesn't tire himself out. We've walked all the way from his house this morning, so apologies for our lateness."

"Not at all." Nina waved away the apology. "That's brilliant news!"

Dan reached his seat and lowered himself gingerly into it before relaxing and smiling widely. Sweat beaded his forehead but he looked well, and Nina felt a surge of joy to see evidence of his continuing recovery.

"Thanks for the company and the chair, Bille," he addressed Kjeldsen. "Sorry I made you late for work."

"Pfft," replied Kjeldsen, mirroring Nina's earlier hand movement. "There are more important things than punctuality."

After the laughter that followed this out of character statement had died away, Nina told them about the message. She dialled it up to play on Liu's console, to save him having to move again, and they all closed in to watch.

"I think I'll save all the communications in the database, but locked away in the military section so they aren't available for general access," Nina mused. "That'll save difficult questions if we get any that we don't want to be accessible to everyone later on."

"That sounds sensible, Captain." Kjeldsen nodded. "Would you like me to have a look at the regulations document for you?"

"Would you?" Nina replied gratefully. "I didn't want to ask as it'll be such a dull job, but it probably needs doing."

"Not a problem. I can set up an algorithm to compare it to the last such document we had and highlight any changes, which will speed it up considerably."

"You're a lifesaver, Bille, thank you," Nina sighed in relief.

Kjeldsen was as good as their word and by the end of the following day, Nina had in her possession a brief summary of the changes that had occurred in the military while they were en route. It was a much smaller institution now than the one she had joined but with more outposts; a number of new space stations close to Earth had been built, as well as more capsules on the moon and Mars, and Camelot had started a small military training centre. Nina considered this and thought it might be a good idea to do something similar on Demeter; there would be a number of teenagers reaching adulthood soon amongst the colonists and the military might be a good option for employment for some of them. She resolved to ask the rest of the Union their opinion at their next meeting, which was due to take place later in the week.

They had been attempting to meet every couple of weeks, though the schedule was fairly flexible and this one had been delayed by a week because of the general meeting last Monday night. Nina skimmed the rest of the document, relieved to find nothing that would indicate she was no longer allowed to wear her new summer uniform, and put it aside to go over more thoroughly another day.

The Union meeting was scheduled for Friday at 14.00, so after lunch with Dan and Sarah, Nina headed over to the community centre, prepared for a long afternoon. The meetings had been getting longer and longer and she had a nasty feeling this one was going to break the record. It was stiflingly hot today, with dark ominous clouds hanging low overhead and Nina expected the heavens to open at any second. Heavy rain had been becoming more frequent recently and Nina was starting to worry they'd settled somewhere with a monsoon season, though Leclerc was so far loath to use that label. Nina headed upstairs to the small meeting room that had been booked for the session, label affixed neatly to the door by the new centre manager, and slid into a chair amidst the buzz of chatter. She made conversation with Ana Romero, who confided that she was busy but not enough to cause her concern, until everyone had arrived and the meeting began.

Jerry had been elected as the chair, due to his administrative background, and he read out the agenda as Nina ran her eyes over the rest of the group at the table. They all looked well, she was pleased to see, mostly relaxed and not outwardly showing any sign of dread at being cooped up indoors all afternoon while the air thickened with moisture.

The Johnsons went first. A few people had come forward since to say they had home-brewing experience, so they were forging ahead with setting up one of the barns as an experimental drinks station while the brewers set up for more conventional drink-making on their own premises. They had also woken some more animals, after the success of the first batch, and Nina could only imagine the scenes as they had tried to herd cows and sheep into the transport. Overall they were progressing well, although some of the newly installed sheep weren't adapting as well as they had hoped and were having to be kept in one of the barns for monitoring.

"Sheep are like that, though," said Jarli, shrugging. "Healthy one second, dead the next." Anabelle smacked him lightly on the arm, laughing at the expressions of horror on the faces of some of the more urban-minded members of the Union.

Leclerc went next, updating everyone on the many scientific discoveries she and Robert were still making. They had now identified almost five hundred species of aquatic life, both in the sea and the lakes and rivers they had found inland.

"Oh!" she turned to Nina. "We think we have identified the large aquatic carnivore we spotted early on."

"Really?" Nina wasn't sure she wanted to hear this; if it was anything like the predator that had attacked Liu, she thought she might rather stay ignorant.

Leclerc grinned. "It's a whale."

Nina raised her eyebrows. "A whale?"

Leclerc waggled her head in concession. "Well, a whale is the closest Earth equivalent we can think of. Very large, but probably not a danger to humans."

"Probably," Saima repeated drily, picking up on the word.

"Well, we haven't had any volunteers to test the theory yet," admitted Leclerc.

She had also been working closely with the cartographers, who had mapped the river almost to the estuary from the tracking droid Leclerc had set off on the expedition four weeks ago. Her expression told Nina all she needed to know about what

Monique thought of the cartographers, even if their expertise in their field wasn't in question.

"We've also made some progress with land-dwelling mammals, and we think there might actually be two distinct subspecies of rat-dog; some of them are much darker in colour and appear to get larger than their lighter counterparts, and there may be even more variation across different continents. There are striations on the backs of the larger ones and they have different shaped ears, which could indicate a wider range of them than we initially thought." Nina suppressed her smirk; maybe they could name one of them after Dan after all. "There are also some smaller mouse-like creatures that look like they might burrow, which we've seen scurrying past some of the field cameras, and one or two larger things that we have yet to identify. What I'd really like to do is start sending some more expeditions out into the field, as there's only so much I can do remotely."

"What progress have you made with the creature that attacked Commander Liu?" Jerry asked, worry etching lines deeper into his face. "We need to be sure that it's safe before we send more people out."

"I believe we've identified it successfully, and now that we know what it looks like, we can make more estimates as to what will keep us safe. I am confident that it would not be able to penetrate our trucks, for example, so I have no reservations about sending teams out in those. I would recommend we send armed security with all missions and nobody goes anywhere unaccompanied. Other than that, I cannot know anymore until we gather more information, which we will need to go out into the field to do. None of the cameras I have set up to catch sight of it have logged anything, so I really have no other options."

Nina could see that Jerry still looked concerned, so jumped in. "I have full confidence in the abilities of my security officers to protect all the team members on a mission. It's what they're trained to do, after all. From now on, we will make sure that at least two security officers accompany each mission and that all the members of a team are armed and trained in how to use their weapons. I understand there are risks, but we need to understand more about this planet in order to minimise them. Every member of my crew who signed on for this mission knew what they were signing on for and it is imperative that we continue our exploration for the success of the colony. Hiding in town without knowing what's out there is only going to do us more damage in the long run."

Heads nodded all around the table, some more reluctantly than others. Nina sat back, satisfied that everyone was in agreement.

"Alright," said Jerry, nodding slowly. "Mr Lovell? How has the second week of school been?"

"Good, thank you." Nehemiah sat up straighter in his chair and Nina was reminded again how tall he was. "Some of the children who were a little unsettled at first have really started to get the hang of things this week and everyone seems to be feeling much more comfortable. School drop-offs and pick-ups are just like I remember them being back on Earth." He smiled. "The children seem to be making friends in their peer groups, but because they're small years, they're also socialising a lot with children not exactly the same age as them and there's a lot of activity in the playground. It's very nice to see."

"How are they getting on with their studies?" Ana asked.

"The older year groups have got stuck straight in, and I believe it's helping them a lot to have something familiar to come back to. After all, a lot *is* still the same and reminding themselves that things like gravity work the same on Demeter as on Earth is reassuring for some of them."

A thought struck Nina. "*Is* gravity the same on Demeter as on Earth?" she asked Leclerc.

Leclerc grinned. "More or less. It's a tiny bit less strong here, but not enough that you would notice."

"Huh," remarked Saima, sitting back in her chair. The corner of her mouth quirked. "You learn something new every day."

"What about the younger children?" Sarah asked and Nina remembered, with an odd lurch in her stomach, that Sarah would have been through something similar as a parent.

"They are mostly reacting as they normally would on starting school—some of them are excited to go every morning and others still cry as they leave their parents. They are forming good friendships though, and there aren't any that I'm particularly worried about."

"Maria is in school most days and has been touching base with both Nehemiah and Patrin," said Ana, leaning forward.

"When is the next batch of children starting school?" Mira asked.

"Two weeks from Monday," Nehemiah answered. "There is talk of class meet-ups before the new groups start school, so that they have a chance to meet some of their peers beforehand, but this would be entirely voluntary and up to the individuals concerned."

Nehemiah answered a few more questions before passing the baton to Saima.

"I've had a really enthusiastic response to my survey," she said, dialling up some information on her notepad. "Over half of the adult population replied and a good few of the younger members got in touch too." She paused, frowning, and skimmed through some information before looking back up at them. "So, by far the most popular thing that people seem to want is music. About seventy-five percent of the respondents have said they'd be really keen to have some kind of music available. There's a huge variety in what people want though; some people would like to have weekly recitals in the community centre, others think that ambient music in the Plasa would be nice. Others would like proper gigs to go to and some said they don't mind what, they'll listen to anything!

"There's also been some pretty enthusiastic responses about getting some sports going, so I'm going to start conferring with André and see what he thinks. People have suggested all sorts—football, cricket, pétanque in the Plasa, beach volleyball..." she trailed off, eyes on her notepad.

"It all sounds great, Saima," Nina volunteered.

"Anything to start getting a bit of community spirit going and get people some entertainment before it starts feeling like a penal colony!" Lowanna chuckled. "Though I might pass on the beach volleyball myself."

Everyone laughed, and Saima grinned.

"That feels like a good note to end on," Jerry commented. "Any other business before we wrap it up for the time being?"

"I did have one thought, actually," Nina said quickly. "Sorry everyone. It actually links back into Saima's bit slightly—I was wondering about setting up an organisation of cadets. Eventually we'll want to be able to offer military training to young people leaving school, but I thought it might be worth seeing if there was any interest in setting up a troupe amongst the children and teens."

"It's definitely worth considering," agreed Nehemiah. "Extra-curricular activities like that are so good for the development of young people. I think it could be a very good idea."

"I'll add it to the list," Saima agreed, "and we can keep it as one of our options as we develop everything. It's so good for the kids to have something they can focus on other than school—I was never a girl scout myself, I was far too busy dancing, but my sister raved about the things she did with her lot."

"Excellent," said Jerry. "Let's leave it there for now and if anyone else has any more ideas for Saima, they can bring them up next time."

"Or send me a message," Saima added. "I'm more than happy to meet up and chat through anything anyone thinks of, just let me know."

The meeting adjourned and Nina found herself walking out of the building with Nehemiah. She noted with bleak amusement it had lasted just under five minutes longer than the previous meeting.

"Any plans for the weekend, Captain?" Nehemiah asked, as they stepped out into the overpowering mugginess of the afternoon.

"Not really," she replied. "I'll probably just read over some paperwork." She didn't say that she still wasn't used to having proper days off to know what to do with them, but she got the impression from the twinkle in Nehemiah's eye that he knew anyway.

"Why don't you come to the beach with us tomorrow?" he suggested. "The safe area is nice and big now and Kezia's learning to swim. We're planning on taking some food down from the canteen and making a day of it."

"I wouldn't want to intrude," she demurred, and he waved her away with a flap of his hand.

"Not at all," he dismissed. "Kezia is so excited to know a real space Captain, she'd be over the moon if you joined us. Although, if that's reason enough for you to stay away, I won't be at all offended." He laughed.

"Actually, that does sound nice. I haven't even been in the water yet," she admitted. "Though I'm not sure the weather will be on your side."

Nehemiah laughed again. "Kezia's seven; she'll be in that sea no matter what the weather. But if it's pouring with rain, we'll let you off."

"You're so kind." Nina grinned.

Chapter Twenty-One

It started raining before Nina made it back from the meeting and by the time she got home, she was soaked to the skin. The downpour continued all through the rest of the evening, and she could still hear it drumming against her roof when she went to bed. It was an odd sound, unfamiliar due to the large amount of time she had spent in the vacuum of space, and it took her a while to relax enough to fall asleep.

When she woke up the next morning, however, the sky was almost completely clear and the few clouds that dotted the horizon were small and fluffy. Nina dressed herself in a light shirt and long shorts, putting her exercise clothes on underneath; they would double as swimwear in the absence of anything more appropriate.

The canteen was surprisingly empty, possibly due to people getting up slightly later on a Saturday, so she snagged a small table outside and watched as people drifted across the Plasa while she ate. The settlement tried to run to a five-day week, giving the majority of colonists two regular days off in a row; Nina and the rest of the Union were conscious of not letting people burn out by trying to do too much early on in the development of the colony. Like Lowanna had said, this was supposed to be a new world, not a penal colony, and giving people enough downtime to spend with their friends and families was an essential part of that. Nina ate slowly, enjoying her granola in the warmth of the morning sun, before clearing her empty bowl and making her way across the Plasa to the bay.

The beach was almost busier than the canteen, though it was hard to tell with the way people were strewn across the sand. Nehemiah had been right; the safe area for swimming was now large enough to give a good area of beach for people to enjoy without crowding together like tourists in the height of summer. Nina smiled to herself as she remembered her crew messing around in the water when it was first being set up; was that really only a few weeks ago? She ambled slowly along the top of the slope, just before the dry grass-like vegetation underfoot began to give way to the black sand that made up the beach.

After a minute or so, she spotted Patrin, already dressed in a pair of blue swimming trunks, sitting on a rug halfway down towards the sea, and just as she turned to make her way down, he looked up and spotted her. Smiling, he waved his arm over his head. Nina raised a hand in reply and started to pick her way between the other beachgoers towards him.

"Good morning," she greeted, as she reached the rug. "Where are Nehemiah and Kezia?"

Patrin pointed down the slope. "Paddling already." Nina followed his finger and saw Kezia splashing around with a few other children a few metres away, in water that just reached her knees. Their shrieks of joy floated up the beach towards them. Nehemiah stood to one side, also in swim-shorts, chatting to another parent. "Please, sit down."

Nina sat and pulled off her sandals. "I can't remember the last time I went to the beach," she sighed, digging her toes into the sand.

Patrin raised an eyebrow. "Your house is right on the seafront, isn't it?"

"You know what I mean," she said, wiggling her toes and watching the sand slide off them. "Walking past it every morning doesn't count."

"True," agreed Patrin. "Well, I'm glad you joined us today, then."

A shadow fell over Nina, followed a second later by some droplets of water.

"Kezia! Stand further back, you'll soak her!"

Nina looked up and saw the small figure of Kezia standing over her, Nehemiah grimacing apologetically just behind. Kezia was beaming, dressed in a turquoise swimsuit with purple bubbles all over it that already shone with water and a large floppy hat covered in monsters. The hat was so big that all Nina could see of her face was her smile, until Patrin reached out and pushed it further back on her head. Kezia's eyes lit up at the sight of Nina.

"Captain! Daddy said you'd be coming, if there weren't any emergencies in space. I'm so glad there weren't."

Nina smiled. "Me too. Have you been for a swim already?"

Kezia sighed hugely. "Not yet. Dad says I have to wait until my breakfast has gone down until I go swimming, so I've just been paddling to a-climb-ties before I get in properly."

Nina smiled at how the girl pronounced the word, wrapping her tongue around the unfamiliar syllables proudly in a way that told Nina she had just learnt it.

She nodded sagely. "Very sensible. Why don't you come and sit down and tell me all about what you've learnt in school this week while you wait for your breakfast to finish going down?"

Kezia vibrated with excitement, seating herself across the rug from Nina with crossed legs and launching into a detailed explanation of her current topic, but wriggling so much that the blanket rucked underneath her and Nina felt in constant danger of getting toes up her nostrils. Nehemiah folded himself down next to Patrin and the two of them looked at their daughter fondly as she spoke, occasionally interjecting with a correction or a suggestion. Nina listened with unfeigned interest; Kezia spoke with such liveliness and passion, and such entertaining facial expressions, that Nina found herself really enjoying talking to her. After a while, Patrin looked at his wrist unit and announced that Kezia was allowed to swim now, if she wanted to.

Kezia let out a yell and leapt into the air, bounding down to the water's edge with a speed that surprised Nina and hovering with her toes just out of reach of the waves. Nehemiah and Patrin shared a look, clearly weighing up whose turn it was to go with her this time, and Nina found herself volunteering.

"I don't mind going in with her," she said. "You two sit down for a bit."

"Are you sure?" they asked, practically in unison and with matching quizzical expressions. Nina waved them off as she got to her feet, shedding her shirt and shorts as she did so.

"Of course. You deserve a minute to sit down; I bet you never get a chance for a break normally. Besides, it's been years since I went in the sea. Kezia can show me what to do."

Moving at a far more sedate pace than Kezia had done, Nina strolled towards the water. The waves were gentle, white foam pushing lazily against the dark sand and tickling the ends of Kezia's toes. She giggled and jumped out of their way whenever they came too close.

"Mind if I join you?" Nina asked as she reached the girl, and again Kezia's face lit up. "I bet you're a much better swimmer than I am, will you help me?"

Kezia nodded solemnly. "I'm a really good swimmer." She held out a small hand to Nina, who took it, and together they stepped into the waves. Nina exaggerated her reaction to the slightly cold water with a shriek and Kezia dissolved into giggles. When the water was up to Kezia's waist, they turned to look back at her parents. They waved and she waved back, jumping up and down and splashing Nina, who shrieked again.

"Let's see this swimming then," she said, and Kezia launched herself into the water without further ado. She hadn't been lying; she was a good swimmer, confident and practised, if a lot more splashy than Nina. Nina mostly stood and watched, enjoying the sun on her skin contrasting with the coolness of the water lapping against her, though she did duck under once just so she could say she had. It was a pleasant temperature, making a nice contrast to the muggy air, and once she had acclimatised properly, she felt like she could stay in for hours.

"Captain!"

Nina turned and saw Pete Stafford wading into the water behind her wearing brightly coloured swimming shorts with large tropical flowers on. Sophia held his hand and for once, wasn't clutching her cuddly octopus.

"Hi Pete, hi Sophia," she greeted, standing up from where she had been crouching under the water. Refreshing drips trickled down her back. "Please, call me Nina; I'm definitely not on duty right now."

"I don't know, I'd say you're on some kind of duty." He gave a low chuckle, looking past her to where Kezia was practicing her duck dives by retrieving stones from the seabed. He looked more relaxed than Nina had ever seen him.

"True," she acknowledged with a grin.

"Hi, Sophia." Kezia bounced past Nina, greeting the other child with what must have been a very wet hug. Sophia squealed loudly.

"Of course, they must be in the same class," Nina realised, and Pete nodded.

"Yeah, they just about squeezed into the same group, though Kezia is old for the year and Sophia is one of the youngest. It's really helped Sophia settle in, having someone she already knew in the class. We had a few play-dates after they woke up and they get on really well."

"That's so nice," Nina said, smiling at the playing girls. "It must be such a relief for you."

"Definitely," he agreed. "She was always shy back on Earth, so I was worried she'd get left on the fringes out here, but they've become firm friends really fast."

"How about your mum and brother?" Nina asked. "Are they settling in okay?"

"Yeah, great!" he enthused, and Nina realised this was probably the main reason for his change in demeanour. It made such a difference to people to have support and she vowed to have a chat with Ana about giving her the authority to bump other people up the waking list if it would help her patients. "It's been so nice. I even left Sophia with Mum one night and me and Davy went to the canteen. Not quite the same as the pub, but nice to get some time to myself."

"I bet," replied Nina with a grin.

"That's them over there," he pointed out, waving to a woman and a man sitting on a rug not far from the Lovells. Nina was too far away to make them out clearly, but she waved a hand as they responded to Pete. She noticed that the beach was a lot more crowded than it had been earlier, with later risers obviously making their way down while she had been in the water with Kezia. She chatted a while longer with Pete, who enthused about the rugby team he was setting up with André, until she noticed Nehemiah slowly wending his way to the water's edge. When he caught her eye, he smiled and jerked his head back towards the picnic rug, so Nina splashed her way over to where Kezia was playing sharks with Sophia.

"Time to get out, Kezia," she called, not daring to get too close. Kezia groaned and pulled a face but complied, swimming towards the shore until it got too shallow and wading splashily

285

through the water from there. Nina realised she was breathing heavily and felt a start of guilt for not keeping a closer eye on her.

"You've been in there for ages!" Nehemiah said as she reached him.

"I'm not tired at all," the girl panted, and Nehemiah laughed outright at the bare-faced lie.

"Of course not. It's a good thing you had Sophia to play with, or poor Nina would have been exhausted! Time for a snack and then you need to sit down and get some more sun-cream on."

"I'm sorry, did I let her stay in too long?" Nina asked anxiously as Kezia hared off up the beach.

"Not at all," Nehemiah replied, his deep voice reassuring Nina. "She'd stay in there all day if she could, but she does use a lot of energy splashing around. Maybe we'll finally get her to bed before nine tonight." He laughed.

"Fingers crossed," Nina replied, as they reached the picnic rug.

Kezia dug into an already half-empty pot of dried fruit, and Patrin offered Nina something as she sat down. "No thank you, I haven't used nearly as much energy as this young shark here."

Kezia giggled, her mouth full of fruit.

"Thank you so much for taking her in," Patrin said, and Nehemiah murmured his agreement. "I got to read some of my book, and Nehemiah and I had an actual conversation!"

"You're very welcome," Nina responded sincerely. "We had a great time, didn't we?"

Kezia nodded enthusiastically. "Can you come to the beach with us every week, Captain Nina?"

"We'll see," said Nehemiah diplomatically. "The captain is very busy and important, you know."

"Oh pooh," dismissed Nina, waving a hand and smiling at Kezia's renewed giggles. "We're all equally important on this planet, and I imagine you're busier than I am at the moment. I spend most of my time these days twiddling my thumbs and watching other people do their jobs."

Patrin gave her a knowing look. "Itching to get back in the saddle?"

"Maybe." Nina smiled. "I'm not good at sitting still."

Kezia nodded wisely. "That's because you're an explorer," she said, with an air of explaining the obvious. "Explorers need to be out exploring, otherwise they get bored."

"Very true," agreed Nina. "Maybe I'll get to go out exploring again soon."

After the required waiting period following the application of sun-cream, all three of the Lovells went in the water, leaving Nina to relax by herself on the rug. She made the acquaintance of Pete's relatives; his brother Davy, who was a musician by trade, and his mum Elaine. Both of them were currently helping out with getting the fishing operation up and running, as Elaine had considerable experience back home and Davy was mostly without a job at the moment. Still, as he remarked to Nina with a cheery grin, after the general meeting the week before he was hopeful that he might be able to get his creative juices flowing again soon. Saima had already approached him about a couple of projects and he was keen to see what else she was cooking up. Both of them were pleasant, mild-mannered people and Nina heaved a sigh of relief that Pete and Sophia finally had a bit more of a support group around them.

They had a picnic lunch on the beach; Patrin headed up to the canteen and came back with a hamper filled with enough food for all of them. Nina noted with interest that a fair amount of it was local produce and recognised a few items from their taste test. Seeing the way Kezia was looking at a blue fruit she remembered Taylor trying, Nina told her it was called a 'glum' and that she'd explain why after she'd had one. Patrin looked at Nina with a newfound respect as Kezia devoured the whole thing, and Nina accordingly explained that one of her crew had named it after deciding it tasted like a cross between a grape and a plum. Some of the orange shoots that Nina had particularly liked were included too and they all enjoyed Kezia trying to guess what they might be called, until Nina took pity on her and told her they were Pavlov shoots.

"Why?" asked Kezia, her face scrunching in confusion.

"Because my Chief Engineer Elena Pavluhkin tried them first," Nina explained, popping another one into her mouth.

After lunch, there was a card game while they waited for their food to go down and then yet more swimming. Nina went over to say hi to Robert, who she had noticed on the other side of the beach with his wife, mother-in-law and two small children, and got introduced to the whole family. By now the day was extremely hot, the early morning clouds long gone, and the beach was full of families. She borrowed some of Kezia's sun-cream to put on her shoulders, which were starting to go pink, and regretted not bringing a hat. They all had a game of frisbee in the water and Nina couldn't remember the last time she had had such a fun day.

Eventually, when the sun had travelled right across the sky and they were all sticky, sandy and worn out, Nehemiah announced that it was time for them to head home and get some supper. Nina bade them farewell, thanking them profusely for inviting her along and promising to join them again soon. They traipsed off, an exhausted Kezia starting to droop between her parents, and Nina headed in the opposite direction to her house for a much-needed shower before she met Sarah for dinner.

Chapter Twenty-Two

Nina spent the night at Sarah's, after a quiet dinner at one of the outdoor tables at the canteen, and they woke up late on Sunday. Sarah had Sunday off too, so they had a nice, lazy day after Nina's energetic Saturday and by the time Nina got into work on Monday morning, she felt more refreshed than she had in a long time. However, she was also more than a little twitchy and decided that it was definitely time she went on another exploratory mission. There were two expeditions planned for this week, the first to be sent out after the hiatus following Liu's injury, and Nina wanted to make sure she was part of one of them. First, though, there was another message from Earth. Nina smiled wryly. How convenient of the Admiralty to make sure that their messages arrived in the early hours of Monday morning, ready for perusal at the start of the working week. She knew that it was complete coincidence, but the whimsy still made her smile.

This message was similar to the previous week's in that it didn't contain much information. Park had received their third communication, and was pleased with how they were progressing and how much they were managing to achieve. She had passed on the scientific information to the relevant people her end, who were dissecting it now and were likely to have questions next week. She indicated with some amusement that there had been some in-fighting amongst the scientists, all of whom were desperate to be the first to get their hands on fresh information about extra-terrestrial life.

Nina snorted and made a mental note to let Leclerc know; the woman was rightly proud of her role here on Demeter and would be highly entertained to know she was causing such a stir back on Earth. Park closed by wishing them success with their next batch of waking sleepers, which Nina realised with a start would have been the Union. It was very strange indeed to have such a long lag between messages and she wondered how they'd ever manage to keep up a proper dialogue. She supposed it was not unlike the sending of letters in the olden days, and that once the growth of the colony slowed down a little, it would get easier. She realised now that she had been waiting for a message to give her orders, but that that would actually be unfeasible at this point. It reassured her to know that at this stage, at least, she still more or less had autonomy and that they were trusting her and the rest of the Union to build the colony in the way that worked best for them.

Her correspondence dealt with, she turned to the planning of the upcoming expeditions. She had a meeting on the subject this morning, so at 11.00 she found herself in the meeting room with Liu, Dr Caimile, Leclerc, Sakamoto and the cartographers. Tumelo looked marginally less sullen than she remembered but Niamh, in contrast, kept a frown on for the entire meeting. As before, they were sending out two teams in opposite directions, but each team would now need to drive a much further distance than before to get to the next area for charting.

The previous missions had mapped far enough that a whole day's drive would be necessary before the teams reached uncharted land, so these trips had to be accordingly longer. They agreed that a week-long mission would commence on Wednesday, giving the teams five whole days to investigate new territory to make up for the day of travelling either end. Niamh's expression turned even sourer at the decision and Nina wondered why the woman had chosen the job, given that she seemed to take no enjoyment at all from it.

"What about our days off?" she grumbled.

"How about the teams take four days off in a row after the mission, so have the Thursday and the Friday as well as Saturday and Sunday, to make up for the lost weekend in the middle?" Liu suggested. Nina nodded and the rest of the group agreed eagerly, but Niamh seemed barely appeased.

"Why does she do this job if she dislikes it so much?" Nina asked Dan later, puzzled.

"I don't think it's just the job," he replied. "She doesn't seem particularly keen on anything, really. Last week I overheard her complaining at the canteen that there isn't enough variety in the food and that nothing tastes like it did back home."

"Maybe I should get her referred to Ana," Nina said thoughtfully. "Perhaps she's just not settling well, and she's

293

slipping under the radar because nobody wants to get close enough to her to help."

Liu had not been pleased about the fact that he was unable to go on this occasion but was sensible enough to realise why and knew that there was no use moaning about it. His recovery was coming along well, and he was walking without help more than before, but he wasn't fool enough to risk it all by trying to run before he could walk. Instead, he backed up Nina's suggestion that she should go and professed himself more than willing to deputise for her while she was away.

"It's about time you got to do some proper exploring," he grinned, slapping her on the back. "Just watch out for turtles."

Sarah was less happy about her going away for such a long time, but Nina knew she would never come between her and something she wanted to do. She swung between surly and affectionate and Nina was patient with her, knowing it must be bringing back bad memories and how scared Sarah was of losing her. She couldn't promise to come back but made sure to spend as much time with her as she could, letting her hold her as tight as she wanted in bed the night before they left.

They had breakfast quietly in the canteen together, holding hands across the table, and Sarah came with her to the lab to see them off. It was easy to get involved in the hustle and bustle of the mission preparations and before they knew it, it was time to go. Nina came to give her one last squeeze and a goodbye kiss and Sarah waved her off with a passable imitation of her normal manner. Liu moved to stand next to her, giving Nina a nod and a salute as the trucks rolled off. Her insides squeezed with anticipation, even as guilt surged up her throat as she watched

Sarah grow smaller. She swallowed the feeling down; Dan knew everything that she knew about Sarah's past and she knew that between him and Serena, she would be in good hands.

It was a long day, so they took it in turns to drive. After a quick stop on the way out of town for Leclerc to check on the cameras near the coast, they sped up and maintained a steady pace. Nina's team consisted of herself, Tumelo, Taylor as medic, Leclerc, Sakamoto and another security officer, Palani Kamaka, who Nina hadn't met before. He was young and enthusiastic, with dark skin and long hair braided back in a matching style to Sakamoto. He clearly looked up to her and Nina wondered privately if he had done his hair to match hers. Taylor buzzed with excitement at getting out of town, having been splitting his time between the cryobay on the ship and the medical centre in the bay, and he had kissed Fraser and Kjeldsen goodbye with an enormous grin on his face.

The chat in the truck gradually died away as the day ticked past. Nina read several chapters of her book before putting it away and staring out of the window again. It was happily cloudy, so the truck was cooler than it could have been, but the air was still thick and Nina's shirt stuck to her back against the seat. They stopped for an hour for lunch and to stretch their legs, but other than that they kept driving. After the attack on Liu, Pavluhkin and Chaudhary had fitted both trucks with internal bathroom units to avoid unnecessary and dangerous trips outside at night, so they didn't even need to stop for toilet breaks. The upside of this was that they had also installed a small shower cubicle, so Nina's fears about not getting a proper wash for a week had turned out to be unfounded.

Nina dozed for a while in the afternoon, took a turn driving and just as she was contemplating getting her book out again, the navigation unit on the truck chimed. Taylor, who was driving, breathed a sigh of relief.

"Nearly there," he said, looking over with a smile. Nina pulled herself up and looked out of the window.

They were headed south, so had been driving parallel to the sea for most of the day. It was still visible outside but now they were raised above it, looking down on the sparkling peaks of green-tinged water from on high. To Nina's left, huge boulders and chunks of rock littered the ground and she guessed they fell away to cliffs behind. Taylor drove a sensible distance away from the edge, navigating around the occasional rock that had made its way inland, so Nina couldn't tell how high up they were, only that the sea looked a long way away and the stony ground leading to the edge looked far less hospitable than the beautiful bay they had made their home. When they eventually stopped about five minutes later, Leclerc did a quick scan to make sure there wasn't anything unusual and they all jumped out.

The wind hit Nina like a physical blow. Her hair whipped instantly into her face and she ducked back into the shelter of the van to tie it back before braving the open again. It wasn't cold but the strength of the breeze whisked any warmth away before it sank in, and Nina was glad of the sturdy fabric of her uniform for the first time in months. Clouds raced across the sky, throwing shadows briefly over them as they blocked the sun, then moved out of the way again just as quickly.

"Makes you realise just how sheltered our bay is, doesn't it?" shouted Sakamoto as she approached.

The group stood fairly close together, clothes flapping around them, rolling their shoulders and waggling legs that weren't used to staying still for so long. Nina envied the tight braids of the security pair; strands were already coming out of her hastily-styled ponytail and catching her painfully in the eyes. She nodded fervently and stretched her arms up over her head, rotating slowly to look around her.

Fifty metres or so from where they stood, the ground appeared to end abruptly and Nina was sure it dropped sharply down to the sea. She vowed to steer well clear until Leclerc had taken as many readings as possible and she knew it wasn't going to collapse the second she went near it. On the other side of the truck, heading inland, were more rocky escarpments. The land they currently stood on was undulating and the rocks Nina had observed out of the truck window were scattered everywhere. It reminded her of some of the coastal walks she had been on as a child; very impressive scenery, but not particularly amicable.

Leclerc, Taylor and Tumelo started lugging their kit out of the back of the truck and Sakamoto sent Kamaka to give them a hand. She herself stayed alert, standing to attention in what Nina tried very hard not to think of as her meerkat pose, eyes roving over the unfamiliar landscape. Nina joined them and a few minutes later, all the equipment they needed tonight was out. Tumelo got started with some kit that Nina didn't recognise and Leclerc began on the routine of taking samples and setting up cameras, as well as laying out various humane traps to see if anything wandered in overnight. Nina first offered to give Tumelo a hand, but he declined with a distracted expression, so she joined in with taking samples under Leclerc's direction until it was time to call back to base and check in for the evening. She clambered back into the truck and took a seat, glad to be out of the wind.

"Captain!" greeted Kjeldsen, smiling as if they were especially pleased to see her. They must be relieved to hear from her with Taylor in the party, Nina guessed. "Punctual as usual. Do you need me to put you through to Commander Liu?"

"Not unless he needs to talk to me about something in particular. I haven't got anything unusual to report, just checking in. We've arrived at our designated campsite, which is fairly unpleasant after spending the last few months in our lovely new hometown, and we're taking the usual samples and getting on with bits."

"Excellent." Kjeldsen nodded. "Nothing to report here either; Liu is happy that everything is under control."

"Thanks, Bille. That's always good to hear," Nina replied, tension she hadn't realised she was carrying slipping from her shoulders. She loved getting away on exploratory missions like this, but there was always an extra layer of worry as ship's captain and now a member of the Demetrian Union. She signed off and climbed back out, observing the team for a moment before deciding on her next move.

Heading round to the back of the truck, she started digging out food parcels to prepare an evening meal, rightly guessing that everyone else would be so involved in their tasks that they would forget about food until much later.

After half an hour, Nina had not only sorted out rations but also converted the seats in the passenger portion of the truck into berths for the night, and pulled out the folding table and chairs in the cargo section to build a makeshift kitchen. After trying and failing to call everyone in from the safety of the truck, she jumped down and went to round them up. They were all astounded by how much time had passed and that dinner was ready already, and by the time Nina had repeated herself for the fourth time, her amusement was giving way to irritation and hunger. Sakamoto made sure everyone else was safely inside the truck before climbing in herself and raising the tailgate, protecting them from both the wind and any hidden dangers. The hot rations restored the team, some of whom were surprised by how much a day in a truck had taken out of them, and they retired to bed in mostly good spirits.

The next day was easier than the first, now that the largest chunk of travelling was out of the way. They rose early and Kamaka prepared breakfast while Leclerc checked the traps. Nina laughed out loud when one of the larger ones turned out to contain a small rat-dog, which sniffed at Leclerc's feet in puzzlement before taking off into the bushes nearby.

"Is there anywhere these things don't live?" Leclerc fumed, while Nina laughed.

The rest of the traps, on the other hand, contained enough to appease her. They found several small mouse-like creatures, confirming Leclerc's theories about how common they might be, and something that looked a bit like a newt. Leclerc was extremely interested in this, as it was the first live specimen of amphibious life that she had seen, and she spent a while studying it before reluctantly releasing it where she had found it. It scuttled off with surprising speed in the direction of the cliffs, blending in with the orangey brown scrubland before it had gone further than three metres.

"Things are far too good at camouflage here." Leclerc frowned, staring at the spot where the newt had disappeared.

"How are you naming everything?" Nina asked, the thought suddenly occurring to her. "You must be discovering hundreds of new species. How on Earth are you cataloguing them all?"

Leclerc shrugged. "At the moment they mostly just have numbers. All the fish, especially. Some, like the rat-dogs, acquired names through colloquial usage, and others have particularly distinguishing features. But yes, at some point, they will all need naming."

"Perhaps you should get the schoolchildren involved?" Nina suggested. "I'm sure they'd love that. Get them to study an animal and come up with a name for it?"

Leclerc raised an eyebrow. "We might end up with some oddly named creatures."

Nina laughed. "True. But I'm sure you can invoke your rights as Chief Scientist and veto anything too strange."

"It's a good suggestion," Leclerc conceded, "especially for the older children that are studying biology. It might help get them more invested in their lessons."

They made four stops that day and by the time the truck pulled up for the final time that night, Nina was ready for a break. They had covered far less ground, as the aim was to map thoroughly not generally, and had gone through the same routine of samples, cameras and mapping at each location. Nina wondered again how many cameras they had, and Leclerc had revealed that they did in fact have a large supply but that they were currently reusing ones that had initially been set up closer to the settlement that had outlived their usefulness. They set the traps up again overnight, Leclerc muttering dire threats under her breath about what she was going to do to any rat-dogs that she found in the morning, and retired to bed.

The next few days passed swiftly, forming a kind of pattern. They took it in turns to prepare meals, drive and to convert the truck into its various modes as needed. The two security officers traded off standing guard and assisting with the experiments, and Nina learnt how to operate some of the scanners more thoroughly. They were each allocated three minutes of hot water every day, which was just enough for a very speedy shower, and Nina appreciated the luxury of not still wearing several days dirt when she got up in the morning, though it was a tough choice between using it then or in the evening after a long day's work.

The team mostly got on well, and if Tumelo was occasionally still sullen and uncommunicative, it was better than being outright nasty. Nina wondered how the other team was getting on and if Niamh was behaving any better; she didn't envy them spending a week in a cramped truck with the crotchety woman. It was on the fourth night of the mission that Nina's wrist unit buzzed, about an hour after her usual check in, and, worried that something had happened, she climbed through into the cab of the truck, shutting the compartment door behind her for a bit of privacy. It wasn't Liu's face that appeared on the screen when she answered, however, but Dr Caimile's.

"Doctor! Is anything wrong?"

Sarah's face scrunched in confusion. "No, should there be?"

Nina laughed and relaxed. "Not at all. I was just worried you were calling with bad news."

Sarah shook her head. "No, not calling in an official capacity, just calling my girlfriend to see how her trip is going."

Nina felt a smile creep onto her face at the term and tried not to act like a teenager. "That's okay then. Maybe we should have separate work and personal units, so we know what capacity the call is in before we answer it."

Sarah nodded seriously. "That's a good idea. Then you can pick up your calls naked when I ring without worrying it's going to be about work."

Nina flushed bright red but couldn't keep the grin off her face. "Sarah! Do you know how small these trucks are?"

Sarah dropped the mock professional demeanour and grinned too. "Sorry. But I miss you."

"I miss you too," replied Nina, sincerely. "How are you?"

"I'm okay," Sarah shrugged. "Focusing on work mainly. Serena's taken me for dinner a couple of times. Oh!" she interjected. "Don't tell anyone yet, but we have our first confirmed pregnancy on Demeter!"

"That's great news!" said Nina, sitting up straighter. "Who is it?"

Sarah shook her head. "I can't tell you. She's only eight weeks pregnant so she wants to keep it quiet for a while. But it's very exciting. The midwifery team are practically falling over each other to attend her, and they're working extra hard to get their centre up and running now they've got a deadline. They want to encourage everyone to have their babies at home or in the midwife unit rather than the med centre, as long as there are no complications, so they need to make sure it's all up to par."

They chatted for a bit longer and Nina was happy to see the almost invisible lines of tension leaking out of Sarah as she saw for herself that Nina was okay. She was keen to hear how Taylor was doing and pleased when Nina reported how helpful and pleasant he was making himself to everyone. Sarah wasn't officially his line manager anymore now that the settlement had grown; while working in the medical centre he had a nursing supervisor to report to, while she oversaw the junior doctors. However, the two of them still worked closely together as they remained the official medics of the ship, and as such, Sarah continued to take an interest in him, knowing that they would be working together again whenever they got back to the ship.

For the first time in what felt like ages, Nina thought of the ship and wondered about it. She hadn't even cleared out her room, as she'd assumed she'd be heading back up frequently for a long time to come. How quickly they had all settled down after a lifetime of constant moving!

After fifteen minutes or so, Sarah said that she supposed she had better let Nina get back and Nina reluctantly agreed.

"I'll be back in a few days now," Nina reassured her as they signed off. "Four evenings from now, I'll be having the longest bath I can manage before I turn into a prune, and letting you ply me with wine."

Sarah laughed and blew her a kiss before ending the call.

Nina headed back through and, after reassuring everyone that everything was okay, climbed into her bunk for some much-needed rest.

The morning after, they had planned to turn inland. The problem was, finding terrain that was navigable by the truck. For the first hour they continued winding slowly southwards, going up and down steeper and steeper inclines, with Tumelo registering what he could hanging out of the window. Eventually, they found a gap in the endless stone and through sheer determination, Sakamoto managed to plot a route inland. Nina found herself gripping the edge of the seat as the truck ascended far steeper slopes than she was comfortable with, twisting and turning to pass boulders bigger than her house, and more than once, they had to turn back and try a different path.

After several hours of white-knuckle route-finding, they emerged, the engine of the truck straining, onto a plateau high above their starting point. They powered down the truck a safe distance from the edge and all jumped out, Nina's heart still hammering.

"That was the most stressful drive I've ever been on," Taylor said with a grimace as he climbed down after her. "And here I thought my Dad's driving was bad."

Nina forced a laugh, though she was still on edge. Leclerc scanned their surroundings and after a few minutes, they had all calmed enough to start their usual routines. Kamaka took first guard while Sakamoto took a few minutes breather; Nina had not envied her position as designated driver that morning and made sure she had plenty of time to wind down before doing anything else. Finding a safe route had taken so long that it was already lunchtime, so once the gear had been unloaded, Nina jumped straight in with preparing a rather heartier meal than they would usually have at this point in the day. Everyone crammed it down somewhat faster than usual and by the time the last plate had been scraped clean, Nina felt almost back to normal.

"Please tell me you got all of that, Tumelo," she addressed the cartographer. "I never want to go anywhere near that cliff face again."

Tumelo grinned and nodded. "Seconded. In fact, I'd suggest next time you want to take a look along this coast, you take a shuttle."

"Amen to that," agreed Kamaka, and they all laughed.

Unpleasant as the morning had been, it had given them some valuable information about the geological formations along the coastline and Leclerc had even spotted some new species of birds that appeared to be nesting in the cliffs, so it hadn't been a complete waste of time. Still, she wasn't the only one to breathe a sigh of relief when they all climbed back into the passenger cabin of the truck after lunch and saw that their route for the afternoon took them straight across the flattest stretch of land she had seen on this continent yet. Where behind them the cliffs fell away sharply, ahead there appeared to be almost no variation in contours at all. Nina thought that if she squinted, she could see blue shapes on the horizon that might be the shadows of hills, but in front of them stretched mile upon mile of flat plains. They set off at a good pace and before long, the sea and the terrifying experiences of the morning were far behind them.

At the next two stops of the afternoon, Leclerc spent longer than usual with her equipment, as the terrain was so vastly different from anything they had seen before. The plateau had appeared pale purple when viewed from a distance, but closer up there was a huge range of colours in the vegetation. The most common varieties seemed to be a kind of lilac-hued long grass, which rippled gently in the light wind, and some tufty, heather-like clumps. The vegetation was a bit less orange here than in some of the other spots they had visited, and Nina found it rather refreshing.

Everybody mucked in to gather samples, including Tumelo, who had very little to do with such flat, featureless ground. The equipment in the truck recorded mileage and height variations automatically, so when there were not additional observations for him to log, he found himself somewhat at a loss. As there was a bit of crossover with his field, he took over taking soil samples for Leclerc and she concentrated on gathering bits of everything else she could lay her hands on.

They were still working at their last stop when Nina called back to Bayville and got Liu instead of Kjeldsen.

"It's their day off," answered Liu, when Nina asked. "Today is Sunday, although I can see why you'd forget that out in the wilderness where you are. How is everything going?"

Nina recounted her tale of terror from the morning and he listened sympathetically. She also advised him that they might be running a few hours behind schedule, due to the extra time they'd had to take to navigate a safe path inland, and not to worry if they were a bit late arriving back on the last day. Liu accepted this with a nod and Nina hoped he'd pass it on to Sarah so that she wouldn't worry either. After signing off, she set immediately to making up the beds before joining the rest of her team for a quick evening meal.

They were delayed in setting off again the next day, as Leclerc had found some more interesting species in traps that morning. Alongside the inevitable rat-dog and some almost-mice, there was a small lizard-like creature that Nina thought very similar to the newt-thing they had found nearer the coast.

"Please can we name these things soon?" she asked Leclerc wearily, as they both squatted to look at it. It sat perfectly still inside the trap, as if hoping they wouldn't notice it if it stayed still enough.

"Certainly we can," Leclerc agreed. "This will be Reptile 0073."

Nina glared. "You know perfectly well that's not what I mean."

Leclerc shrugged. "I have more than enough to do without naming everything as well, Captain," and Nina had to concede the point.

"Alright," she said, "what's so special about this one then?"

"Can you not tell? The resemblance to the creature that attacked Liu is extremely pronounced." Nina started back instinctively, and Leclerc laughed. "Don't worry, it's a completely different species. But there are some interesting points about it that indicate a similar evolutionary line."

Nina nodded along as Leclerc explained, pointing at the lizard as she went, and Nina admitted that it did look fairly similar. But, she thought privately as they eventually got back in the truck, so did all reptiles. She wasn't foolish enough to voice the thought out loud, fearing a lecture from Leclerc on the subject of reptilian diversity, so she kept it to herself as they eventually started out on their day's journey.

By the time they stopped for the night, Nina was finding it hard to keep track of their progress. Every single point they had stopped at had looked exactly the same to her untrained eye, and even Leclerc had admitted that it was quite similar. The soil was all sandy in texture and light in colour, and the ground continued to be covered in lilac grass, scrubby orange bushes and stumpy little trees. Leclerc theorised that the trees indicated subterranean water pockets and so far, that seemed to be corroborated by the larger amount of wildlife found near them, but they had yet to find any standing water at surface level. Tumelo had taken to scanning the horizon wildly at intervals, as if hoping something worth charting was going to leap out and hit him, but mostly kept to himself or helped Leclerc out with an air of resignation.

At least the wind had dropped from the punishing level at the coast, but the respite from the constant gale meant an increase in insect levels and Nina was constantly slapping small flying things from her arms and legs as they worked. Mindful of the biting insects that had been causing problems back in town, she was again grateful for the long sleeves of her uniform, although it caused her to sweat more than she liked and suddenly, three minutes a day in the shower didn't seem like nearly enough. They were late to bed again that evening and Nina found herself looking forward to this time in two days, when she would be back by herself in her own spacious double, not a cramped bunk in an overheated crowded truck.

She laughed slightly at herself; it wasn't long ago she'd been unable to imagine ever settling down and here she was, on her first exploratory mission in weeks, eagerly anticipating her return to civilisation. She wriggled down under the covers and got as comfortable as possible before falling quickly asleep.

The next day was their last full day of tracking before they started on the long drive home the following morning. Nina, resigned to another day of dust and dryness, was pleasantly surprised when, after the first stop, the ground started to slope gradually downwards and the vegetation got more verdant. Her interest in the mission rekindled, she peered out of the window as they passed more and more trees and larger bushes, with more green plants than she had seen since they landed. Tumelo let out an exclamation and they all turned to look at him.

"I think we're coming up on a large body of water, an inland lake or something? We should reach the closest edge in about a kilometre."

Leclerc, peering over his shoulder to look at his screen, nodded and sat up straight. "I was sure there must be some around here—we saw them on our flybys—but I wasn't expecting to hit one so soon. This could be a real development."

Nina noted the light shining in Leclerc's eyes that indicated she was excited almost to the point of fanaticism and smiled to herself. She really couldn't have picked someone better suited for this job; Leclerc's enthusiasm and skill far outstripped that of any of the other scientists Nina had ever worked with.

After a slow approach, as Kamaka had to navigate the truck through the ever-increasing flora, Nina caught a flash from the sun sparkling off a large body of water ahead. It came and went, disappearing as their view was obscured by a large bush or a tree before reappearing suddenly from behind a different one. Nina was mesmerised, and when the trees finally thinned enough to make it out, steel blue and twinkling, she let out a soft "ooh" of appreciation. The next second, Kamaka slammed on the brakes and they all jolted forwards in their seats.

"Sorry about that, folks," he apologised as they all grimaced, rubbing their chests and sides where the restraints had caught them. "The water snuck up on me faster than I was expecting."

They all unbuckled, and Nina crept forward to look out of the front window. True enough, the water was visible immediately in front of them, with the tree line extending a good few metres into the water itself. Nina understood.

"Not to worry, Kamaka. I'd have expected the trees to stop before the water too. Good job not plunging us straight into it." She patted him on the shoulder and he smiled awkwardly, then they joined the rest of the team in exiting the vehicle.

The ground was slightly squishy underfoot, which felt odd after months of treading on compacted dry ground and solar paving. The lake in front of them, as Nina decided it must be, was huge, stretching as far as she could see in all directions. It was currently a light grey colour, though a moment ago before the sun had disappeared behind a cloud, it had been sparkling and blue. The trees surrounding them were mostly green, as were the wide variety of bushes interspersed between them. It was the most Earth-like place Nina had been since their arrival and she found herself unexpectedly nostalgic as she surveyed the vista. She had got used to Demeter and she enjoyed living here, but it was nice to see a landscape without any orange for a change.

Nina dragged herself out of her thoughts and went to join the others. There were so many new things to catalogue that Nina wasn't surprised in the least when Leclerc pulled her aside half an hour later.

"We need more time," she stated bluntly. "Literally everything here is new, and there's at least three times as much variety in plant life as at the last few stops. There's no way we're going to be able to get all this logged if we stick to the schedule."

Nina nodded. "Alright. You crack on and I'll have a look at the maps and work something out. It's going to take us a while to work out how to get round this, anyway."

"Thanks, Captain. I appreciate it." Leclerc grinned briefly, letting her excitement show, then stepped away to continue her work. Nina made her way down to the water's edge where Tumelo stood, surrounded by his own equipment.

"Is now a good time?" she asked tactfully, aware that the cartographer was still the prickliest member of the team and required different handling to her military crew. He finished inputting something on one of his screens and turned to her; to her relief, he was smiling. She smiled back. "We finally found something worth mapping, eh?"

"This is a really, really interesting body of water," he said, and Nina grinned at the enthusiasm in his voice. "It might take me a while to get what I need—it'd be great if I could get at least a preliminary survey of what's underneath the surface done as well."

"You're in luck. Leclerc's asked for more time as well so we're likely to be here for a while, if that's okay with you?"

"That would be brilliant, thank you Captain," he said, with more sincerity than Nina remembered hearing from him.

"Not a problem," she replied honestly. "What are your thoughts on how we proceed from here, whenever that may be? Obviously going straight ahead isn't looking like such a good option now."

Tumelo nodded seriously. "Once I've got a bit more data and I've got the underwater mapping kit set up, I'll be able to take a look at it. For now, your guess is as good as mine."

"I'll let you get on, then," Nina said. "Let us know if we can do anything to help you out at all."

"Thanks, Captain." He turned back towards his equipment and Nina headed back towards the truck, pleased with the progress the man was making towards becoming someone she might voluntarily spend time with.

Chapter Twenty-Three

Nina spent the next two hours digging, snipping, scooping and all manner of things to get Leclerc's samples collected as quickly as possible. There was such a wide variety of specimens here that when they were still only halfway through after several hours, they decided to stop for lunch and do the rest after a meal. Nina breathed a sigh of relief at the decision; although the trees gave them some shade, which was refreshing after the last couple of days on the plateau, it was still hot work and she was more than ready for a rest. She scraped her hair off her forehead, sighing as she peeled her shirt from her back.

After the team had eaten a swift meal, the security officers switched roles and Sakamoto stood watch while Kamaka got his hands dirty. Nina climbed back into the truck to have a look at the maps and to give Commander Liu a call.

They didn't actually have far to go, she realised. The route they had taken had up until now been more or less as planned and they were less than a day's drive, with work stops taken into account, from where they were due to stop making investigations and return straight home. However, there was now a rather large obstruction in their way and they still had no idea as to how large it was. Nina checked the maps one more time, then dialled up a connection to Bayville.

"Good afternoon, Captain; this is unexpected," Kjeldsen said upon answering. "Is everything okay?"

"Everything's fine," Nina reassured them, "we've just hit a bit of a snag. Is Commander Liu there? I'd like to talk to him as well."

"I'm here," Nina heard him say, and a moment later his face appeared next to Kjeldsen's on her screen. "What's going on, Captain?"

Nina filled them in on the developments, and Liu nodded.

"Do you have enough supplies to keep you going if the mission runs a bit longer than anticipated?" he asked.

"We do," confirmed Nina. "Chaudhary sent us off with at least a week's extra because he always plans for everything to go wrong. It's at times like this that I'm grateful for his paranoia."

"He's going to be very smug about it though," sighed Liu, and Kjeldsen grinned. "Don't forget we've got the shuttles too, so if you have an emergency, we can come and lift you out, or drop extra supplies. Whatever you need."

Nina thanked him, then turned the comm unit so they could see out of the window. They both made noises of interest.

"That's a little weird, actually," Liu said. "I've got so used to orange."

Nina laughed. "I know what you mean. Anyway, I'd better go and get my hands dirty again. Can you let Dr Caimile know that plans have changed for me? I'll try to give her a call tonight, but I don't want her worrying unnecessarily if I don't manage to."

Liu's face softened. "Not a problem, Nina. She's doing okay, actually. But I'll let her know for you."

"Thanks, Dan. Brooke out."

The gathering of specimens took almost the whole of the rest of the afternoon and when Leclerc finally announced that she was finished, they had a brief conflab about whether it was worth moving on this late or if they should remain where they were for the night. In the end they decided to move; the team agreed they didn't mind working a bit later today if it meant they might get back earlier, and it seemed a bit of a waste to stay at one site longer than necessary. They piled back into the truck and Nina took her turn driving.

It was incredibly slow work. The plants by the water's edge stood so close together, and the line of the water meandered up and down so that they needed to head out to be able to navigate a path. Their plan was to head east along the edge of the lake, and hopefully reach a point where they could turn north and start their trip back to town. It wasn't quite what you'd call a forest, Nina thought as she drove; there weren't enough trees. Instead, creeping tendrils snaked between large bushes, weaving across the gaps between them in a complicated web. She bounced the word 'mangrove' around in her head, dimly aware of pictures of similar looking locations from old Earth, before she realised she was getting distracted and pulled her mind back to the task at hand. The spongy ground was hard to drive on and she worried that the truck might sink if it got any boggier. After two hours, Tumelo estimated that they had driven about five kilometres and they agreed to stop for the night.

It was already past the point when they normally had their evening meal so the team split into groups; while Sakamoto stood guard, Leclerc and Taylor started the experiments, Tumelo got out his scanners and Nina and Kamaka got to work on preparing dinner. Nina checked quickly that they were still well stocked and breathed a sigh of relief to find she had been right; Chaudhary had sent far more food than they needed for the original mission and they still had enough for almost another whole week. She made a mental note to thank him again for always being so prepared when they made it back to town, and returned to setting up the truck for dinner and bed.

Thankfully, it didn't take them nearly as long to gather specimens at this site as it had done at the previous one. Leclerc had been banking on a large amount of crossover, given that the locations were almost identical, and her educated guess had been right. Instead of gathering samples of everything, she merely scanned most of the plants and got a bleep of confirmation, meaning that they had already identified one of these and had now logged this one. Nina was gaining more scientific knowledge than she had ever expected to from this mission and was more impressed than ever at the slick way Leclerc ran her operations. By the time Nina and Kamaka had served up dinner, Leclerc had reached a convenient point to sit down and eat and was happy to leave the rest until afterwards.

"So, extra time with you lot, huh?" Kamaka said with a grin, scraping the last bits of sauce from the sides of his bowl. "What did I do to deserve this?"

"Ah, you love us," Taylor threw back. "What could be better than more time in a cramped van, navigating through uncertain conditions, with the same people you've already spent a week with?"

They all laughed, and Nina cleared her throat. "I'd like to thank everyone for the way you're all responding to these unexpected circumstances, and I'm sorry about this turn of events. Kjeldsen will be informing whoever you put down on your contact forms of our late return, but if anyone would like to make a personal call this evening to reassure someone yourselves, feel free to use the console in the cab to do so."

The wrist units that most people wore on Demeter weren't as advanced as the installs and didn't have the capability to send calls outside a certain range. Nina knew from experience how much nicer it was to get a call regarding changed plans in person rather than an official notification, and didn't begrudge using military kit on occasions like this for uses that were not strictly regulation. A few of them took her up on her offer and Tumelo went first; as the only member of the team who wasn't military, he hadn't signed up for this in quite the same way the others had. Taylor went next and came back looking much more refreshed after speaking to his significant others, followed by Kamaka and Leclerc. By the time Nina was free to use the console, it was getting dark and she wondered if it was too late to call. She decided to try anyway; Nina had told Liu that she would try to call, and she didn't want Sarah to worry if she didn't.

When she picked up almost immediately, Nina knew she had made the right choice.

"Hey," she said softly. "Are you okay?"

"Better now I've seen you," Sarah replied truthfully. She looked agitated; her lips looked like she had been biting them and her shoulders hunched around her ears. Nina wished she could reach through the screen and give her a hug. "Dammit Nina, I didn't sign on for emotions like this!"

"I'm sorry," Nina said sincerely. "I had to let the rest of the team call home first. We're absolutely fine, you know, we're just having to find a different route back."

"I know," Sarah snapped. "Logically, I know that. And logically I know that's a perfectly normal and expected thing to happen on a mission like this. But I was expecting this to be my last evening without you and now I don't know if it is or not, and I don't like not knowing."

"I know. If it helps, I'm not enjoying it much myself. I'm getting far too old for sleeping in crew quarters like this. Monique was right on that first jaunt—Sakamoto does snore, and Taylor mumbles."

Something like a smile crossed Sarah's face. "You'd better hurry back then."

"I'll be there as soon as I can," promised Nina.

The next morning they were all up early. After the customary scans, which showed nothing immediately outside the truck, they jumped down and went to check the traps. Nina headed towards the water, passing by a large bush on her way, and froze in her tracks. The ground here was more mud than anything else and large footprints showed clearly, less than a metre away from her and heading from the water into the bushes. They were quite round, with scaly indents visible across the pads of them and the imprints of long sharp claws outlined at the top.

"Leclerc!" she called urgently. "Come here!"

Before she had even finished speaking, there was a rustle in the bushes and Nina immediately realised her mistake. A head poked out of the undergrowth less than three metres away from her, much higher up than she expected, with a sharp powerful-looking beak and suspicious dark eyes.

"Oh shit," she swore, fumbling for the weapon strapped to her belt.

Before she could get it out of its holster, the thing lunged, propelling itself forwards with incredible speed on huge muscular legs, mouth wide and front claws raised to strike. Nina yelled, finally pulling her gun free, knowing even as she swung to face it that she was too late. A shot sounded behind her and the animal crumpled. Nina turned and saw Sakamoto, her weapon trained on the now motionless creature, and Leclerc behind her, her face white.

"Are you alright, Captain?" Sakamoto asked, never taking her eyes off the thing now lying less than a foot from Nina. She was amazed that its momentum hadn't carried it forward onto her, but the force of Sakamoto's bullet must have countered it.

"I'm okay," she replied, breathing heavily. "Thank you."

"Is that it?" asked another voice behind her, and Nina turned to see the rest of the team peering through the bushes; they had all come running at the sound of the shot firing. Kamaka crept forward, his own weapon drawn. "I mean, is that the predator that attacked Commander Liu?"

"I don't know if it's the same animal, but it's certainly the same species," Leclerc answered. "Is it dead, Sakamoto?"

Sakamoto, gun still trained on the animal, had knelt down next to it. "I would be very surprised if it isn't," she answered. "I can't feel a pulse and it looks dead, but I'm not going to say I'm a hundred percent certain because, well, it is an alien."

That broke some of the tension and Nina chuckled shakily. Keeping her gun out, she moved forward to look at the animal. It was huge, much bigger than she had thought even as it leapt at her, with strong thick limbs, a long muscular neck and a massive tail. It looked built for agility, speed and power and was definitely the same creature as the one in the image that they had managed to extract from the camera still. Its skin was a greenish grey, mottled and bumpy, which explained the indents in the footprints Nina had seen, and the sharpness of its beak gave her shivers. Its eyes stared ahead unseeing, with none of the spark that had been there a moment ago.

"It looks pretty dead to me. Can you believe I actually feel bad about that?"

Leclerc shook her head, looking steadier. "Respect for life is important. That's how we got into trouble back on Earth. But you shouldn't feel bad because we killed an animal that was about to kill you. And we will certainly make use of the incident to study and learn more about the creature, so that we can avoid causing more deaths in the future. Ours and theirs," she clarified.

Nina nodded. "Let's get to work, then. Sakamoto, I'd like you to stay here. Kamaka, go and keep Tumelo company, in case there are others."

They nodded and took up positions, but Taylor came over to Nina and took her by the elbow. "They can get to work, and you can join them after you've had a cup of tea and a sit down."

Nina started. "What? No, I'm fine."

Taylor raised his eyebrows. "Do you want me to have to report back to Dr Caimile that you ignored medical advice after a near death experience?"

Nina glared at him but allowed herself to be guided back to the truck. "You are spending far too much time with her."

Taylor ignored her. "Sit down in here and I'll get you a drink and something to eat. Even captains can go into shock, you know."

Nina sat down and realised as she did so that she was shaking. Taylor's use of the phrase 'near death experience' had helped to hammer home the fact that she had very nearly had an accident at least as serious as Commander Liu's, possibly even worse. She had been foolish to go through that clump of bushes on her own, and even more foolish to do it without a drawn weapon. She started running through scenarios in her head, thoughts whirling faster and faster until she felt Taylor press a mug into her hands.

"Here," he said gently. "Drink this."

Nina looked up at him. "How could I have been so stupid?" she asked, and was surprised to find her eyes brimming with tears.

"Try not to over-analyse it. You're okay and that's what matters. Drink your tea."

Nina took a sip; it was incredibly sugary. "I hate sweet tea," she grumbled, and Taylor laughed.

"Sorry," he said. "But you'll feel better after it."

Nina drank the mug slowly, munching on the biscuits he had brought her, and found that she did feel better after all.

"Thanks, Stephen," she said, getting to her feet to return the mug.

"I'm just glad all I had to do was treat for emotional shock rather than anything else," he said seriously.

They tidied up and headed around to join Leclerc, a move Nina immediately regretted. As Nina watched, Leclerc withdrew a hand from inside the creature, clutching an unidentifiable organ. Blood oozed out of it onto the ground and Nina felt her stomach roil. Taylor looked between them and instantly sent Nina off to help Tumelo. She thanked him with a silent smile; she wasn't normally squeamish, but dissection after a big shock wasn't her idea of a good morning.

Tumelo was doing well; he had come to investigate with the others when he heard the commotion, but after everything had calmed down, he had returned to his equipment and was making some good discoveries.

"I'm reading higher ground off to the east," he said, "which indicates that the edge of the lake isn't too far in that direction. It definitely continues for at least another three kilometres, but it starts getting noticeably shallower after two so I'm hopeful that we'll round the edge of it in the next stage of our journey."

"That's excellent news," Nina said, with relief. "After this morning's fun and games, I'm ready to be rid of this lake as soon as possible."

Tumelo frowned. "Even if we reach the eastern side of it, we're likely to still continue along it on the northern-wards part of our journey," he replied. "I'm afraid we've probably still got a good day's worth of travel at least before we hit familiar territory."

Nina sighed. "Okay. At least we're learning all the time," she remarked, and Tumelo grinned.

"I've learnt a lot this trip. Most of my work before we arrived here was in far more controlled environments. It's actually kind of thrilling to be out on the frontier like this, exploring and mapping as we go. It's given me a bit of a taste for it."

Nina smiled at the sincere enthusiasm in Tumelo's voice. "I'm glad. I'm sure there'll be much more for you to do over the coming years."

"I hope so," he replied.

It took several more hours for Leclerc to get to the point where she felt she had learned everything she could from the specimen. Nina could see her regret that she couldn't take the whole thing with her, as they definitely did not have the storage facilities on board to transport an entire creature the size of a small cow, and offered to get Fraser to come out with a shuttle.

"It's not necessary, Captain," she said, shaking her head. "I've got everything I really need, it just seems such a shame not to take it with us."

"Ah yes," agreed Taylor, shaking his head sadly, "I too am really disappointed not to be sharing the truck with a dismembered carcass for the rest of the journey home."

Leclerc swatted him but couldn't keep the grin off her face. "What I will do is set up a camera here, to see what happens to remains left this close to the water and what kind of creatures come out to feed on it."

"Has anyone ever told you you're a little bit ghoulish, Monique?" Taylor questioned.

It didn't take Leclerc long to set her camera up so they were on their way shortly afterwards, hoping to make it to the edge of the lake in time for a late lunch. Nina peered eagerly out of the window but almost an hour and a half passed before Tumelo announced that he was picking something up. The water was getting rapidly shallower and soon the edge of the lake started winding almost imperceptibly around to point towards the north.

"Let's stop here," Nina decided, "mainly because I'm starving and it's well past lunchtime." The others agreed, so they pulled up and assembled a hasty lunch before taking another look at the maps.

"We're definitely on the right track," Tumelo explained, to general enthusiasm once everyone had eaten. "What it looks like is that the edge of the lake gradually meanders up to the north, and off to the east is the opposite side of the ridge that we drove past when we first got down here. There should be a passable route of sorts between the edge of the lake before the ground starts heading sharply upwards, and if we follow that, it'll take us back up to where we need to be."

"That sounds plausible," Kamaka commented. "I'm up for that. Leclerc, are we getting our science on here?"

Thoroughly enjoying the look of scandalised outrage on Leclerc's face, Nina got stuck in with the rest of the team in making as quick a job of 'getting their science on' as possible. The vegetation was starting to thin out a little, so she was relieved to find everything taking less time than they had begun to expect. Nina had just scanned a small greenish-blue bush with large orange flowers when the comm unit in the truck started bleeping. She checked her wrist unit; they weren't due a check in for hours yet. Frowning, she pulled herself up into the cab and answered it. Sarah appeared on the screen and Nina smiled to see her. Then she registered the serious look on her face and heart sank.

"What's happened?" she asked, lead lining her stomach. "Is it Liu?"

Dr Caimile shook her head. "No, he's fine. It's Pavluhkin." Relief and dread coursed through Nina in equal measure. "She's had a severe reaction to a bite from one of the insects. She went into anaphylactic shock and we had to perform CPR. She's in hospital now."

"Will she be okay?" Nina swallowed.

"I don't know," Sarah said, her voice cracking even through her professional mask.

"Oh god," said Nina. There was a lump in her throat that felt like it was the size of a football. "We're still at least a day away; I can't leave the team here."

"I know." Sarah nodded. "But I thought I should tell you, and Leclerc might want to come back to see her."

"Leclerc?" Confusion cut through Nina's distress.

"She's down as Pavluhkin's next of kin on her contact forms. We can send Fraser out to pick her up if she wants to come back."

"Okay." Nina steeled herself. "I'll go and get her. One moment."

Action helped her focus, and Nina took a deep breath as she climbed out of the truck. Leclerc knelt a few metres away, laughing with Taylor over something one of them had found. Nina felt her gut clench as she approached and touched her gently on the elbow.

"Monique, can you come with me for a moment?" Confusion rode over Leclerc's face, but she put down her tools and followed Nina to the truck. "I'm afraid Dr Caimile has some bad news. You can take the call in the cab."

Worry replaced confusion on Leclerc's face, and Nina felt sick as she watched her climb into the front seat to talk to Sarah. She turned away to give her some privacy, but couldn't help overhearing Leclerc's exclamations of dismay. When she emerged a few moments later, she was choking back tears.

"I need to go back," she said, voice shaking.

Nina nodded. "Of course. Did they say how soon the shuttle will be here?"

"Soon," Leclerc replied, after a moment. She stood, gazing limply into the distance.

"I'm so sorry," Nina said. "I knew you two were close, but I don't think I realised how close."

Leclerc gave a watery smile. "She's everything to me. I've never had a friend like her before. I don't know what I'll do if..." She hiccupped and covered her mouth with her hand.

Nina guided her to a seat and beckoned Taylor over, quietly explaining the situation. He made a cup of strong sweet tea for the second time that day and Nina briefed the rest of the team on the situation. Then they sat, Leclerc gazing into her mug, while they waited for Fraser to arrive.

The sound of an aircraft approaching made them all look up, eyes scanning the sky through the trees for any sight of it. To Nina's surprise, when they eventually spotted the ship, it was her tandem, not the shuttle. She understood immediately; landing the shuttle in the thick vegetation here would be difficult even for an accomplished pilot like Fraser. The ship squeezed through a gap in the trees and landed delicately a few metres from the truck. Leclerc rose wordlessly to approach and Nina followed.

"Captain, Leclerc," Fraser greeted them through the open hatch. She wore a sombre expression and nodded at Nina as Leclerc climbed in.

"Send her my best," Nina said. "We'll be back as soon as we can."

"Understood, Captain," Fraser replied.

"Look after her," Nina said in an undertone, casting her eyes over the still silent Leclerc in the back, now staring down at her knees.

Fraser nodded fervently. "We will. See you in a couple of days."

She closed the hatch and Nina stepped back, saluting as the little craft took off. Then, feeling slightly lost, she made her way back to the rest of the group.

The team were quiet when they got back in the van, and Nina knew she wasn't the only one worrying. They then began the process of cautiously navigating their way east, trying to find a break from the constant bushes and trailing vines without starting to ascend what turned out to be the fairly steep slopes that ran up the side of the ridge. They picked up pace fairly swiftly, and managed to find a channel between the two where they could maintain a decent speed. By the time they reached the usual time for their final stop of the night, they had made it much farther north than they had anticipated, and the morale of the team had risen accordingly.

"How's it looking, Tumelo?" asked Nina aside, after the usual ablutions were complete. "Reckon we might make it back tomorrow?"

"If we don't hit any more complications, then yes." He nodded, a serious look on his face. "What worries me is that we're between the lake and the sea and in my experience, there's normally something linking those two things."

"But we didn't drive past any rivers on the way here," Nina frowned.

"I know," said Tumelo. "It's entirely possible the lake empties out south of where we were and heads out to sea that way. But I'm still not one hundred percent certain that we're going to have a clear run from here."

"That makes sense," agreed Nina. "Is it possible it goes underground?"

"That's an option too. But until we get past it, I really don't know what we're going to find."

"I appreciate your honesty," Nina said. "Fingers crossed we get lucky."

They had barely finished setting up for the night when Nina started drooping. Try as she might to hide it, Taylor caught her yawning and frowned.

"You should get to bed, Captain. It's been a long day and the stress is probably catching up with you. Get some rest and I promise you'll feel better in the morning."

Nina stifled another yawn. "I just need to check in with Commander Liu and then I'll go."

"With all due respect Captain, you need to rest. Can someone else check in for you?"

Nina shook her head. "He'll get worried if I don't call in person."

Taylor's frown deepened. "Go to bed, Captain. I'll call Commander Liu and tell him you've gone to bed on my medical advice and you can fill him in on the rest tomorrow."

The look on his face prevented Nina from arguing further. Resolving to let him spend less time with Dr Caimile, she dragged herself into her bunk. She had barely managed to take her boots off and wriggle out of her uniform before her eyes closed and she fell deeply asleep.

Chapter Twenty-Four

Nina woke the next morning feeling a thousand times better. She hadn't even realised how much she was carrying when she went to bed, preferring generally to put that sort of thing out of her mind and carry on, but now she noticed the improvement. The worry over Pavluhkin still niggled at her, but it felt manageable. She made a mental note to send a commendation to Taylor's supervisor when she got back; it couldn't have been easy for him to stand up to a senior officer with the few years of experience he had, but he had done so, so firmly that she had been unable to argue and proved himself right. She emerged from her bunk and went in search of breakfast.

"Good morning, Captain. How are you feeling?" Taylor greeted her, his cheery words almost completely covering up the fact he was scanning her with a professional gaze.

"Much better, thank you," she replied, clapping him on the shoulder. "I wanted to thank you for making sure I did the right thing last night; I feel like a new woman."

Taylor relaxed and grinned. "Just doing my job."

"How did your call to Commander Liu go?" she asked as she helped herself to coffee.

"All fine," he replied, "I think he guessed that something had happened, but he didn't ask questions and I said you'd check in today."

"Thanks, Stephen. I'll give him a buzz now." Nina climbed into the front of the truck, careful not to spill her coffee, and dialled up the comm centre. As usual, Kjeldsen answered.

"Good morning, Captain. We thought you might call this morning," they greeted and a moment later, Liu joined them, his eyes anxious.

"Captain. Is everything alright? Taylor said you'd gone to bed early on medical advice but wouldn't elaborate."

Nina held up a hand. "I'm fine, Dan. There was a bit of an incident in the morning; nobody was hurt but it was quite a shock. I'll fill you in on everything in person, hopefully later today."

Kjeldsen's face brightened. "Are you expecting to be back tonight, then?"

"I'm cautiously optimistic," Nina hedged. "There's still the possibility that the lake might throw us off or we encounter a river, but if everything goes smoothly we should be with you before it gets dark."

"Good to know, Captain," Liu said. "Let us know if anything changes, otherwise we'll expect you at some point this evening."

"Will do." She paused, not knowing if she actually wanted to hear the answer to her next question. "How is Pavluhkin?"

"She's okay," Liu replied, his face cracking into a smile. "Dr Caimile is keeping her in for observation, but it's all under control."

Nina sagged with relief. "Thank god. I'll tell the rest of the team, they'll be so pleased to hear."

By the time Nina had finished her call, the traps had been checked, emptied and everything stowed, ready to set off. Nina beamed with pride at how the team had come together in Leclerc's absence, working harder than ever. They piled into the truck, Nina driving again, and made their way as consistently northwards as the ever-changing landscape let them. The going was good, for the most part; the hills sloped sharply up to the east, climbing to the peaks they had seen from the other side, and the lake continued to the west. They had a horrible moment of doubt when the lake started extending back towards the east again and Nina followed the line around, sharing uneasy glances with Tumelo, before it twisted sharply back on itself and disappeared off to the west. Nina breathed a sigh of relief, thankful that Tumelo's possible river hadn't appeared, and set the truck back onto a northerly course.

They soon left the lake behind them and the landscape started getting less verdant and more orange. By the time they stopped mid-morning, it was just a shimmer on the horizon. Nina took a look at Tumelo's map and saw the point they had curved around trailing back up gradually northwest, until it reached a point where it was no longer charted.

"We're going to have to come back and look at this again, aren't we?" Nina asked him.

"Definitely," Tumelo agreed. "I want to know how far it extends inland and where its source is. It's possible it's fed from the hills where we're setting up the hamlet, but there might be more rivers further south that it comes from too. I'm also really interested by how deep it gets and what's underneath it."

Nina laughed. "Well, I'm glad you've got yourself a bit of a project."

"This whole planet is a project!" Tumelo enthused, and Nina marvelled at how much he had changed in the past week. "Before this trip, I wasn't really sure how everything was going to work. It seemed like way too much work for me and Niamh to handle together, but now I really feel like I've hit my stride." His expression clouded. "I just hope she has too."

"We'll find out soon, hopefully," Nina said.

The morning's tests didn't take long to complete; the landscape was more familiar than it had been for days and most of the species they encountered were already in the database. Sakamoto called Nina over for a moment and enthused over a nest of insects that had apparently so far only been seen individually, but apart from that, no new discoveries were made. When they got back in the truck there was a palpable air of excitement; as long as nothing went wrong from now on, there was only one more stop to go before they would be back on already charted territory.

"Not that I'm not having fun, mind," said Kamaka, as they strapped themselves in. "I'd just really like to have a shower that lasts longer than three minutes at some point in the near future."

336

"Yeah, we'd all like you to as well," quipped Taylor, holding his nose and leaning away from him.

"You should get Sakamoto to tell you about some of the missions we've done in the past." Nina laughed. "What's the record for the longest you've been without a shower, Nanako?"

"You really don't want to know," retorted Sakamoto drily.

The last stop rolled around quickly; they all jumped out and split into groups to prepare lunch at the same time as doing the experiments. By the time they had finished eating, the atmosphere was buoyant. Taylor held his cup out to clink and the rest of the team bumped theirs together.

"Here's to the last science stop being successfully completed! How far until we're back in known lands now?" Taylor asked.

"Five kilometres," Tumelo replied with a grin. "If we don't hit anything else unusual, we're on target to get home about sunset tonight."

Taylor whooped and the group laughed. As they climbed back into the truck, however, Nina saw Sakamoto narrowing her eyes at the horizon. Following the other woman's gaze, she saw dark clouds gathering there.

"Are we in for trouble?" Nina asked her, quietly enough that nobody else could hear.

"I don't know," Sakamoto replied, worrying her lip. "Meteorology isn't one of my specialities, but those look pretty ominous, even to me. I'd prefer it if we can make it home before they reach us, if they're headed this way."

Nina held her finger up to check for wind direction. "They probably are. Let's floor it and hope for the best."

They shared another anxious glance, then climbed back in and took their seats. Sakamoto was designated driver for this stretch, so they didn't have to share their concerns with anyone else just yet and Nina caught the look of determination on her face as she settled behind the console. In a matter of minutes, they passed the imaginary boundary that marked previously explored territory and some of the team cheered. Nina smiled tightly and tried not to dampen the jubilant mood.

Sakamoto drove fast and some of the team commented. After several hours driving, they stopped to switch drivers and stretch their legs briefly and Nina's heart sank. The clouds had gained on them and, while the sky was still a patchy blue ahead of them, the swirling grey masses behind were well on their way to overtaking them. Nina thought she could see dense swathes of rain and wondered if they were in for a thunderstorm. Sakamoto looked up as soon as she exited the truck and grimaced.

"We need to keep going. It's nearly on us and that is not going to be fun to drive in."

"Agreed," Nina nodded. "Alright everyone, back in the truck I'm afraid. We need to try to stay ahead of those clouds or we might not make it back tonight." Everyone looked up and various expressions of disgust crossed faces.

"That's incentive enough for me," Taylor said promptly, vaulting back into the truck and strapping himself into the driver's seat. "Come on, folks. Let's see if we can race the clouds home."

They set off again. Taylor set a pace to rival Sakamoto's, but the light level soon started dropping and the sky ahead of them lost any remaining patches of blue. He switched on the lights on the truck and less than an hour after they started again, the first drops of rain started falling on the windscreen. Taylor cursed and Nina leaned against the window to peer up at the sky. It was dark enough to pass for dusk; some of the clouds looked blacker than she had yet seen on this planet and she shivered.

"Keep it up, Taylor," Nina encouraged, and he looked over at her and grimaced. The rain turned heavy, hammering on the roof of the truck and forcing Taylor to slow his speed to see through the streams ahead. Nina, sitting up front next to him, dialled up the truck's route-finding program and made a face. "I'm going to give them a ring," she decided, and called up the command centre on the console.

"Good afternoon, Captain," greeted Kjeldsen as the call connected.

"Is it?" retorted Taylor loudly from next to her, glaring through the windscreen at the sheeting rain. Kjeldsen started at the sound of his voice.

"We've run into a bit of weather," she said, shooting a look at Taylor. Just then, the first roll of thunder echoed through the truck and Nina had to admire its timing. If she was going for dramatic effect, she couldn't have picked a better moment.

Kjeldsen bit back a smile. "So I hear. I wasn't even sure if we had thunderstorms on this planet yet."

"Well, apparently we do, and this one is a belter. We've had to reduce our speed considerably to be able to drive safely, so we're going to be later than anticipated."

"Understood, Captain," they responded, serious again. "Do you have a current ETA?"

Nina exhaled. "If we keep going at this rate, we're about five hours away."

Kjeldsen's eyebrows raised but they didn't comment. "Good luck, Captain. I'll pass that on to all the relevant parties and we hope to see you soon."

"Thanks, Kjeldsen. Brooke out."

The next few hours were some of the tensest that Nina had experienced since landing on Demeter. The rain didn't let up and the thunder continued to rumble around them, punctuated by blinding flashes of lightning. Nina guessed that as they were travelling in the same direction as the storm, they were spending more time directly under it and more than once, she wondered if it wouldn't be better to stop and wait it out. When she tentatively vocalised the point, after a particularly deafening rattle shook them all, the team shook their heads.

"With all due respect, Captain, I'd rather do a bit more driving in this and be back in my own bed," Taylor said, and the rest of the group agreed.

They stopped once more to switch drivers after he had done three hours, avoiding opening the door by a lot of scrambling, and once free of the front, he collapsed gratefully in a passenger seat with his eyes closed. Kamaka took over for the last stretch and Tumelo dug out some rations for them all to munch on in lieu of dinner. Nina kept checking the map every few minutes until, irritated at herself, she turned the console off and switched to staring out of the front instead.

After what seemed like an age, and half the team had dozed off in the back of the truck, Kamaka let out a sound.

"I think we're nearly home," he murmured, and not long afterwards the beams of the truck's headlights reflected off the first building Nina had seen in a week.

"Thank god," she sighed, slumping in her chair in relief. "Good work, Palani. Let's go to the command centre first to make sure there aren't people waiting there."

Kamaka nodded and they slowly navigated their way through the dark houses. It was nearly one o'clock in the morning and Nina didn't see a single light until they pulled up outside the command centre in the Plasa. It was still pouring, the rain lit up in the light spilling from the windows of the centre, and the shape of the building was barely discernible through the rods of grey water. Kamaka switched off the engine and Nina turned to wake the sleepers.

"We're home, everybody."

Those who had been asleep shook off their grogginess at the sound of these words and grins slowly broke out on faces.

"We made it!" Taylor yelled.

"I'll head into the centre to let them know we're back, then we can drop everybody off in the truck. No sense in us all getting soaked if we can avoid it." Nina paused and grinned. "Well done, team."

There were some more whoops, then Nina zipped her jumpsuit up as high as it would go, opened the truck door and jumped down. She was soaked in seconds, despite Kamaka parking as close to the building as he could safely get. By the time she made it through the door, her hair was plastered flat to her head and rain was collecting in her eyebrows. Five pairs of eyes looked up at the sound of her entry and Nina had a brief moment to smile at the figures sitting around a table playing cards before one of them leapt to her feet and charged across the room to her.

"Nina!" Sarah enveloped her in a tight hug before immediately letting go and stepping back. "Eurgh. You're soaking."

Nina laughed. "Sorry. It's a tad damp out there."

"You get unbelievably British when you talk about the weather," Liu remarked. He had risen in a slightly more leisurely fashion, followed by Kjeldsen and Fraser, and they were all ranged behind Sarah with matching smiles on their faces. "Welcome home, Captain."

"Thank you, Commander," she returned with equal formality. "It's good to be home." She turned to the remaining person in the room who she didn't know, standing a little back from the crew.

"Ah yes," said Liu, noticing her gaze. "This is Ms Kamaka, Palani's mother. She wanted to be here to welcome him home."

"It's a pleasure to meet you, Ms Kamaka," Nina greeted, shaking hands. "I'm sorry we're so late."

"Not at all," replied Ms Kamaka. She was a tall strong looking woman, with grey-streaked hair reaching almost to her waist and laugh lines that suggested she smiled a lot. "I know I shouldn't worry, but it's hard not to."

"Tell me about it!" agreed Sarah, exhaling a huff of air.

Nina smiled at her in what she hoped was a reassuring way, then looked back at Liu. "Might I suggest we leave the formal debrief until tomorrow, or rather, later today, and all get home to bed?"

"That sounds like an excellent plan, Captain," agreed Liu.

"We've parked the truck just outside so we could drop everybody off—if you run for it, you'll only get a little wet."

Liu eyed her soaking uniform and dripping hair in a way that implied disbelief, but didn't say anything. Nina opened the command centre door and ran for it, heading for the entrance to the passenger compartment of the truck and fumbling with the handle for a moment before it slid open. She was outside for less than ten seconds but managed to completely drench herself from head to foot again; the rain, it seemed, hadn't let up in the slightest. The others followed close behind her and they all climbed quickly into the truck, shrieking and cursing as they too were soaked through. There were cries of delight from Taylor and Kamaka as they recognised their people come to meet them, and they exchanged damp hugs and kisses as Sakamoto climbed back into the front and started the engine to head to their first drop off.

Nina waved goodbye to the various members of her team and her crew, offering words of thanks and congratulations as they all left in turn, until only Nina, Sarah, Dan and Sakamoto were left.

"Let's park outside mine, since that's in the middle of our houses," Nina suggested as they waved off Tumelo. Sakamoto shot a curious glance at Sarah but didn't say anything.

"Thanks, Captain," she agreed. She guided them slowly around the sleeping houses until they came to a stop outside Nina's cottage. "Last stop, everybody out," she joked, then climbed through the seats to join them in the passenger compartment. With a goodnight greeting, she picked up her duffel bag from the storage area before battling with the door and heading out into the night. Dan picked up Nina's bag and handed it to her.

"Thanks, Dan. Let's make a run for it, and see you in the morning."

He nodded, threw a quick farewell back at them and leapt out of the door. Nina marvelled at how much he had improved even in the week she had been away.

"He'll be back on missions in no time," Sarah commented, picking up on Nina's train of thought.

"Let's hope so," Nina remarked. "How's Pavluhkin?"

Sarah exhaled. "She's okay. She'll pull through."

"Thank goodness," Nina said, nodding in relief. A thought occurred to her. "I'd assumed you were staying at mine tonight, but is that okay?"

Sarah smiled. "Yes please." Nina shouldered her bag, took Sarah's hand and they ran together for the front door of her cottage.

In her haste, Nina swiped so wildly at the security pad by the front door that she had to do it three times before it picked her chip up, and they fell through the door laughing. Nina dropped her bag on the floor and plucked at the damp fabric of her uniform in disgust.

"I need to get out of this," she said, unzipping as she spoke. "Then warm pyjamas and bed, if that's okay?"

"Sounds perfect," Sarah smiled, heading through to Nina's bedroom. By the time Nina joined her, making a brief stop in the bathroom to towel off, Sarah was already in bed. She smiled and grabbed a pair of clean pyjamas from her chest of drawers. She hadn't been wearing proper pyjamas to bed much recently, preferring shorts and a tank top in the summer heat, but the storm had cut through some of the heat and that, coupled with her tiredness and three soakings in a short space of time made her want something snuggly to sleep in. She dragged her limbs through the soft material, climbed into bed and, after a quick cuddle, fell more or less straight asleep.

Chapter Twenty-Five

Nina woke gradually the next morning, slowly becoming aware of the birds chirping outside her window and the brightness sneaking in around the blind. She stretched, enjoying the space around her and the knowledge that she didn't need to be anywhere until later, and immediately panicked and checked the clock. It showed just after 10.00 and she relaxed again; she had told the entire team and the crew that had been up late to spend the morning catching up on sleep, and that they would convene after lunch at 14.00 in the meeting room at the command centre. Her movement woke Sarah, who snuggled in closer.

"Are you working today?" Nina asked quietly.

"Nope," answered Sarah, smugly popping the 'p' without opening her eyes.

Nina let her hands explore her girlfriend, revelling in the luxury of a lazy morning in bed without anywhere to be.

Eventually, however, her stomach gave a hungry growl and she sat up.

"First things first, I want a proper shower. I'm amazed you want to be anywhere near me after a week washing in that contraption that Chaudhary cooked up."

Sarah smiled. "I've seen you in worse situations. Go wash. I'll be here when you get back."

Nina climbed out of bed and sauntered through to the bathroom. She took her time washing, relishing the steady stream of hot water and thoroughly scrubbing her scalp as she washed her hair. When she emerged, she sighed happily and headed back into the bedroom to get dressed, still wrapped in a towel. Sarah took her place in the bathroom and Nina sat on the bed for a moment before pulling on a clean uniform. After far less time than Nina had taken, Sarah returned from the bathroom and dressed in clothes from her designated drawer. Nina smiled at the domesticity, warmth unfurling in her stomach; she had never had a partner she felt comfortable enough with to get to the stage of leaving clothes at the other's house before. Sarah caught her looking and glared suspiciously.

"What?" she asked.

"Nothing." Nina grinned. "Let's get some breakfast." She checked her wrist unit with a laugh. "Or brunch, I suppose!"

They walked in silence to the canteen, smiling and nodding at the few people they passed. The storm had broken the back of the heat and the air was far less muggy now, though still pleasantly warm. Nina eventually worked out it was Friday morning, and the lateness of the hour meant that most people were already at work but not yet heading out for lunch. She and

Sarah helped themselves to omelettes, made with fresh eggs from the farm's chickens instead of the dried substitutes used on ships, and found a seat in a quiet corner outside.

"I need to tell you about some things that happened on the mission before the briefing," Nina said as they dug in. Sarah nodded and Nina tentatively started. She skimmed over the general mission, knowing that Sarah would find out about that later, but she wanted her to hear about the creature attacking her by the lake from her in private before she had to tell everyone else. As Nina had suspected, Sarah tried to cover her reactions, saying little and nodding while Nina talked.

"So, how are you feeling?" Nina asked, once they had finished eating and Sarah had still said nothing. Surprise flickered in Sarah's eyes but she covered it quickly. "Oh come on. Even before this, you've been quiet since I got back, and unusually docile. Talk to me."

Sarah sighed and looked away. Nina waited, and after a moment Sarah broke the silence. "You're right. Of course I had feelings about you going away, and being late back, and eventually getting back in the middle of the night in a thunderstorm. And now you tell me you were attacked by the same creature that almost paralysed Dan and that I might have actually lost you." She breathed in sharply and reached for Nina's hand across the table. "At the moment I'm just glad you're back."

"Me too," agreed Nina. "It was great to get out and explore but I'm glad that's not the only part of my job now. I'm getting too old to be on the road the whole time, and the attack definitely helped put things in perspective."

Sarah looked at the table. "I was worried you'd enjoy it so much you'd decide you wanted to go out on missions every week."

"Definitely not," Nina said firmly. "Even if I wanted to, I have too many other responsibilities on this planet and I can't neglect them." She paused, tapping her fingers on the table. "On the other hand, I'm never going to stop exploring; it's far too engrained in me and I'd go stir crazy if I never got to go on another mission again. But I think I'd like to do less going out in trucks and more exploring from the shuttle again. Land based missions just aren't as much fun."

Sarah looked up at her and smiled. "I'd never want you to stop doing something you enjoyed. But I'm glad I'm not going to have to go back to only seeing you very occasionally. I've got used to having you around, Nina, and I like it. I like you."

Nina grinned. "I like you too, Sarah. And I'm glad you like having me around. I like being around you."

Sarah looked away again. "I was worried that this mission was going to change things between us and that they'd go back to how it was before. And I don't think I knew if I could deal with being in a relationship where the other person kept going away. But," Sarah took a deep breath and looked Nina in the eye, "you're worth it, Nina. I don't want our jobs to come between us again, whether that means me getting used to you being away for a few days sometimes or you dealing with my shift patterns. I want this relationship and I want to make it work, and I want to still be making it work in fifty years."

Nina had never heard Sarah talk in such depth about her feelings, and she leaned over to kiss her. After a moment's hesitation, Sarah kissed her back, hard.

"I want that too, Sarah," she said, breathless, when they pulled away. "I love you."

Sarah's eyes softened. "I love you too, Nina," she responded, and leaned back in to kiss her again with a smile.

By the time they made it to the briefing, Nina's smile had only just died down. She felt ridiculous, getting so giddy about her feelings, but being with Sarah made her feel like a teenager, and they both had little enough experience with serious relationships that in some ways they almost were. They arrived at the command centre just before the hour struck. The rest of the team drifted in slowly, looking refreshed after a morning off, some real food and a proper wash. They hung around in groups chatting until Nina cleared her throat to kick them off at 14.00 and everyone took their seats. The whole of the mission team was there, as was the entirety of Nina's crew, with the exception of Pavluhkin, who was still in hospital. Leclerc had left her side for long enough to attend the meeting, and would be returning to help her move home when she was discharged later that day. Nina exchanged a few words with her briefly and was relieved to hear they were both doing well.

"Thank you all for coming along today. I know the idea was to have the debriefing when we arrived so you could get four days off in a row afterwards, so I appreciate you being flexible about it, especially given the unexpected extension to the mission in the first place. What we'll do instead is give you four days starting from tomorrow, so you'll get Saturday and Sunday as planned, then Monday and Tuesday on top. Is that alright with everyone?" There were murmurs of assent, nods and grins around the table. "Great. Leclerc, do you want to start us off?"

They started with the basics; Leclerc talked science and Tumelo covered the geographic discoveries. The debriefing went smoothly until they got to the part with Nina's attack. Nina tried not to watch Sarah too obviously, but her eyes kept flicking towards her. She stared fixedly at the table while Nina spoke, her knuckles turning white as she gripped the edge. Liu was understandably also agitated, and asked a lot of questions.

"We took pictures and a lot of samples, Commander," said Leclerc, at her most diplomatic. Nina admired her ability to focus on the job, given the fact her best friend was still in hospital. "We hope to learn as much as we can about the creature and now we have the opportunity to do that as safely as possible."

"I just don't understand how it got that close to Nina," he asked, visibly concerned.

"It was my fault, Dan," Nina said. "I just didn't think. I went through the bushes by myself and I've definitely learned from the experience. I think we need to run drills and extra training before we send out missions in the future; I know that I'm out of practise from three months of living landside and working a desk job. I'd like to make our military protocols more prevalent in our daily routines from now on and make sure that everyone going out on missions is fully prepared."

"I agree, Captain," nodded Sakamoto. "This life is very different from what we've done before and while we need to adapt, we need to make sure that we remain ready for all the different parts of our job."

"Great," Nina said. "Let's talk afterwards about mixing up the schedules to allow for that." She turned to Liu. "Did anything else happen that we need to be aware of while we were away?"

352

Liu nodded, obviously dragging his mind off Nina's attack. "We received another transmission, presumably from Earth, but we couldn't open it as it's coded to your credentials."

Nina frowned. "We should probably ask them to change that. If something happens to me, you still need to be able to communicate with HQ. I'll put something to that effect in the next drop. Anything else?"

Sarah cleared her throat. "We're in the process of contacting people listed as having allergies to bees or wasps in their medical files to make sure they have adrenaline auto-injectors, and that they keep them on them at all times. Without ambulances, our response times aren't as fast as they could be and we're lucky Pavluhkin was so close to the medical centre, otherwise things might have been very different."

Leclerc made a distressed noise.

"Thanks, Sarah," she said, trying to communicate with her eyes not to delve into more detail. "We'll have a think about what we can do to sort that out; maybe Ramin can find us a ground vehicle that'll work as an ambulance."

"Definitely," Chaudhary agreed, for once his face not lifted in a smile.

Nina wrapped things up. "Great. Thanks, everyone. Finish up anything urgent today, then take some time off. Dismissed."

Chatter broke out around the table and Nina exchanged some small talk with people before heading next door to her console. She settled into her seat, noticing at once the now familiar flashing light that indicated a message. Letting the scanner read her chip, she fired up the system and accessed the message. Park's cheery face filled her screen and Nina wondered if the woman was always like this, or if she made a special effort for her communications.

"Good morning, Captain and thank you for your latest message. It sounds like you've been busy there—we're all very impressed. I can't believe how much you've got sorted already, it sounds like you're well on the way to establishing a thriving community."

The message continued in this vein and Nina sighed, realising she'd been hoping for something a bit more. Was the only purpose of the communications with Earth for them to be commenting on things she'd done two months ago? She knew they weren't going to be sending her orders for a long time yet; there would be no point with the time lag, but it still felt slightly hollow to come back from a successful research mission and find a message talking about what she'd done ten weeks ago.

The message ended and Nina busied herself with composing a reply, making sure that she included the request for Liu and Kjeldsen to also be able to access the communications in case of an incident. She also gathered the information she wanted to include in Monday's drop, as technically she would still be off duty on Monday morning. When she had finished that, she reviewed all the information from the previous week to make sure she hadn't missed anything, then called Liu over. The message from Earth had reminded her of something that had been nagging at the back of her mind for a while now.

"Have you got a minute for a chat before you leave?" she asked, and he agreed. They headed into the lesser used smaller room, which comfortably seated up to four in seats that reminded her of the old armchairs in the galley back on the *Posterity*. They could bring some of the decorations down to make it feel more lived in, she realised as she looked around. It would be nice to make things feel a bit more permanent. They lowered themselves into their seats and Nina got straight to the point.

"I'm thinking of separating the ship," she stated bluntly. "We're well on the way to being an established settlement and it seems pointless to keep wasting resources heading back up into space every time we need to wake people up. There's plenty of room to the south of Bayville we can land the sleeper section in, and it'd make life much easier for everyone if we're not having to run several shuttle trips a day to the ship." She paused, gathering her thoughts. "I think I'd sort of been waiting for orders from home to tell us when to do it, but actually the lag is too great and that's not going to happen. So it's up to us to decide."

Liu nodded slowly. "I'd been wondering the same thing myself. I thought to start with that it would be obvious when the 'right' time was, but now I'm not sure I think there is such a thing as the right time. There's so much going on in different areas that it's hard to know, but I think it makes a lot more sense to have people waking up planet-side rather than in orbit and having to transfer."

"I agree. For us, getting in the shuttle wasn't a big deal but for the people we're waking up now who are less used to space travel, I'm starting to wonder if it's a big thing to put them through when they're freshly woken."

"Probably," Liu said, grinning. "A gentle truck drive through beautiful surroundings is probably much more soothing for people who aren't mad enough to sign up for the military."

"I think so," said Nina, smiling too. "So we're in agreement?" Liu nodded. "That's great. Where are we now, then?" She consulted her wrist unit, and looked back up at Dan. "Let's do it a week today, next Friday. That should give everyone ample time to prepare, even people who are supposed to be having four days off in a row."

"You do need time off, Nina." Dan frowned at her. "You'll crash and burn if you don't give yourself time to recover, even I know that."

"I know, I know," Nina waved him off impatiently.

Dan returned to the subject of the ship. "Are you thinking of landing the passenger section of the *Posterity*?" he asked.

"I don't think so," Nina mused. "I'd rather keep that in space for now; its useful to have a base of operations in orbit and we don't have a station up there. Maybe we can place it in a geostationary orbit above Bayville—I know we've been using it to take readings, but I can't imagine anything more that can be taken from up there when we've got so much on the ground now."

"We can always set a couple of satellites up to keep an orbital eye on the planet, if we need to," Liu offered, and Nina agreed.

"Exactly. That's a good idea, actually. Can you get Kjeldsen to prepare something, whenever it's not their days off—I'm starting to lose track of who's working when. And we'll need to check with Mira about location for the sleeper section—she might have some ideas and we don't want to mess up her town planning."

"Leave it to me." Dan nodded. "And try not to think about it too much on your days off. Are you coming to the crew dinner tonight? Fraser's hosting, and you missed last week's because of the mission."

"Oh!" Nina had completely forgotten about it. "Yes, of course I'll be there. I'll see you later then, in that case."

Nina arrived at Fraser's later that evening, wearing an olive-green shirt and black trousers, pleased to have the opportunity to relax in a way that she knew how to. She had never been one for sitting still, but socialising with her crew had always been one of her favourite ways to spend her downtime. Fraser greeted her enthusiastically and she joined the rest of the team who were spread out on rugs and scattered cushions across the floor of the garden. Fraser had hung little globes of light around the place; some hanging off the walls, others dangling from sticks dug into the ground, and the effect was cosy and magical. Nina accepted a beer and found herself a cushion by Leclerc and Pavluhkin, who was propped up on what looked like a deckchair.

"I'm fine." She smiled, replying to Nina's query. "Monique can stop flapping, honestly."

"I do not flap!" Leclerc's expression of outrage made Nina laugh out loud and she relaxed, finally feeling the weight of the previous few days lifting.

"I've got an idea for a game we could play tonight," Fraser suggested, after everyone had eaten as much tagine as they could. "We go around the group and everyone comes up with one thing that they miss from Earth, and one thing they prefer here." Worried looks appeared on some faces, and a couple of people exchanged glances. "I'm not meaning anything too deep," she added hastily, "just little things that you never realised you took for granted. For example, I have never gone this long without eating a kiwi fruit and I am having serious cravings!" There was general laughter as the group cottoned on. "As for things I prefer here, well, life wouldn't be the same without my two partners in crime." She caught the eyes of Taylor and Kjeldsen and grinned shyly and they both smiled back, Kjeldsen blushing deeply. Nina found herself rather touched.

The game continued, now that Fraser had set the parameters, and the confessions ranged from amusing to sentimental. Sakamoto made everyone laugh by announcing that she missed the range of cheese available back home, and Nina had to agree with her. Pavluhkin rather sweetly said that her favourite thing about being here was making friends with Leclerc, and the two squeezed hands with a smile. Nina was a little stumped when it came to her turn, before eventually confessing to missing drinking proper cider in a nice pub but that she much preferred the lack of pollution on Demeter. Nina enjoyed the sense of togetherness that the game gave them all and gave Fraser an approving smile when she caught her eye. Liu's idea of crew dinners seemed to be working out for everyone; there were more hugs than usual when it was time to go at the end of the evening, and Nina felt a surge of happiness as she waved goodbye to her host, walking the short walk back to her own home with Sarah by her side.

Chapter Twenty-Six

Friday morning the following week came around quickly. Nina made a quick stop by the school gates on the Monday, despite it being her day off, to watch the next batch of children starting. There were slightly fewer children than there had been on the very first day and the majority of them had met some of their peer group beforehand, so the scene was much less chaotic than the last time. Patrin had suggested a mentoring system where new starters got paired with a child that had already been attending for a few weeks, so they had someone to show them around and sit with them. Nina thought it was an excellent idea as she watched the proud 'mentors' greeting their buddies and helping them into the school, some holding hands, others chattering away excitedly.

"Giving them a little responsibility can do the world of good to some children," Patrin commented quietly, smiling at the children from his place by Nina at the gates.

The rest of the week contained little except preparations for separation. She spent a long time in consultation with Chaudhary about what stock should be moved into the sleeper section for easier access from the planet; it had a small amount of storage space so could be used to store those things that were more frequently required. Fabric and clothes took up the majority of the area, as Leclerc was expecting the weather to turn soon and they had no idea how cold it would get.

Nina headed back up to the ship for the first time in weeks on the Wednesday and walked the quiet corridors in awe. How quickly she had adapted to living on the surface! She stopped by her quarters; her bed was still made with her pyjamas under the pillow from the last night she had spent there, an empty cup of water on the bedside table next to the picture of her, Dan and Sarah taken at the party to celebrate Dan's promotion. She collected her few personal belongings to take back down to her cottage on the surface, which now felt more like home than anywhere she had lived since childhood.

Friday morning at 10.00 found Nina on the bridge, surrounded by her crew. She smiled at them all, aware of how far they'd come since the last time they had been here together.

"Welcome back, everyone. Let's get this show on the road. Fraser, can you put us into a geo-stationary orbit over Bayville please?"

"Aye, Captain." Fraser swung around and ran her fingers over her console, and Nina felt the answering thrum of the engines firing through her chair. The images on the screen shifted and Fraser steered them expertly until they were in place. "Orbit locked in, Captain."

"Excellent. Head down to the sleeper section and prepare for separation. Dr Caimile, you too."

The doctor nodded and followed Fraser off the bridge. They had agreed in advance that she should be present in the cryobay in case any complications arose during separation or landing, and Nina hoped beyond hope it was just a precaution. She didn't know what they'd do if something happened to wake up everyone else still in cryogenic storage in one go, or even worse, if they lost people. Shaking away such unhelpful thoughts, Nina forced herself to return to the present and waited for confirmation that her people were in place. Moments later, Dr Caimile announced her arrival, followed almost immediately by Fraser.

"Standing by and awaiting your orders, Captain," Fraser's voice announced through the intercom.

"Thank you. Pavluhkin, please begin the separation sequence."

"Aye, Captain," confirmed the engineer. A request for authorisation pinged up on Nina's screen and she lifted her palm to the scanner to confirm; separating the ship required authorisation from both the Captain and the Chief Engineer simultaneously. "Separation beginning in three, two, one…"

The ship thrummed again and Nina thought she felt the distant clunks as the clamps connecting the two sections of the ship disengaged. A moment later, Pavluhkin looked back up. "Separation complete."

"Excellent. Fraser, can you confirm you have control?"

"Aye, Captain," Fraser replied. "We are nearly at a safe distance from the main ship and will start our descent when we are." There was silence for a moment, then Fraser continued. "Minimum safety range attained. We are starting our descent."

Nina turned her gaze to her console and watched as the proximity sensors showed the sleeper section moving away. It was slow going, as the sleeper section was only fitted with basic navigational tools, meant for exactly the purpose they were currently using them for. After a few moments, Fraser's voice came back over the intercom. "Now entering the atmosphere. Beginning final descent."

"All systems remain normal," contributed Pavluhkin, still monitoring the sleeper section from her console to Nina's left. Nina tried not to hold her breath.

"Approaching landing site," Fraser said. "Initiating landing sequence."

The sleeper section was equipped with old fashioned landing feet, which Nina imagined emerging from the bottom of the cylindrical vessel now. She remembered the feeling of the legs thunking out of the very first ship she ever flew in and how it had settled surprisingly softly onto the spring-loaded contraptions when they touched down.

"Legs are out," confirmed Pavluhkin.

"We have touchdown," came Fraser's jubilant voice a moment later. "The sleeper section is down."

Nina exhaled. "Well done, everyone—several thousand people safely delivered to the planet. Particularly you, Fraser; I know how finicky those controls can be. Power down the navigation systems and we'll be down soon so Pavluhkin can do her final checks."

"Aye, Captain," Fraser returned, and Nina could hear the smile in her voice.

There was an extra note of celebration at the crew dinner that night and Nina brought along some sparkling wine she had been saving for a special occasion. The crew laughed and talked, jubilant about another successful mission and another step on the long journey to making this planet their new home. Nina stood on the edge of the party, watching them fondly, until Liu sought her out.

"Cheers, Captain," he greeted, clinking glasses with her. He followed her gaze towards the team they had built, letting out a sigh. "It really does feel like the end of an era, doesn't it?"

"End?" said Nina, smiling. "No. This is just the beginning."

The End

Acknowledgements

So many people have helped with this book that I couldn't thank them all, but a few names jump out as needing a bit of extra recognition.

To Jen, without whom this book would have got stuck at less than ten thousand words, who encouraged me to get creative and draw some maps when I confessed I couldn't imagine the planet; it's fair to say this book wouldn't have happened without you!

Also to Jenn, who gave me the benefit of her wisdom regarding publishing in general and excellent, more specific advice on an early draft of Posterity.

The amazing team at Gurt Dog Press also deserve a huge thank you, for taking me on and putting so much effort into making Posterity the best it can be.

To Su, who read it first, for their never-ending encouragement on my work and their helpful and intuitive feedback.

And Colin, who has listened to me wittering about writing endlessly; thank you for supporting me in following this dream and believing in me even when I wasn't sure myself.

If you enjoyed this book, head on over to my website www.jessnewton.org and sign up to my newsletter to keep up to date.

About the Author

Jess fell into writing as a teenager, tempted by the dark world of fanfiction, but it wasn't until she hit her thirties that she started seriously writing original works. She has a tendency towards science fiction, although lately she has also started to dabble in fantasy and romance.

Her stories are the ones she wished she could have read as a teenager, when as the only queer kid with lesbian mums in an all girls' school, she often struggled to find characters she could identify with. Her motto is that everyone should be able to find themselves on the page of a book, no matter who they are. Outside of writing she enjoys theatre, music and dancing, sitting in the garden of a pub with a pint, and has two children.

A Gurt Dog Press

Publication 2021